## ONE FOR THE MONEY

Thirteen of the finest spellbinders that Agatha Christie ever wrote.

## TWO FOR THE SHOW

Here is the pleasure of the marvelous plotmaking of the mistress of mystery coupled with the irresistible personalities of her star sleuths.

## THREE TO GET READY

You'll want to lock, bolt, and chain your door for a triple guarantee that no one will interrupt your enjoyment of these riveting gems of suspense.

## FOUR TO GO

Hercule Poirot, Miss Jane Marple, Harley Quin, and Mr. Parker Pyne join forces to form a matchless quartet of crime solvers supremely qualified to be your guide through the darkest realms of evil and most dazzling triumphs of mind over menace.

# Surprise! Surprise!

# AGATHA CHRISTIE

A DELL BOOK

Published by
DELL PUBLISHING CO., INC.
1 Dag Hammarskjold Plaza
New York, New York 10017

ISBN: 0-440-18389-8

Reprinted by arrangement with
Dodd, Mead & Company, Inc.
Printed in the United States of America
Previous Dell Edition #8389
New Dell Edition
First printing—January 1979

# Contents

# PREFACE

IN THIS UNIQUE COLLECTION of mystery stories, a superb raconteur presents thirteen surprise-ending masterpieces. In each of them she leads the reader gently down the garden path of her tale, planting clues right and left before his eyes while she deftly diverts his attention elsewhere. And each conclusion comes as a surprise, as logical as it is unexpected. Young people, good and bad as in real life, play an important part in these stories, and young readers will enjoy matching wits with them in these thirteen baffling mysteries.

R.T.B.

# DOUBLE SIN

I HAD CALLED in at my friend Poirot's rooms to find him sadly overworked. So much had he become the rage that every rich woman who had mislaid a bracelet or lost a pet kitten rushed to secure the services of the great Hercule Poirot. My little friend was a strange mixture of Flemish thrift and artistic fervor. He accepted many cases in which he had little interest owing to the first instinct being predominant.

He also undertook cases in which there was a little or no monetary reward sheerly because the problem involved interested him. The result was that, as I say, he was overworking himself. He admitted as much himself, and I found little difficulty in persuading him to accompany me for a week's holiday to that well-known South Coast resort, Ebermouth.

We had spent four very agreeable days when Poirot came to me, an open letter in his hand.

"*Mon ami,* you remember my friend Joseph Aarons, the theatrical agent?"

I assented after a moment's thought. Poirot's friends are so many and so varied, and range from dustmen to dukes.

"*Eh bien,* Hastings, Joseph Aarons finds himself at Charlock Bay. He is far from well, and there is a little affair that it seems is worrying him. He begs me to go over and see him. I think, *mon ami,* that I must accede to his request. He is a faithful friend, the good Joseph Aarons, and has done much to assist me in the past."

"Certainly, if you think so," I said. "I believe Charlock Bay is a beautiful spot, and as it happens I've never been there."

"Then we combine business with pleasure," said Poirot. "You will inquire the trains, yes?"

"It will probably mean a change or two," I said with a grimace. "You know what these cross-country lines are. To go from the South Devon coast to the North Devon coast is sometimes a day's journey."

However, on inquiry, I found that the journey could be accomplished by only one change at Exeter and that the trains were good. I was hastening back to Poirot with the information when I happened to pass the offices of the Speedy cars and saw written up:

Tomorrow. All-day excursion to Charlock Bay. Starting 8:30 through some of the most beautiful scenery in Devon.

I inquired a few particulars and returned to the hotel full of enthusiasm. Unfortunately, I found it hard to make Poirot share my feelings.

"My friend, why this passion for the motor coach? The train, see you, it is sure? The tires, they do not burst; the accidents, they do not happen. One is not incommoded by too much air. The windows can be shut and no drafts admitted."

I hinted delicately that the advantage of fresh air was what attracted me most to the motor-coach scheme.

"And if it rains? Your English climate is so uncertain."

"There's a hood and all that. Besides, if it rains badly, the excursion doesn't take place."

"Ah!" said Poirot. "Then let us hope that it rains."

"Of course, if you feel like that and . . ."

"No, no, *mon ami*. I see that you have your heart set on the trip. Fortunately, I have my great coat with me and two mufflers." He sighed. "But shall we have sufficient time at Charlock Bay?"

"Well, I'm afraid it means staying the night there. You see, the tour goes round by Dartmoor. We have lunch at Monkhampton. We arrive at Charlock Bay about four o'clock, and the coach starts back at five, arriving here at ten o'clock."

"So!" said Poirot. "And there are people who do this for pleasure! We shall, of course, get a reduction of the fare since we do not make the return journey?"

"I hardly think that's likely."

"You must insist."

"Come now, Poirot, don't be mean. You know you're coining money."

"My friend, it is not the meanness. It is the business sense. If I were a millionaire, I would pay only what was just and right."

As I had foreseen, however, Poirot was doomed to fail in this respect. The gentleman who issued tickets at the Speedy office was calm and unimpassioned but adamant. His point was that we ought to return. He even implied that we ought to pay extra for the privilege of leaving the coach at Charlock Bay.

Defeated, Poirot paid over the required sum and left the office.

"The English, they have no sense of money," he grumbled. "Did you observe a young man, Hastings, who paid over the full fare and yet mentioned his intention of leaving the coach at Monkhampton?"

"I don't think I did. As a matter of fact . . ."

"You were observing the pretty young lady who booked No. 5, the next seat to ours. Ah! Yes, my friend, I saw you. And that is why when I was on the point of taking seats No. 13 and 14—which are in the middle and as well sheltered as it is possible to be—you rudely pushed yourself forward and said that 3 and 4 would be better."

"Really, Poirot," I said, blushing.

"Auburn hair—always the auburn hair!"

"At any rate, she was more worth looking at than an odd young man."

"That depends upon the point of view. To me, the young man was interesting."

Something rather significant in Poirot's tone made me look at him quickly. "Why? What do you mean?"

"Oh! Do not excite yourself. Shall I say that he interested me because he was trying to grow a mustache and as yet the result is poor." Poirot stroked his own magnificent mustache tenderly. "It is an art," he murmured, "the growing of the mustache! I have sympathy for all who attempt it."

It is always difficult with Poirot to know when he is serious and when he is merely amusing himself at one's expense. I judged it safest to say no more.

The following morning dawned bright and sunny. A really glorious day! Poirot, however, was taking no chances. He wore a woolly waistcoat, a mackintosh, a heavy overcoat, and two mufflers, in addition to wearing his thickest suit. He also swallowed two tablets of "Anti-grippe" before starting and packed a further supply.

We took a couple of small suitcases with us. The pretty girl we had noticed the day before had a small suitcase, and so did the young man whom I gathered to have been the object of Poirot's sympathy. Otherwise, there was no luggage. The four pieces were stowed away by the driver, and we all took our places.

Poirot, rather maliciously, I thought, assigned me the outside place as "I had the mania for the fresh air" and himself occupied the seat next to our fair neighbor. Presently, however, he made amends. The man in seat 6 was a noisy fellow, inclined to be facetious and boisterous, and Poirot asked the girl in a low voice if she would like to change seats with him. She agreed gratefully, and the change having been effected, she entered into conversation with us and we were soon all three chattering together merrily.

She was evidently quite young, not more than nineteen, and as ingenuous as a child. She soon confided to us the reason for her trip. She was going, it seemed, on business for her aunt who kept a most interesting antique shop in Ebermouth.

This aunt had been left in very reduced circumstances on the death of her father and had used her small capital and a houseful of beautiful things which her father had left to start in business. She had been extremely successful and had made quite a name for herself in the trade. This girl, Mary Durrant, had come to be with her aunt and learn the business and was very excited about it—much preferring it to the other alternative—becoming a nursery governess or companion.

Poirot nodded interest and approval to all this.

"Mademoiselle will be successful, I am sure," he said gallantly. "But I will give her a little word of advice. Do not be too trusting, mademoiselle. Everywhere in the world there are rogues and vagabonds, even it may be on this very coach of ours. One should always be on the guard, suspicious!"

She stared at him open-mouthed, and he nodded sapiently.

"But yes, it is as I say. Who knows? Even I who speak to you may be a malefactor of the worst description."

And he twinkled more than ever at her surprised face.

We stopped for lunch at Monkhampton, and, after a few words with the waiter, Poirot managed to secure us a small table for three close by the window. Outside, in a big courtyard, about twenty *char-a-bancs* were parked—*char-a-bancs* which had come from all over the county. The hotel dining room was full, and the noise was rather considerable.

"One can have altogether too much of the holiday spirit," I said with a grimace.

Mary Durrant agreed. "Ebermouth is quite spoiled in the summers nowadays. My aunt says it used to be quite different. Now one can hardly get along the pavements for the crowd."

"But it is good for business, mademoiselle."

"Not for ours particularly. We sell only rare and valuable things. We do not go in for cheap bric-a-brac. My aunt has clients all over England. If they want a particular period table or chair, or a certain piece of china, they write to her, and, sooner or later, she gets it for them. That is what has happened in this case."

We looked interested and she went on to explain. A certain American gentleman, Mr. J. Baker Wood, was a connoisseur and collector of miniatures. A very valuable set of miniatures had recently come into the market, and Miss Elizabeth Penn—Mary's aunt had purchased them. She had written to Mr. Wood describing the miniatures and naming a price. He had replied at once, saying that he was prepared to purchase if the miniatures were as represented and asking that some one should be sent with them for him to see where he was staying at Charlock Bay. Miss Durrant had accordingly been dispatched, acting as representative.

"They're lovely things, of course," she said. "But I can't imagine any one paying all that money for them. Five hundred pounds! Just think of it! They're by Cosway. Is it Cosway I mean? I get mixed up in these things."

Poirot smiled. "You are not experienced, eh, mademoiselle?"

"I've had no training," said Mary ruefully. "We weren't brought up to know about old things. It's a lot to learn."

She sighed. Then suddenly, I saw her eyes widen in surprise. She was sitting facing the window, and her glance now was directed out of that window, into the courtyard. With a hurried word, she rose from her seat and almost ran out of the room. She returned in a few moments, breathless and apologetic.

"I'm so sorry rushing off like that. But I thought I saw a man taking my suitcase out of the coach. I went flying after him, and it turned out to be his own. It's one almost exactly like mine. I felt like such a fool. It looked as though I were accusing him of stealing it."

She laughed at the idea.

Poirot, however, did not laugh. "What man was it, mademoiselle? Describe him to me."

"He had on a brown suit. A thin weedy young man with a very indeterminate mustache."

"Aha," said Poirot. "Our friend of yesterday, Hastings. You know this young man, mademoiselle. You have seen him before?"

"No, never. Why?"

"Nothing. It is rather curious—that is all."

He relapsed into silence and took no further part in the conversation until something Mary Durrant said caught his attention.

"Eh, mademoiselle, what is that you say?"

"I said that on my return journey I should have to be careful of 'malefactors,' as you call them. I believe Mr.

Wood always pays for things in cash. If I have five hundred pounds in notes on me, I shall be worth some malefactor's attention." She laughed but again Poirot did not respond. Instead, he asked her what hotel she proposed to stay at in Charlock Bay.

"The Anchor Hotel. It is small and not expensive, but quite good."

"So!" said Poirot. "The Anchor Hotel. Precisely where Hastings here has made up his mind to stay. How odd!"

He twinkled at me.

"You are staying long in Charlock Bay?" asked Mary.

"One night only. I have business there. You could not guess, I am sure, what my profession is, mademoiselle?"

I saw Mary consider several possibilities and reject them —probably from a feeling of caution. At last, she hazarded the suggestion that Poirot was a conjurer. He was vastly entertained.

"Ah! But it is an idea that! You think I take the rabbits out of the hat? No, mademoiselle. Me, I am the opposite of a conjurer. The conjurer, he makes things disappear. Me, I make things that have disappeared, reappear." He leaned forward dramatically so as to give the words full effect. "It is a secret, mademoiselle, but I will tell you, I am a detective!"

He leaned back in his chair pleased with the effect he had created. Mary Durrant stared at him spellbound. But any further conversation was barred for the braying of various horns outside announced that the road monsters were ready to proceed.

As Poirot and I went out together I commented on the charm of our luncheon companion. Poirot agreed.

"Yes, she is charming. But, also rather silly?"

"Silly?"

"Do not be outraged. A girl may be beautiful and have auburn hair and yet be silly. It is the height of foolishness to take two strangers into her confidence as she has done."

"Well, she could see we were all right."

"That is imbecile, what you say, my friend. Anyone who knows his job—naturally he will appear 'all right.' That little one she talked of being careful when she would have five hundred pounds in money with her. But she has five hundred pounds with her now."

"In miniatures."

"Exactly. In miniatures. And between one and the other there is no great difference, *mon ami*."

"But no one knows about them except us."

"And the waiter and the people at the next table. And, doubtless, several people in Ebermouth! Mademoiselle Durrant, she is charming, but, if I were Miss Elizabeth Penn, I would first of all instruct my new assistant in the common sense." He paused and then said in a different voice: "You know, my friend, it would be the easiest thing in the world to remove a suitcase from one of those *char-a-bancs* while we were all at luncheon."

"Oh! Come, Poirot, somebody will be sure to see."

"And what would they see? Somebody removing his luggage. It would be done in an open and aboveboard manner, and it would be nobody's business to interfere."

"Do you mean—Poirot, are you hinting— But that fellow in the brown suit—it was his own suitcase?"

Poirot frowned. "So it seems. All the same, it is curious, Hastings, that he should have not removed his suitcase before, when the car first arrived. He has not lunched here, you notice."

"If Miss Durrant hadn't been sitting opposite the window, she wouldn't have see him," I said slowly.

"And since it was his own suitcase, that would not have mattered," said Poirot. "So let us dismiss it from our thoughts, *mon ami*."

Nevertheless, when we had resumed our places and were speeding along once more, he took the opportunity of giving Mary Durrant a further lecture on the dangers of indiscretion which she received meekly enough but with the air of thinking it all rather a joke.

We arrived at Charlock Bay at four o'clock and were fortunate enough to get rooms at the Anchor Hotel—a charming old-world inn in one of the side streets.

Poirot had just unpacked a few necessaries and was applying a little cosmetic to his mustache preparatory to going out to call upon Joseph Aarons when there came a frenzied knocking at the door. I called "Come in," and, to my utter amazement, Mary Durrant appeared, her face white and large tears standing in her eyes.

"I do beg your pardon—but—but the most awful thing has happened. And you did say you were a detective?" This to Poirot.

"What has happened, mademoiselle?"

"I opened my suitcase. The minatures were in a croco-dile dispatch case—locked, of course. Now, look!"

She held out a small square crocodile-covered case. The lid hung loose. Poirot took it from her. The case had been forced; great strength must have been used. The marks were plain enough. Poirot examined it and nodded.

"The miniatures?" he asked, though we both knew the answer well enough.

"Gone. They've been stolen. Oh! What shall I do?"

"Don't worry," I said. "My friend is Hercule Poirot. You must have heard of him. He'll get them back for you if anyone can."

"Monsieur Poirot. The great Monsieur Poirot."

Poirot was vain enough to be pleased at the obvious rev-erence in her voice. "Yes, my child," he said. "It is I, my-self. And you can leave your little affair in my hands. I will do all that can be done. But I fear—I much fear—that it will be too late. Tell me, was the lock of your suitcase forced also?"

She shook her head.

"Let me see it, please."

We went together to her room, and Poirot examined the suitcase closely. It had obviously been opened with a key.

"Which is simple enough. These suitcase locks are all much of the same pattern. *Eh, bien,* we must ring up the police and we must also get in touch with Mr. Baker Wood as soon as possible. I will attend to that myself."

I went with him and asked what he meant by saying it might be too late. *"Mon cher,* I said today that I was the opposite of the conjurer—that I make the disappearing things reappear—but suppose someone has been beforehand with me. You do not understand? You will in a minute."

He disappeared into the telephone box. He came out five minutes later looking very grave. "It is as I feared. A lady called upon Mr. Wood with the miniatures half an hour ago. She represented herself as coming from Miss Elizabeth Penn. He was delighted with the miniatures and paid for them forthwith."

"Half an hour ago—before we arrived here."

Poirot smiled rather enigmatically. "The Speedy cars are quite speedy, but a fast motor from say, Monkhampton, would get here a good hour ahead of them at least."

"And what do we do now?"

"The good Hastings—always practical. We inform the police, do all we can for Miss Durrant, and—yes, I think decidedly, we have an interview with Mr. J. Baker Wood."

We carried out this program. Poor Mary Durrant was terribly upset, fearing her aunt would blame her.

"Which she probably will," observed Poirot, as we set out for the Seaside Hotel where Mr. Wood was staying. "And with perfect justice. The idea of leaving five hundred pounds' worth of valuables in a suitcase and going to lunch! All the same, *mon ami,* there are one or two curious points about the case. That dispatch box, for instance, why was it forced?"

"To get out the miniatures."

"But was not that a foolishness? Say our thief is tampering with the luggage at lunch time under the pretext of getting out his own. Surely it is much simpler to open the suitcase, transfer the dispatch case unopened to his own suitcase, and get away, than to waste the time forcing the lock?"

"He had to make sure the miniatures were inside."

Poirot did not look convinced, but, as we were just being shown into Mr. Wood's suite, we had no time for more discussion.

I took an immediate dislike to Mr. Baker Wood.

He was a large vulgar man, very much overdressed and wearing a diamond solitaire ring. He was blustering and noisy.

Of course, he'd not suspected anything amiss. Why should he? The woman said she had the miniatures all right. Very fine specimens, too! Had he the numbers of the notes? No, he hadn't. And who was Mr.—er—Poirot, anyway, to come asking him all these questions?

"I will not ask you anything more, monsieur, except for one thing. A description of the woman who called upon you. Was she young and pretty?"

"No, sir, she was not. Most emphatically not. A tall woman, middle-aged, grey hair, blotchy complexion and a budding mustache. A siren? Not on your life."

"Poirot," I cried, as we took our departure. "A mustache. Did you hear?"

"I have the use of my ears, thank you, Hastings."

"But what a very unpleasant man."

"He has not the charming manner, no."

"Well, we ought to get the thief all right," I remarked. "We can identify him."

"You are of such a naive simplicity, Hastings. Do you not know that there is such a thing as an alibi?"

"You think he will have an alibi?"

Poirot replied unexpectedly: "I sincerely hope so."

"The trouble with you is," I said, "that you like a thing to be difficult."

"Quite right, *mon ami.* I do not like—how do you say it —the bird who sits!"

Poirot's prophecy was fully justified. Our traveling companion in the brown suit turned out to be a Mr. Norton Kane. He had gone straight to the George Hotel at Monkhampton and had been there during the afternoon. The only evidence against him was that of Miss Durrant who declared that she had seen him getting out his luggage from the car while we were at lunch.

"Which in itself is not a suspicious act," said Poirot meditatively.

After that remark, he lapsed into silence and refused to discuss the matter any further, saying when I pressed him, that he was thinking of mustaches in general, and that I should be well advised to do the same.

I discovered, however, that he had asked Joseph Aarons —with whom he spent the evening—to give him every detail possible about Mr. Baker Wood. As both men were staying at the same hotel, there was a chance of gleaning some stray crumbs of information. Whatever Poirot learned, he kept to himself, however.

Mary Durrant after various interviews with the police, had returned to Ebermouth by an early morning train. We lunched with Joseph Aarons, and, after lunch, Poirot announced to me that he had settled the theatrical agent's problem satisfactorily, and that we could return to Ebermouth as soon as we liked. "But not by road, *mon ami;* we go by rail this time."

"Are you afraid of having your pocket picked, or of meeting another damsel in distress?"

"Both those affairs, Hastings, might happen to me on the train. No, I am in haste to be back in Ebermouth, because I want to proceed with our case."

"Our case?"

"But, yes, my friend. Mademoiselle Durrant appealed to me to help her. Because the matter is now in the hands of the police, it does not follow that I am free to wash my hands of it. I came here to oblige an old friend, but it shall never be said of Hercule Poirot that he deserted a stranger in need!" And he drew himself up grandiloquently.

"I think you were interested before that," I said shrewdly. "In the office of cars, when you first caught sight of that young man, though what drew your attention to him I don't know."

"Don't you, Hastings? You should. Well, well, that must remain my little secret."

We had a short conversation with the police inspector in charge of the case before leaving. He had interviewed Mr. Norton Kane, and told Poirot in confidence that the young man's manner had not impressed him favorably. He had blustered, denied, and contradicted himself.

"But just how the trick was done, I don't know," he confessed. "He could have handed the stuff to a confederate who pushed off at once in a fast car. But that's just theory. We've got to find the car and the confederate and pin the thing down."

Poirot nodded thoughtfully.

"Do you think that was how it was done?" I asked him, as we were seated in the train.

"No, my friend, that was not how it was done. It was cleverer than that."

"Won't you tell me?"

"Not yet. You know—it is my weakness—I like to keep my little secrets till the end."

"Is the end going to be soon?"

"Very soon now."

We arrived in Ebermouth a little after six and Poirot drove at once to the shop which bore the name "Elizabeth Penn." The establishment was closed, but Poirot rang the bell, and presently Mary herself opened the door, and expressed surprise and delight at seeing us.

"Please come in and see my aunt," she said.

She led us into a back room. An elderly lady came forward to meet us; she had white hair and looked rather like a miniature herself with her pink-and-white skin and her blue eyes. Round her rather bent shoulders she wore a cape of priceless old lace.

"Is this the great Monsieur Poirot?" she asked in a low charming voice. "Mary has been telling me. I could hardly believe it. And you will really help us in our trouble. You will advise us?"

Poirot looked at her for a moment, then bowed.

"Mademoiselle Penn—the effect is charming. But you should really grow a mustache."

Miss Penn gave a gasp and drew back.

"You were absent from business yesterday, were you not?"

"I was here in the morning. Later I had a bad headache and went directly home."

"Not home, mademoiselle. For your headache you tried the change of air, did you not? The air of Charlock Bay is very bracing, I believe."

He took me by the arm and drew me toward the door. He paused there and spoke over his shoulder.

"You must comprehend, I know everything. This little—farce—it must cease."

There was a menace in his tone. Miss Penn, her face ghastly white, nodded mutely. Poirot turned to the girl.

"Mademoiselle," he said gently, "you are young and charming. But participating in these little affairs will lead to that youth and charm being hidden behind prison walls —and I, Hercule Poirot, tell you that that will be a pity."

Then he stepped out into the street and I followed him, bewildered.

"From the first, *mon ami,* I was interested. When that young man booked his place as far as Monkhampton only, I saw the girl's attention suddenly riveted on him. Now why? He was not of the type to make a woman look at him for himself alone. When we started on that coach, I had a feeling that something would happen. Who saw the young man tampering with the luggage? Mademoiselle and mademoiselle only, and remember she chose that seat—a seat facing the window—a most unfeminine choice.

"And then she comes to us with the tale of robbery—the dispatch box forced which makes not the common sense, as I told you at the time.

"And what is the result of it all? Mr. Baker Wood has paid over good money for stolen goods. The miniatures will be returned to Miss Penn. She will sell them and will have made a thousand pounds instead of five hundred. I make the discreet inquiries and learn that her business is in a bad state—touch and go. I say to myself—the aunt and niece are in this together."

"Then you never suspected Norton Kane?"

"*Mon ami!* With that mustache? A criminal is either clean shaven or he has a proper mustache that can be removed at will. But what an opportunity for the clever Miss Penn—a shrinking elderly lady with a pink-and-white complexion as we saw her. But if she holds herself erect, wears large boots, alters her complexion with a few unseemly blotches and—crowning touch—adds a few sparse hairs to her upper lip. What then? A masculine woman, says Mr. Wood, and—'a man in disguise' say we at once."

"She really went to Charlock yesterday?"

"Assuredly. The train, as you may remember telling me, left here at eleven and got to Charlock Bay at two o'clock.

Then the return train is even quicker—the one we came by. It leaves Charlock at four:five and gets here at six:fifteen. Naturally, the miniatures were never in the dispatch case at all. That was artistically forced before being packed. Mademoiselle Mary has only to find a couple of mugs who will be sympathetic to her charm and champion beauty in distress. But one of the mugs was no mug—he was Hercule Poirot!"

I hardly liked the inference. I said hurriedly:

"Then, when you said you were helping a stranger, you were willfully deceiving me. That's exactly what you were doing."

"Never do I deceive you, Hastings. I only permit you to deceive yourself. I was referring to Mr. Baker Wood—a stranger to these shores." His face darkened. "Ah! When I think of that imposition, that iniquitous overcharge; the same fare single to Charlock as return, my blood boils to protect the visitor! Not a pleasant man, Mr. Baker Wood, not, as you would say, sympathetic. But a visitor! And we visitors, Hastings, must stand together. Me, I am all for the visitors!"

# THE ARCADIAN DEER

HERCULE POIROT stamped his feet, seeking to warm them. He blew upon his fingers. Flakes of snow melted and dripped from the corners of his mustache.

There was a knock at the door and a chambermaid appeared. She was a slow-breathing, thickset country girl and she stared with a good deal of curiosity at Hercule Poirot. It was possible that she had never seen anything quite like him before.

She asked, "Did you ring?"

"I did. Will you be so good as to light the fire?"

She went out and came back again immediately with paper and sticks. She knelt down in front of the big Victorian grate and began to lay a fire.

Hercule Poirot continued to stamp his feet, swing his arms, and blow on his fingers.

He was annoyed. His car—an expensive Messarro Gratz —had not behaved with that mechanical perfection which he expected of a car. His chauffeur, a young man who enjoyed a handsome salary, had not succeeded in putting things right. The car had staged a final refusal in a secondary road a mile and a half from anywhere with a fall of snow beginning. Hercule Poirot, wearing his usual smart patent leather shoes, had been forced to walk that mile and a half to reach the riverside village of Hartly Dene—a village which, though showing every sign of animation in summertime, was completely moribund in winter. The Black Swan had registered something like dismay at the arrival of a guest. The landlord had been almost eloquent as he pointed out that the local garage could supply a car in which the gentleman could continue his journey.

Hercule Poirot repudiated the suggestion. His Latin thrift was offended. Hire a car? He already had a car—a large car—an expensive car. In that car and no other he proposed to continued his journey back to town. And in any case, even if repairs to it could be quickly effected, he was not going on in this snow until next morning. He demanded a room, a fire, and a meal. Sighing, the landlord showed him to the room, sent the maid to supply the fire, and then retired to discuss with his wife the problem of the meal.

An hour later, his feet stretched out toward the comforting blaze, Hercule Poirot reflected leniently on the dinner he had just eaten. True, the steak had been both tough and full of gristle, the Brussels sprouts had been large, pale, and definitely watery, the potatoes had had hearts of stone. Nor was there much to be said for the portion of stewed apple and custard which had followed. The cheese had been hard and the biscuits soft. Nevertheless, thought Hercule Poirot, looking graciously at the leaping flames, and sipping delicately at a cup of liquid mud euphemistically called coffee, it was better to be full than empty, and after tramping snowbound lanes in patent leather shoes, to sit in front of the fire was Paradise!

There was a knock on the door and the chambermaid appeared.

"Please, sir, the man from the garage is here and would like to see you."

Hercule Poirot replied amiably, "Let him mount."

The girl giggled and retired. Poirot reflected kindly that her account of him to her friends would provide entertainment for many winter days to come.

There was another knock—a different knock—and Poirot called:

"Come in."

He looked up with approval at the young man who entered and stood there looking ill at ease, twisting his cap in his hands.

Here, he thought, was one of the handsomest specimens of humanity he had ever seen, a simple young man with the outward semblance of a Greek god.

The young man said in a low, husky voice, "About the car, sir, we've brought it in. And we've got at the trouble. It's a matter of an hour's work or so."

Poirot said, "What is wrong with it?"

The young man plunged eagerly into technical details. Poirot nodded his head gently, but he was not listening. Perfect physique was a thing he admired greatly. There were, he considered, too many rats in spectacles about. He said to himself approvingly, *Yes, a Greek God—a young shepherd in Arcady.*

The man stopped abruptly. It was then that Hercule Poirot's brows knitted themselves for a second. His first reaction had been esthetic, his second was mental. His eyes narrowed themselves curiously as he looked up.

He said, "I comprehend. Yes, I comprehend." He paused and then added, "My chauffeur, he has already told me that which you have just said."

He saw the flush that came to the other's cheek, saw the fingers grip the cap nervously.

The young man stammered, "Yes—er—yes, sir. I know."

Hercule Poirot went on smoothly: "But you thought that you would also come and tell me yourself?"

"Er—yes, sir, I thought I'd better."

"That," said Hercule Poirot, "was very conscientious of you. Thank you."

There was a faint but unmistakable note of dismissal in the last words but he did not expect the other to go and he was right. The young man did not move.

His fingers moved convulsively, crushing the tweed cap, and he said in a still lower, embarrassed voice:

"Er—excuse me, sir—but it's true, isn't it, that you're the detective gentleman—you're Mr. Hercules Pwarrit?" He said the name carefully.

Poirot said, "That is so."

Red crept up the young man's face.

He said, "I read a piece about you in the paper."

"Yes?"

The boy was now scarlet. There was distress in his eyes—distress and appeal. Hercule Poirot came to his aid.

He said gently, "Yes? What is it you want to ask me?"
The words came with a rush now.

"I'm afraid you may think it's awful cheek of me, sir. But your coming here by chance like this—well, it's too good to be missed. Having read about you and the clever things you've done, anyway, I said as after all I might as well ask you. There's no harm in asking, is there?"

Hercule Poirot shook his head. He said, "You want my help in some way?"

The other nodded. He said, his voice husky and embarrassed, "It's—it's about a young lady. If—if you could find her for me."

"Find her? Has she disappeared, then?"

"That's right, sir."

Hercule Poirot sat up in his chair.

He said sharply, "I could help you, perhaps, yes. But the proper people for you to go to are the police. It is their job and they have far more resources at their disposal than I have."

The boy shuffled his feet.

He said awkwardly, "I couldn't do that, sir. It's not like that at all. It's all rather peculiar, so to speak."

Hercule Poirot stared at him. Then he indicated a chair.
*"Eh bien,* then, sit down—what is your name?"

"Williamson, sir, Ted Williamson."

"Sit down, Ted. And tell me all about it."

"Thank you, sir." He drew forward the chair and sat down carefully on the edge of it. His eyes had still that appealing doglike look.

Hercule Poirot said gently, "Tell me."

Ted Williamson drew a deep breath.

"Well, you see, sir, it was like this. I never saw her but the once. And I don't know her right name nor anything. But it's queer like, the whole thing, and my letter coming back and everything."

"Start," said Hercule Poirot, "at the beginning. Do not hurry yourself. Just tell me everything that occurred."

"Yes, sir. Well, perhaps you know Grasslawn, sir, that big house down by the river past the bridge?"

"I know nothing at all."

"Belongs to Sir George Sanderfield, it does. He uses it in the summertime for week-ends and parties—rather a gay lot he has down as a rule. Actresses and that. Well, it was in last June—and the radio was out of order and they sent me up to see to it."

Poirot nodded.

"So I went along. The gentleman was out on the river with his guests and the cook was out and his manservant had gone along to serve the drinks and all that on the launch. There was only this girl in the house—she was the lady's-maid to one of the guests. She let me in and showed me where the set was, and stayed there while I was working on it. And so we got to talking and all that. Nita her name was, so she told me, and she was lady's-maid to a Russian dancer who was staying there."

"What nationality was she, English?"

"No, sir, she'd be French, I think. She'd a funny sort of accent. But she spoke English all right. She—she was friendly and after a bit I asked her if she could come out that night and go to the pictures, but she said her lady would be needing her. But then she said as how she could get off early in the afternoon because as how they wasn't going to be back off the river till late. So the long and the short of it was that I took the afternoon off without asking (and nearly got the sack for it too) and we went for a walk along by the river."

He paused. A little smile hovered on his lips. His eyes were dreamy.

Poirot said gently, "And she was pretty, yes?"

"She was just the loveliest thing you ever saw. Her hair was like gold—it went up each side like wings—and she had a gay kind of way of tripping along. I—I—well, I fell for her right away, sir. I'm not pretending anything else."

Poirot nodded.

The young man went on: "She said as how her lady would be coming down again in a fortnight and we fixed up to meet again then." He paused. "But she never came. I waited for her at the spot she'd said, but not a sign of her, and at last I made bold to go up to the house and ask for her. The Russian lady was staying there all right and her maid, too, they said. Sent for her, they did, but when she came, why, it wasn't Nita at all! Just a dark, catty-looking girl—a bold lot if there ever was one. Marie, they called her. 'You want to see me?' she says, simpering all over. She must have seen I was took aback. I said was she the Russian lady's-maid and something about her not being the one I'd seen before, and then she laughed and said that the last maid had been sent away sudden. 'Sent away?' I said. 'What for?' She sort of shrugged her shoulders and stretched out her hands. 'How should I know?' she said. 'I was not there.'

"Well, sir, it took me aback. At the moment I couldn't think of anything to say. But afterward I plucked up courage and I got to see this Marie again and asked her to get me Nita's address. I didn't let on to her that I didn't even know Nita's last name. I promised her a present if she did what I asked—she was the kind as wouldn't do anything for you for nothing. Well, she got it all right for me—an address in North London, it was, and I wrote to Nita there —but the letter came back after a bit—sent back through the post office with *no longer at this address* scrawled on it."

Ted Williamson stopped. His eyes, those deep blue steady eyes, looked across at Poirot. He said:

"You see how it is, sir? It's not a case for the police. But I want to find her. And I don't know how to set about it. If—if you could find her for me." His color deepened. "I've—I've a bit put by. I could manage five pounds—or even ten."

Poirot said gently, "We need not discuss the financial side for the moment. First reflect on this point—this girl, this Nita—she knew your name and where you worked?"

"Oh, yes, sir."

"She could have communicated with you if she had wanted to?"

Ted said more slowly, "Yes, sir."

Poirot looked at him thoughtfully.

He murmured, "And you still want very much to find her?"

The color surged up in Ted Williamson's face.

He said, "Yes, I do, and that's that! I want to marry her if she'll have me. If you'll only try and find her for me, sir?"

Hercule Poirot smiled. He said to himself, *"Hair like wings of gold." Yes, I think this is the third Labor of Hercules. If I remember rightly, that happened in Arcady.*

Hercule Poirot looked thoughtfully at the sheet of paper on which Ted Williamson had laboriously inscribed a name and address.

*Miss Valetta, 17 Upper Renfrew Lane, N.15.*

He wondered if he would learn anything at that address. Somehow he fancied not. But it was the only help Ted could give him.

Seventeen Upper Renfrew Lane was a dingy but respectable street. A stout woman with bleary eyes opened the door to Poirot's knock.

"Miss Valetta?"

"Gone away a long time ago, she has."

Poirot advanced a step into the doorway just as the door was about to close.

"You can give me, perhaps, her address?"

"Couldn't say, I'm sure. She didn't leave one."

"When did she go away?"

"Last summer it was."

"Can you tell me exactly when?"

A clinking noise came from Poirot's right hand where two half crowns jostled each other in friendly fashion.

The bleary-eyed woman softened in an almost magical manner. She became graciousness itself.

"Well, I'm sure I'd like to help you, sir. Let me see now. August, no, before that—July—yes, July it must have been. About the third week in July. Went off in a hurry, she did. Back to Italy, I believe."

"She was an Italian, then?"

"That's right, sir."

"And she was at one time lady's-maid to a Russian dancer, was she not?"

"That's right. Madame Semoulina or some such name.

Danced at the Thespian in this Bally everyone's so wild about. One of the stars, she was."

Poirot said, "Do you know why Miss Valetta left her post?"

The woman hesitated a moment before saying, "I couldn't say, I'm sure."

"She was dismissed, was she not?"

"Well—I believe there was a bit of a dust up! But mind you, Miss Valetta didn't let on much about it. She wasn't one to give things away. But she looked wild about it. Wicked temper she had—real Eyetalian—her black eyes all snapping and looking as if she'd like to put a knife into you. I wouldn't have crossed her when she was in one of her moods!"

"And you are quite sure you do not know Miss Valetta's present address?"

The half crowns clinked again encouragingly.

The answer rang true enough: "I wish I did, sir. I'd be only too glad to tell you. But there—she went off in a hurry and there it is!"

Poirot said to himself thoughtfully, *Yes, there it is.*

Ambrose Vandel, diverted from his enthusiastic account of the décor he was designing for a forthcoming ballet, supplied information easily enough.

"Sanderfield? George Sanderfield? Nasty fellow. Rolling in money but they say he's a crook. Dark horse! Affair with a dancer? But of course, my dear—with Katrina. Katrina Samoushenka. You must have seen her? Oh, my dear —too delicious. Lovely technique. *The Swan of Tuolela*— you must have seen *that*? My décor! And the other thing of Debussy, or is it Mannine, *'La Biche au Bois'*? She danced it with Michael Novgin. He's so marvelous, isn't he?"

"And she was a friend of Sir George Sanderfield?"

"Yes, she used to week-end with him at his house on the river. Marvelous parties I believe he gives."

"Would it be possible, *mon cher,* for you to introduce me to Mademoiselle Samoushenka?"

"But, my dear, she isn't here any longer. She went to

Paris or somewhere quite suddenly. You know, they do say
that she was a Russian spy or something—not that I believe it myself—you know people love saying things like
that. Katrina always pretended that she was a White Russian—her father was a prince or a grand duke—the usual
thing! It goes down so much better." Vandel paused and
returned to the absorbing subject of himself. "Now as I
was saying, if you want to get the spirit of Bathsheba
you've got to steep yourself in the Semitic tradition. I express it by—"

He continued happily.


The interview that Hercule Poirot managed to arrange
with Sir George Sanderfield did not start too auspiciously.

The "dark horse," as Ambrose Vandel had called him,
was slightly ill at ease. Sir George was a short square man
with dark coarse hair and a roll of fat in his neck.

He said, "Well, M. Poirot, what can I do for you? Er—
we haven't met before, I think?"

"No, we have not met."

"Well, what is it? I confess, I'm quite curious."

"Oh, it is very simple—a mere matter of information."

The other gave an uneasy laugh.

"Want me to give you some inside dope, eh? Didn't
know you were interested in finance."

"It is not a matter of *les affaires*. It is a question of a
certain lady."

"Oh, a woman." Sir George Sanderfield leaned back in
his armchair. He seemed to relax. His voice held an easier
note.

Poirot said, "You were acquainted, I think, with Mademoiselle Katrina Samoushenka?"

Sanderfield laughed. "Yes. An enchanting creature. Pity
she's left London."

"Why did she leave London?"

"My dear fellow, I don't know. Row with the manage-
ment, I believe. She was temperamental, you know—very
Russian in her moods. I'm sorry that I can't help you but I
haven't the least idea where she is now. I haven't kept up
with her at all."

There was a note of dismissal in his voice as he rose to his feet.

Poirot said, "But it is not Mademoiselle Samoushenka that I am anxious to trace."

"It isn't?"

"No, it is a question of her maid."

"Her maid?"

Sanderfield stared at him.

Poirot said, "Do you—perhaps—remember her maid?"

All Sanderfield's uneasiness had returned.

He said awkwardly, "No, how should I? I remember she had one, of course. Bit of a bad lot, too, I should say. Sneaking, prying sort of girl. If I were you I shouldn't put any faith in a word that girl says. She's the kind of girl who's a born liar."

Poirot murmured, "So actually you remember quite a lot about her?"

Sanderfield said hastily, "Just an impression, that's all. Don't even remember her name. Let me see, Marie something or other—no, I'm afraid I can't help you to get hold of her. Sorry."

Poirot said gently, "I have already got the name of Marie Hellin from the Thespian Theater—and her address. But I am speaking, Sir George, of the maid who was with Mademoiselle Samoushenka before Marie Hellin. I am speaking of Nita Valetta."

Sanderfield stared.

He said, "Don't remember her at all. Marie's the only one *I* remember. Little dark girl with a nasty look in her eye."

Poirot said, "The girl I mean was at your house, Grasslawn, last July."

Sanderfield said sulkily, "Well, all I can say is I don't remember her. Don't believe she had a maid with her. I think you're making a mistake."

Hercule Poirot shook his head. He did not think he was making a mistake.

Marie Hellin looked swiftly at Poirot out of small intelligent eyes and as swiftly away again. She said in smooth, even tones:

"But I remember perfectly, Monsieur. I was engaged by Madame Samoushenka the last week in July. Her former maid had departed in a hurry."

"Did you ever hear why that maid left?"

"She went—suddenly—that is all I know! It may have been illness—something of that kind. Madame did not say."

Poirot said, "Did you find your mistress easy to get on with?"

The girl shrugged her shoulders.

"She had great moods. She wept and laughed in turns. Sometimes she was so despondent she would not speak or eat. Sometimes she was wildly gay. They are like that, these dancers. It is temperament."

"And Sir George?"

The girl looked up alertly. An unpleasant gleam came into her eyes.

"Ah, Sir George Sanderfield? You would like to know about him? Perhaps it is that that you really want to know? The other was only an excuse, eh? Ah, Sir George, I could tell you some curious things about him, I could tell you—"

Poirot interrupted. "It is not necessary."

She stared at him, her mouth open. Angry disappointment showed in her eyes.


"I always say you know everything, Alexis Pavlovitch."

Hercule Poirot murmured the words with his most flattering intonation.

He was reflecting to himself that this third Labor of Hercules had necessitated more traveling and more interviews than could have been imagined possible. This little matter of a missing lady's-maid was proving one of the longest and most difficult problems he had ever tackled. Every clue, when examined, led exactly nowhere.

It had brought him this evening to the Samovar Restaurant in Paris whose proprietor, Count Alexis Pavlovitch, prided himself on knowing everything that went on in the artistic world.

He nodded now complacently.

"Yes, yes, my friend, *I* know—I always know. You ask me where she is gone—the little Samoushenka, the exquisite dancer? Ah! she was the real thing, that little one." He kissed his finger tips. "What fire—what abandon! She would have gone far—she would have been the Première Ballerina of her day—and then suddenly it all ends—she creeps away—to the end of the world—and soon, ah! so soon, they forget her."

"Where is she then?" demanded Poirot.

"In Switzerland. At Vagray les Alpes. It is there that they go, those who have the little dry cough and who grow thinner and thinner. She will die, yes, she will die! She has a fatalistic nature. She will surely die."

Poirot coughed to break the tragic spell. He wanted information.

"You do not, by chance, remember a maid she had? A maid called Nita Valetta?"

"Valetta? Valetta I remember seeing a maid once—at the station when I was seeing Katrina off to London. She was an Italian from Pisa, was she not? Yes, I am sure she was an Italian who came from Pisa."

Hercule Poirot groaned.

"In that case," he said, "I must now journey to Pisa."

Hercule Poirot stood in the Campo Santo at Pisa and looked down on a grave.

So it was here that his quest had come to an end—here by this humble mound of earth. Underneath it lay the joyous creature who had stirred the heart and imagination of a simple English mechanic.

Was this perhaps the best end to that sudden, strange romance? Now the girl would live always in the young man's memory as he had seen her for those few enchanted hours of a July afternoon. The clash of opposing nationalities, of different standards, the pain of disillusionment, all that was ruled out forever.

Hercule Poirot shook his head sadly. His mind went back to his conversation with the Valetta family. The mother, with her broad peasant face; the upright, grief-stricken father; the dark, hard-lipped sister.

"It was sudden, Signore, it was very sudden. Though for many years she had had pains on and off. The doctor gave us no choice—he said there must be an operation immediately for the appendicitis. He took her off to the hospital then and there. *Si, si,* it was under the anesthetic she died. She never recovered consciousness."

The mother sniffed, murmuring, "Bianca was always such a clever girl. It is terrible that she should have died so young."

Hercule Poirot repeated to himself, *She died young.*

That was the message he must take back to the young man who had asked for his help so confidingly.

*She is not for you, my friend. She died young.*

His quest had ended—here where the Leaning Tower was silhouetted against the sky and the first spring flowers were showing pale and creamy with their promise of life and joy to come.

Was it the stirring of spring that made him feel so rebelliously disinclined to accept this final verdict? Or was it something else? Something stirring at the back of his brain —words—a phrase—a name? Did not the whole thing finish too neatly—dovetail too obviously?

Hercule Poirot sighed. He must take one more journey to put things beyond any possible doubt. He must go to Vagray les Alpes.

Here, he thought, really was the world's end. This shelf of snow—these scattered huts and shelters in each of which lay a motionless human being fighting an insidious death.

So he came at last to Katrina Samoushenka. When he saw her, lying there with hollow cheeks in each of which was a vivid red stain, and long, thin, emaciated hands stretched out on the coverlet, a memory stirred him. He had not remembered her name, but he had seen her dance —had been carried away and fascinated by the supreme art that can make you forget art.

He remembered Michael Novgin, the Hunter, leaping and

twirling in that outrageous and fantastic forest that the brain of Ambrose Vandel had conceived. And he remembered the lovely flying Hind, eternally pursued, eternally desirable—a golden beautiful creature with horns on her head and twinkling bronze feet. He remembered her final collapse, shot and wounded, and Michael Novgin standing bewildered, with the body of the slain Deer in his arms.

Katrina Samoushenka was looking at him with faint curiosity.

She said, "I have never seen you before, have I? What is it you want of me?"

Hercule Poirot made her a little bow.

"First, I wish to thank you—for your art which made for me once an evening of beauty."

She smiled faintly.

"But also I am here on a matter of business. I have been looking, for a long time for a certain maid of yours—her name was Nita."

"Nita?"

She stared at him. Her eyes were large and startled.

She said, "What do you know about—Nita?"

"I will tell you."

He told her of the evening when his car had broken down and of Ted Williamson standing there twisting his cap between his fingers and stammering out his love and his pain. She listened with close attention.

She said when he had finished, "It is touching, that—yes, it is touching."

Hercule Poirot nodded.

"Yes," he said. "It is a tale of Arcady, is it not? What can you tell me, Madame, of this girl?"

Katrina Samoushenka sighed.

"I had a maid—Juanita. She was lovely, yes—gay, light of heart. It happened to her what happens so often to those the gods favor. She died young."

They had been Poirot's own words—final words—irrevocable words. Now he heard them again—and yet he persisted.

He asked, "She is dead?"

"Yes, she is dead."

Hercule Poirot was silent a minute, then he said:

"Yet there is one thing I do not quite understand. I asked Sir George Sanderfield about this maid of yours and he seemed afraid. Why was that?"

There was a faint expression of disgust on the dancer's face.

"You just said a maid of mine. He thought you meant Marie—the girl who came to me after Juanita left. She tried to blackmail him, I believe, over something that she found out about him. She was an odious girl—inquisitive, always prying into letters and locked drawers."

Poirot murmured, "Then that explains that."

He paused a minute, then he went on, still persistent:

"Juanita's other name was Valetta and she died of an operation for appendicitis in Pisa. Is that correct?"

He noted the hesitation, hardly perceptible but nevertheless there, before the dancer bowed her head.

"Yes, that is right."

Poirot said meditatively, "And yet—there is still a little point—her people spoke of her, not as Juanita but as *Bianca*."

Katrina shrugged her thin shoulders.

She said, "Bianca—Juanita, does it matter? I suppose her real name is Bianca but she thought the name of Juanita was more romantic and so chose to call herself by it."

"Ah, you think that?" He paused and then, his voice changing, he said, "For me, there is another explanation."

"What is it?"

Poirot leaned forward.

He said, "The girl that Ted Williamson saw had hair that he described as being like wings of gold."

He leaned still a little farther forward. His finger just touched the two springing waves of Katrina's hair.

"Wings of gold, horns of gold? It is as you look at it, it is whether one sees you as devil or as angel! You might be either. Or are they perhaps only the golden horns of the stricken deer?"

Katrina murmured, *"The stricken deer . . ."* and her voice was the voice of one without hope.

Poirot said, "All along Ted Williamson's description

has worried me—it brought something to my mind—that something was you, dancing on your twinkling bronze feet through the forest. Shall I tell you what I think, Mademoiselle? I think there was a week when you had no maid, when you went down alone to Grasslawn, for Bianca Valetta had returned to Italy and you had not yet engaged a new maid. Already you were feeling the illness which has since overtaken you, and you stayed in the house one day when the others went on an all-day excursion on the river. There was a ring at the door and you went to it and you saw—shall I tell you what you saw? You saw a young man who was as simple as a child and as handsome as a god! And you invented for him a girl—not Juanita—but incognita—and for a few hours you walked with him in Arcady."

There was a long pause. Then Katrina said in a low hoarse voice:

"In one thing at least I have told you the truth. I have given you the right end of the story. Nita will die young."

*"Ah, non!"* Hercule Poirot was transformed. He struck his hand on the table. He was suddenly prosaic, mundane, practical.

He said, "It is quite unnecessary! You need not die. You can fight for your life, can you not, as well as another?"

She shook her head—sadly, hopelessly.

"What life is there for me?"

"Not the life of the stage, *bien entendu!* But think, there is another life. Come now, Mademoiselle, be honest, was your father really a prince or a grand duke, or even a general?"

She laughed suddenly.

She said, "He drove a lorry."

"Very good! And why should you not be the wife of a garage hand in a country village? And have children as beautiful as gods, and with feet, perhaps, that will dance as you once danced."

Katrina caught her breath.

"But the whole idea is fantastic!"

"Nevertheless," said Hercule Poirot with great self-satisfaction, "I believe it is going to come true!"

# THE ADVENTURE OF JOHNNIE WAVERLY

"YOU CAN understand the feelings of a mother," said Mrs. Waverly for perhaps the sixth time.

She looked appealingly at Poirot. My little friend, always sympathetic to motherhood in distress, gesticulated reassuringly.

"But yes, but yes, I comprehend perfectly. Have faith in Papa Poirot."

"The police—" began Mr. Waverly.

His wife waved the interruption aside.

"I won't have anything more to do with the police. We trusted to them and look what happened! But I'd heard so much of M. Poirot and the wonderful things he'd done, that I felt he might possibly be able to help us. A mother's feelings—"

Poirot hastily stemmed the reiteration with an eloquent gesture. Mrs. Waverly's emotion was obviously genuine, but it assorted strangely with her shrewd, rather hard type of countenance. When I heard later that she was the daughter of a prominent steel manufacturer of Birmingham who had worked his way up in the world from an office boy to his present eminence, I realised that she had inherited many of the paternal qualities.

Mr. Waverly was a big florid jovial looking man. He stood with his legs straddled wide apart and looked the type of the country squire.

"I suppose you know all about this business, M. Poirot?"

The question was almost superfluous. For some days past the paper had been full of the sensational kidnapping of little Johnnie Waverly, the three-year-old son and heir of Marcus Waverly, Esq., of Waverly Court, Surrey, one of the oldest families in England.

"The main facts I know, of course, but recount to me the whole story, Monsieur, I beg of you. And in detail if you please."

"Well, I suppose the beginning of the whole thing was about ten days ago when I got an anonymous letter— beastly things, anyway—that I couldn't make head or tail of. The writer had the impudence to demand that I should pay him twenty-five thousand pounds—twenty-five thousand pounds, M. Poirot!—Failing my agreement, he threatened to kidnap Johnnie. Of course I threw the thing into the waste paper basket without more ado. Thought it was some silly joke. Five days later I got another letter. 'Unless you pay, your son will be kidnapped on the twenty-ninth.' That was on the twenty-seventh. Ada was worried, but I couldn't bring myself to treat the matter seriously. After all, we're in England. Nobody goes about kidnapping children and holding them up to ransom."

"It is not a common practice, certainly," said Poirot. "Proceed, Monsieur."

"Well, Ada gave me no peace, so—feeling a bit of a fool —I laid the matter before Scotland Yard. They didn't seem to take the thing very seriously—inclined to my view that it was some silly joke. On the 28th I got a third letter. 'You have not paid. Your son will be taken from you at twelve o'clock noon to-morrow, the twenty-ninth. It will cost you fifty thousand pounds to recover him.' Up I drove to Scotland Yard again. This time they were more impressed. They inclined to the view that the letters were written by a lunatic, and that in all probability an attempt of some kind would be made at the hour stated. They assured me that they would take all due precautions. Inspector McNeil and a sufficient force would come down to Waverly on the morrow and take charge.

"I went home much relieved in my mind. Yet we already had the feeling of being in a state of siege. I gave orders that no stranger was to be admitted, and that no one was to leave the house. The evening passed off without any untoward incident, but on the following morning my wife

was seriously unwell. Alarmed by her condition, I sent for
Doctor Dakers. Her symptoms appeared to puzzle him.
Whilst hesitating to suggest that she had been poisoned, I
could see that that was what was in his mind. There was no
danger, he assured me, but it would be a day or two before
she would be able to get about again. Returning to my own
room, I was startled and amazed to find a note pinned to
my pillow. It was in the same handwriting as the others
and contained just three words: 'At twelve o'clock.'

"I admit, M. Poirot, that then I saw red! Someone in
the house was in this—one of the servants. I had them all
up, blackguarded them right and left. They never split on
each other; it was Miss Collins, my wife's companion,
who informed me that she had seen Johnnie's nurse slip
down the drive early that morning. I taxed her with it, and
she broke down. She had left the child with the nursery
maid and stolen out to meet a friend of hers—a man! Pretty goings on! She denied having pinned the note to my pillow—she may have been speaking the truth, I don't know.
I felt I couldn't take the risk of the child's own nurse being
in the plot. One of the servants was implicated—of that I
was sure. Finally I lost my temper and sacked the whole
bunch, nurse and all. I gave them an hour to pack their
boxes and get out of the house.

Mr. Waverly's red face was quite two shades redder as
he remembered his just wrath.

"Was not that a little injudicious, Monsieur?" suggested
Poirot. "For all you know, you might have been playing
into the enemy's hands."

Mr. Waverly stared at him.

"I don't see that. Send the whole lot packing, that was
my idea. I wired to London for a fresh lot to be sent down
that evening. In the meantime, there'd be only people I
could trust in the house, my wife's secretary, Miss Collins,
and Tredwell, the butler, who had been with me since I
was a boy."

"And this Miss Collins, how long has she been with
you?"

"Just a year," said Mrs. Waverly. "She has been invaluable to me as a secretary companion, and is also a very efficient housekeeper."

"The nurse?"

"She has been with me six months. She came to me with excellent references. All the same I never really liked her, although Johnnie was quite devoted to her."

"Still, I gather she had already left when the catastrophe occurred. Perhaps, Monsieur Waverly, you will be so kind as to continue."

Mr. Waverly resumed his narrative.

"Inspector McNeil arrived about 10:30. The servants had all left then. He declared himself quite satisfied with the internal arrangements. He had various men posted in the Park outside, guarding all the approaches to the house, and he assured me that if the whole thing were not a hoax, we should undoubtedly catch my mysterious correspondent.

"I had Johnnie with me, and he and I and the Inspector went together into a room we call the Council Chamber. The Inspector locked the door. There is a big grandfather clock there, and as the hands drew near to twelve I don't mind confessing that I was as nervous as a cat. There was a whirring sound, and the clock began to strike. I clutched Johnnie. I had a feeling a man might drop from the skies. The last stroke sounded, and as it did so, there was a great commotion outside—shouting and running. The Inspector flung up the window and a constable came running up.

" 'We've got him, sir,' he panted. 'He was sneaking up through the bushes. He's got a whole dope outfit on him.'

"We hurried out on the terrace where two constables were holding a ruffianly looking fellow in shabby clothes, who was twisting and turning in a vain endeavour to escape. One of the policemen held out an unrolled parcel which they had wrested from their captive. It contained a pad of cotton wool and a bottle of chloroform. It made my blood boil to see it. There was a note, too, addressed to me. I tore it open. It bore the following words: 'You should have paid up. To ransom your son will now cost you fifty thousand. In spite of all your precautions he has been abducted at twelve o'clock on the 29th as I said.'

"I gave a great laugh, the laugh of relief, but as I did so I heard the hum of a motor and a shout. I turned my head. Racing down the drive toward the South Lodge at a furious speed was a low, long grey car. It was the man who drove it who had shouted, but that was not what gave me a shock of horror. It was the sight of Johnnie's flaxen curls. The child was in the car beside him.

"The Inspector let go a shout.

" 'The child was here not a minute ago,' he cried. His eyes swept over us. We were all there, myself, Tredwell, Miss Collins. 'When did you see him last, Mr. Waverly?'

"I cast my mind back, trying to remember. When the constable had called us, I had run out with the Inspector, forgetting all about Johnnie.

"And then there came a sound that startled us, the chiming of a church clock from the village. With an exclamation the Inspector pulled out his watch. It was exactly twelve o'clock. With one common accord we ran to the Council Chamber, the clock there marked the hour as ten minutes past. Someone must have deliberately tampered with it, for I have never known it gain or lose before. It is a perfect timekeeper."

Mr. Waverly paused. Poirot smiled to himself and straightened a little mat which the anxious father had pushed askew.

"A pleasing little problem, obscure and charming," murmured Poirot. "I will investigate it for you with pleasure. Truly it was planned *à merveille*."

Mrs. Waverly looked at him reproachfully.

"But my boy," she wailed.

Poirot hastily composed his face and looked the picture of earnest sympathy again.

"He is safe, Madame, he is unharmed. Rest assured, these miscreants will take the greatest care of him. Is he not to them the turkey—no, the goose—that lays the golden eggs?"

"M. Poirot, I'm sure there's only one thing to be done—pay up. I was all against it at first—but now! A mother's feelings—"

"But we have interrupted Monsieur in his history," cried Poirot hastily.

"I expect you know the rest pretty well from the papers," said Mr. Waverly. "Of course, Inspector McNeil got on to the telephone immediately. A description of the car and the man was circulated all round, and it looked at first as though everything was going to turn out all right. A car, answering to the description, with a man and a small boy, had passed through various villages, apparently making for London. At one place they had stopped, and it was noticed that the child was crying and obviously afraid of his companion. When Inspector McNeil announced that the car had been spotted and the man and boy detained, I was almost ill with relief. You know the sequel. The boy was not Johnnie, and the man was an ardent motorist, fond of children, who had picked up a small child playing in the streets of Edenswell, a village about fifteen miles from us, and was kindly giving him a ride. Thanks to the cocksure blundering of the police, all traces have disappeared. Had they not persistently followed the wrong car, they might by now have found the boy."

"Calm yourself, Monsieur. The police are a brave and intelligent force of men. Their mistake was a very natural one. And altogether it was a clever scheme. As to the man they caught in the grounds, I understand that his defence has consisted all along of a persistent denial. He declares that the note and parcel were given to him to deliver at Waverly Court. The man who gave them to him handed him a ten shilling note and promised him another if it were delivered at exactly ten minutes to twelve. He was to approach the house through the grounds and knock at the side door."

"I don't believe a word of it," declared Mrs. Waverly hotly. "It's all a parcel of lies."

"*En verité*, it is a thin story," said Poirot reflectively. "But so far they have not shaken it. I understand also that he made a certain accusation?"

His glance interrogated Mr. Waverly. The latter got rather red again.

"The fellow had the impertinence to pretend that he recognized in Tredwell the man who gave him the parcel. 'Only the bloke has shaved off his moustache.' Tredwell, who was born on the estate!"

Poirot smiled a little at the country gentleman's indignation.

"Yet you yourself suspect an inmate of the house to have been accessory to the abduction."

"Yes, but not Tredwell."

"And you, Madame?" asked Poirot, suddenly turning to her.

"It could not have been Tredwell who gave this tramp the letter and parcel—if anybody ever did, which I don't believe— It was given him at ten o'clock, he says. At ten o'clock, Tredwell was with my husband in the smoking room."

"Were you able to see the face of the man in the car, Monsieur? Did it resemble that of Tredwell in any way?"

"It was too far away for me to see his face."

"Has Tredwell a brother, do you know?"

"He had several, but they are all dead. The last one was killed in the war."

"I am not yet clear as to the grounds of Waverly Court. The car was heading for the South Lodge. Is there another entrance?"

"Yes, what we call the East Lodge. It can be seen from the other side of the house."

"It seems to me strange that nobody saw the car entering the grounds."

"There is a right of way through, and access to a small chapel. A good many cars pass through. The man must have stopped the car in a convenient place, and run up to the house just as the alarm was given and attention attracted elsewhere."

"Unless he was already inside the house," mused Poirot. "Is there any place where he could have hidden?"

"Well, we certainly didn't make a thorough search of the house beforehand. There seemed no need. I suppose he might have hidden himself somewhere, but who would have let him in?"

"We shall come to that later. One thing at a time—let us be methodical. There is no special hiding place in the house? Waverly Court is an old place, and there are sometimes 'Priests' Holes,' as they call them."

"By Gad, there *is* a Priest's Hole. It opens from one of the panels in the hall."

"Near the Council Chamber?"

"Just outside the door."

*"Voilà!"*

"But nobody knows of its existence except my wife and myself."

"Tredwell?"

"Well—he might have heard of it."

"Miss Collins?"

"I have never mentioned it to her."

Poirot reflected for a minute.

"Well, Monsieur, the next thing is for me to come down to Waverly Court. If I arrive this afternoon, will it suit you?"

"Oh! as soon as possible, please, Monsieur Poirot," cried Mrs. Waverly. "Read this once more."

She thrust into his hands the last missive from the enemy which had reached the Waverlys this morning and which had sent her post haste to Poirot. It gave clever and explicit directions for the paying over of the money, and ended with a threat that the boy's life would pay for any treachery. It was clear that a love of money warred with the essential mother love of Mrs. Waverly, and that the latter was at last gaining the day.

Poirot detained Mrs. Waverly for a minute behind her husband.

"Madame, the truth, if you please. Do you share your husband's faith in the butler, Tredwell?"

"I have nothing against him, Monsieur Poirot, I cannot see how he can have been concerned in this, but—well, I have never liked him—never!"

"One other thing, Madame, can you give me the address of the child's nurse?"

"149 Netherall Road, Hammersmith. You don't imagine—"

"Never do I imagine. Only—I employ the little grey cells. And sometimes, just sometimes, I have a little idea."

Poirot came back to me as the door closed.

"So Madame has never liked the butler. It is interesting, that, eh, Hastings?"

I refused to be drawn. Poirot has deceived me so often that I now go warily. There is always a catch somewhere.

After completing an elaborate toilet, we set off for Netherall Road. We were fortunate enough to find Miss Jessie Withers at home. She was a pleasant faced woman of thirty-five, capable and superior. I could not believe that she could be mixed up in the affair. She was bitterly resentful of the way she had been dismissed, but admitted that she had been in the wrong. She was engaged to be married to a painter and decorator who happened to be in the neighbourhood, and she had run out to meet him. The thing seemed natural enough. I could not quite understand Poirot. All his questions seemed to me quite irrelevant. They were concerned mainly with the daily routine of her life at Waverly Court. I was frankly bored, and glad when Poirot took his departure.

"Kidnapping is an easy job, *mon ami*," he observed, as he hailed a taxi in the Hammersmith Road and ordered it to drive to Waterloo. "That child could have been abducted with the greatest ease any day for the last three years."

"I don't see that that advances us much," I remarked coldly.

"*Au contraire*, it advances us enormously, but enormously! If you must wear a tie pin, Hastings, at least let it be in the exact centre of your tie. At present it is at least a sixteenth of an inch too much to the right."

Waverly Court was a fine old place and had recently been restored with taste and care. Mr. Waverly showed us the Council Chamber, the terrace and all the various spots connected with the case. Finally, at Poirot's request, he pressed a spring in the wall, a panel slid aside, and a short passage led us into the "Priest's Hole."

"You see," said Waverly. "There is nothing here."

The tiny room was bare enough, there was not even the

mark of a footstep on the floor. I joined Poirot where he was bending attentively over a mark in the corner.

"What do you make of this, my friend?"

There were four imprints close together.

"A dog," I cried.

"A very small dog, Hastings."

"A pom."

"Smaller than a pom."

"A gryphon?" I suggested doubtfully.

"Smaller even than a gryphon. A species unknown to the Kennel Club."

I looked at him. His face was alight with excitement and satisfaction.

"I was right," he murmured. "I knew I was right. Come, Hastings."

As we stepped out into the hall and the panel closed behind us, a young lady came out of a door farther down the passage. Mr. Waverly presented her to us.

"Miss Collins."

Miss Collins was about thirty years of age, brisk and alert in manner. She had fair, rather dull hair, and wore pince-nez.

At Poirot's request, we passed into a small morning room and he questioned her closely as to the servants and particularly as to Tredwell. She admitted that she did not like the butler.

"He gives himself airs," she explained.

They then went into the question of the food eaten by Mrs. Waverly on the night of the 28th. Miss Collins declared that she had partaken of the same dishes upstairs in her sitting room and had felt no ill effects. As she was departing I nudged Poirot.

"The dog," I whispered.

"Ah! yes, the dog!" He smiled broadly. "Is there a dog kept here by any chance, Mademoiselle?"

"There are two retrievers in the kennels outside."

"No, I mean a small dog, a toy dog."

"No—nothing of the kind."

Poirot permitted her to depart. Then, pressing the bell, he remarked to me:

"She lies, that Mademoiselle Collins. Possibly I should also in her place. Now for the butler."

Tredwell was a dignified individual. He told his story with perfect aplomb, and it was essentially the same as that of Mr. Waverly. He admitted that he knew the secret of the Priest's Hole.

When he finally withdrew, pontifical to the last, I met Poirot's quizzical eyes.

"What do you make of it all, Hastings?"

"What do you?" I parried.

"How cautious you become. Never, will the grey cells function unless you stimulate them. Ah! but I will not tease you! Let us make our deductions together. What points strike us specially as being difficult?"

"There is one thing that strikes me," I said. "Why did the man who kidnapped the child go out by the South Lodge instead of by the East Lodge where no one would see him?"

"That is a very good point, Hastings, an excellent one. I will match it with another. Why warn the Waverlys beforehand? Why not simply kidnap the child and hold him to ransom?"

"Because they hoped to get the money without being forced to action."

"Surely it was very unlikely that the money would be paid on a mere threat?"

"Also they wanted to focus attention on 12 o'clock, so that when the tramp man was seized, the other could emerge from his hiding place and get away with the child unnoticed."

"That does not alter the fact that they were making a thing difficult that was perfectly easy. If they do not specify a time or date, nothing would be easier than to wait their chance, and carry off the child in a motor one day when he is out with his nurse."

"Ye—es," I admitted doubtfully.

"In fact, there is a deliberate playing of the farce! Now let us approach the question from another side. Everything goes to show that there was an accomplice inside the house. Point No. 1, the mysterious poisoning of Mrs. Waverly. Point No. 2, the letter pinned to the pillow. Point No. 3, the putting on of the clock ten minutes—all inside jobs. And an additional fact that you may not have noticed. There was no dust in the Priest's Hole. It had been swept out with a broom.

"Now then, we have four people in the house. We can exclude the nurse, since she could not have swept out the Priest's Hole, though she could have attended to the other three points. Four people. Mr. and Mrs. Waverly, Tredwell, the butler, and Miss Collins. We will take Miss Collins first. We have nothing much against her, except that we know very little about her, that she is obviously an intelligent young woman, and that she has only been here a year."

"She lied about the dog, you said," I reminded him.

"Ah! yes, the dog," Poirot gave a peculiar smile. "Now let us pass to Tredwell. There are several suspicious facts against him. For one thing, the tramp declares that it was Tredwell who gave him the parcel in the village."

"But Tredwell can prove an alibi on that point."

"Even then, he could have poisoned Mrs. Waverly, pinned the note to the pillow, put on the clock and swept out the Priest's Hole. On the other hand, he has been born and bred in the service of the Waverlys. It seems unlikely in the last degree that he should connive at the abduction of the son of the house. It is not in the picture!"

"Well, then?"

"We must proceed logically—however absurd it may seem. We will briefly consider Mrs. Waverly. But she is rich, the money is hers. It is her money which has restored this impoverished estate. There would be no reason for her to kidnap her son and pay over her money to herself. Her husband, now, is in a different position. He has a rich wife. It is not the same thing as being rich himself—in fact I have a little idea that the lady is not very fond of parting with her money, except on a very good pretext. But Mr. Waverly, you can see at once, he is *bon viveur*."

"Impossible," I spluttered.

"Not at all. Who sends away the servants? Mr. Waverly. He can write the notes, drug his wife, put on the hands of the clock and establish an excellent alibi for his faithful retainer Tredwell. Tredwell has never liked Mrs. Waverly. He is devoted to his master, and is willing to obey his orders implicitly. There were three of them in it. Waverly, Tredwell, and some friend of Waverly. That is the mistake the police made, they made no further inquiries about the man who drove the grey car with the wrong child in it. He was the third man. He picks up a child in a village near by, a boy with flaxen curls. He drives in through the East Lodge and passes out through the South Lodge just at the right moment, waving his hand and shouting. They cannot see his face or the number of the car, so obviously they cannot see the child's face either. Then he lays a false trail to London. In the meantime, Tredwell has done his part in arranging for the parcel and note to be delivered by a rough looking gentleman. His master can provide an alibi in the unlikely case of the man recognizing him, in spite of the false moustache he wore. As for Mr. Waverly, as soon as the hullabaloo occurs outside, and the Inspector rushes out, he quickly hides the child in the Priest's Hole, and follows him out. Later in the day, when the Inspector is gone and Miss Collins is out of the way, it will be easy enough to drive him off to some safe place in his own car."

"But what about the dog?" I asked. "And Miss Collins lying?"

"That was my little joke. I asked her if there were any toy dogs in the house, and she said no—but doubtless there are some—in the nursery! You see, Mr. Waverly placed some toys in the Priest's Hole to keep Johnnie amused and quiet."

"M. Poirot." Mr. Waverly entered the room. "Have you discovered anything? Have you any clue to where the boy has been taken?"

Poirot handed him a piece of paper.

"Here is the address."

"But this is a blank sheet."

"Because I am waiting for you to write it down for me."

"What the—" Mr. Waverly's face turned purple.

"I know everything, Monsieur. I give you twenty-four hours to return the boy. Your ingenuity will be equal to the task of explaining his reappearance. Otherwise, Mrs. Waverly will be informed of the exact sequence of events."

Mr. Waverly sank down in a chair and buried his face in his hands.

"He is with my old nurse, ten miles away. He is happy and well cared for."

"I have no doubt of that. If I did not believe you to be a good father at heart, I should not be willing to give you another chance."

"The scandal—"

"Exactly. Your name is an old and honored one. Do not jeopardize it again. Good evening, Mr. Waverly. Ah! by the way, one word of advice. Always sweep in the corners!"

# WHERE THERE'S A WILL

"ABOVE ALL, avoid worry and excitement," said Dr. Meynell, in the comfortable fashion affected by doctors.

Mrs. Harter, as is often the case with people hearing these soothing but meaningless words, seemed more doubtful than relieved.

"There is a certain cardiac weakness," continued the doctor fluently, "But nothing to be alarmed about. I can assure you of that. All the same," he added, "it might be as well to have an elevator installed. Eh? What about it?"

Mrs. Harter looked worried.

Dr. Meynell, on the contrary, looked pleased with himself. The reason he liked attending rich patients rather than poor ones was that he could exercise his active imagination in prescribing for their ailments.

"Yes, an elevator," said Dr. Meynell trying to think of something else even more dashing—and failing. "Then we shall avoid all undue exertion. Daily exercise on the level on a fine day, but avoid walking up hills. And, above all, plenty of distraction for the mind. Don't dwell on your health."

To the old lady's nephew, Charles Ridgeway, the doctor was slightly more explicit.

"Do not misunderstand me," he said. "Your aunt may live for years, probably will. At the same time, shock or overexertion might carry her off like that!" He snapped his fingers. "She must lead a very quiet life. No exertion. No fatigue. But, of course, she must not be allowed to brood. She must be kept cheerful and the mind well distracted."

"Distracted," said Charles Ridgeway thoughtfully.

Charles was a thoughtful young man. He was also a young man who believed in furthering his own inclinations whenever possible.

That evening he suggested the installation of a radio set.

Mrs. Harter, already seriously upset at the thought of the elevator, was disturbed and unwilling. Charles was persuasive.

"I do not know that I care for these new-fangled things." said Mrs. Harter piteously. "The waves, you know —the electric waves. They might affect me."

Charles, in a superior and kindly fashion, pointed out the futility of this idea.

Mrs. Harter, whose knowledge of the subject was of the vaguest but who was tenacious of her own opinion, remained unconvinced.

"All that electricity," she murmured timorously. "You may say what you like, Charles, but some people are affected by electricity. I always have a terrible headache before a thunderstorm. I know that." She nodded her head triumphantly.

Charles was a patient young man. He was also persistent.

"My dear Aunt Mary," he said, "let me make the thing clear to you."

He was something of an authority on the subject. He delivered quite a lecture on the theme; warming to his task, he spoke of tubes, of high frequency and low frequency, of amplification and of condensers.

Mrs. Harter, submerged in a sea of words that she did not understand, surrendered.

"Of course, Charles," she murmured, "if you really think—"

"My dear Aunt Mary," said Charles enthusiastically, "it is the very thing for you, to keep you from moping and all that."

The elevator prescribed by Dr. Meynell was installed shortly afterward and was very nearly the death of Mrs. Harter since, like many other old ladies, she had a rooted objection to strange men in the house. She suspected them, one and all, of having designs on her old silver.

After the elevator the radio arrived. Mrs. Harter was left to contemplate the, to her, repellent object—a large, ungainly-looking box, studded with knobs.

It took all Charles's enthusiasm to reconcile her to it, but Charles was in his element, turning knobs and discoursing eloquently.

Mrs. Harter sat in her high-backed chair, patient and polite, with a rooted conviction in her own mind that these newfangled notions were neither more nor less than unmitigated nuisances.

"Listen, Aunt Mary, we are on to Paris! Isn't that splendid? Can you hear the fellow?"

"I can't hear anything except a good deal of buzzing and clicking," said Mrs. Harter.

Charles continued to twirl knobs. "Brussels," he announced with enthusiasm.

"Is it really?" said Mrs. Harter with no more than a trace of interest.

Charles again turned knobs and an unearthly howl echoed forth into the room.

"Now we seem to be on to the Dogs' Home," said Mrs. Harter, who was an old lady with a certain amount of spirit.

"Ha, ha!" said Charles, "you will have your joke, won't you, Aunt Mary? Very good that!"

Mrs. Harter could not helping smiling at him. She was very fond of Charles. For some years a niece, Miriam Harter, had lived with her. She had intended to make the girl her heiress, but Miriam had not been a success. She was impatient and obviously bored by her aunt's society. She was always out, "gadding about" as Mrs. Harter called it In the end she had entangled herself with a young man of whom her aunt thoroughly disapproved. Miriam had been returned to her mother with a curt note much as if she had been goods on approval. She had married the young man in question and Mrs. Harter usually sent her a handkerchief case or a table center at Christmas.

Having found nieces disappointing, Mrs. Harter turned her attention to nephews. Charles, from the first, had been an unqualified success. He was always pleasantly deferential to his aunt and listened with an appearance of intense interest to the reminiscences of her youth. In this he was a great contrast to Miriam who had been frankly bored and showed it. Charles was never bored; he was always good-tempered, always gay. He told his aunt many times a day that she was a perfectly marvelous old lady.

Highly satisfied with her new acquisition, Mrs. Harter had written to her lawyer with instructions as to the making of a new will. This was sent to her, duly approved by her, and signed.

And now even in the matter of the radio, Charles was soon proved to have won fresh laurels.

Mrs. Harter, at first antagonistic, became tolerant and finally fascinated. She enjoyed it very much better when Charles was out. The trouble with Charles was that he could not leave the thing alone. Mrs. Harter would be seated in her chair comfortably listening to a symphony concert or a lecture on Lucrezia Borgia or Pond Life, quite happy and at peace with the world. Not so Charles. The harmony would be shattered by discordant shrieks while he enthusiastically attempted to get foreign stations. But on those evenings when Charles was dining out with friends, Mrs. Harter enjoyed the radio very much indeed. She would turn on the switch, sit in her high-backed chair, and enjoy the program of the evening.

It was about three months after the radio had been installed that the first eerie happening occurred. Charles was absent at a bridge party.

The program for that evening was a ballad concert. A well-known soprano was singing *Annie Laurie*, and in the middle of *Annie Laurie* a strange thing happened. There was a sudden break, the music ceased for a moment, the buzzing, clicking noise continued, and then that, too, died away. There was silence, and then very faintly a low buzzing sound was heard.

Mrs. Harter got the impression, why she did not know, that the machine was tuned into somewhere very far away, and then, clearly and distinctly, a voice spoke, a man's voice with a faint Irish accent.

*"Mary—can you hear me, Mary? It is Patrick speak-*

*ing, . . . I am coming for you soon. You will be ready,
won't you, Mary?"*

Then, almost immediately the strains of *Annie Laurie*
once more filled the room.

Mrs. Harter sat rigid in her chair, her hands clenched on
each arm of it. Had she been dreaming? Patrick! Patrick's
voice! Patrick's voice in this very room, speaking to her.
No, it must be a dream, a hallucination perhaps. She must
just have dropped off to sleep for a minute or two. A curious thing to have dreamed—that her dead husband's
voice should speak to her over the ether. It frightened her
just a little. What were the words he had said?

*"I am coming for you soon. You will be ready, won't
you, Mary?"*

Was it, could it be a premonition? Cardiac weakness.
Her heart. After all, she was getting on in years.

"It's a warning—that's what it is," said Mrs. Harter,
rising slowly and painfully from her chair, and added char-
acteristically, "All that money wasted on putting in an
elevator!"

She said nothing of her experience to anyone, but for
the next day or two she was thoughtful and a little
preoccupied.

And then came the second occasion. Again she was
alone in the room. The radio, which had been playing an
orchestral selection, died away with the same suddenness
as before. Again there was silence, the sense of distance,
and finally Patrick's voice, not as it had been in life—but a
voice rarefied, faraway, with a strange unearthly quality.

*"Patrick speaking to you, Mary. I will be coming for
you very soon now—"*

Then click, buzz, and the orchestral selection was in full
swing again.

Mrs. Harter glanced at the clock. No, she had not been
asleep this time. Awake and in full possession of her fac-
ulties, she had heard Patrick's voice speaking. It was no
hallucination, she was sure of that. In a confused way she
tried to think over all that Charles had explained to her
of the theory of ether waves.

Could it be that Patrick had really spoken to her? That his actual voice had been wafted through space? There were missing wave lengths or something of that kind. She remembered Charles speaking of "gaps in the scale." Perhaps the missing waves explained all the so-called psychological phenomena? No, there was nothing inherently impossible in the idea. Patrick had spoken to her. He had availed himself of modern science to prepare her for what must soon be coming.

Mrs. Harter rang the bell for her maid, Elizabeth.

Elizabeth was a tall, gaunt woman of sixty. Beneath an unbending exterior she concealed a wealth of affection and tenderness for her mistress.

"Elizabeth," said Mrs. Harter when her faithful retainer had appeared, "you remember what I told you? The top lefthand drawer of my bureau. It is locked—the long key with the white label. Everything there is ready."

"Ready, ma'am?"

"For my burial," snorted Mrs. Harter. "You know perfectly well what I mean, Elizabeth. You helped me to put the things there yourself."

Elizabeth's face began to work strangely. "Oh, ma'am," she wailed, "don't dwell on such things, I thought you was a sight better."

"We have all got to go sometime or another," said Mrs. Harter practically. "I am over my three years and ten, Elizabeth. There, there, don't make a fool of yourself. If you must cry, go and cry somewhere else."

Elizabeth retired, still sniffing.

Mrs. Harter looked after her with a good deal of affection.

"Silly old fool, but faithful," she said, "very faithful. Let me see, was it a hundred pounds, or only fifty I left her? It ought to be a hundred."

The point worried the old lady and the next day she sat down and wrote to her lawyer asking if he would send her her will so that she might look it over. It was the same day that Charles startled her by something he said at lunch.

"By the way, Aunt Mary," he said, "who is that funny

old josser up in the spare room? The picture over the mantelpiece, I mean. The old johnny with the beaver and side whiskers?"

Mrs. Harter looked at him austerely.

"That is your Uncle Patrick as a young man," she said.

"Oh, I say, Aunt Mary, I am awfully sorry. I didn't mean to be rude."

Mrs. Harter accepted the apology with a dignified bend of the head.

Charles went on rather uncertainly, "I just wondered. You see—"

He stopped undecidedly and Mrs. Harter said sharply, "Well? What were you going to say?"

"Nothing," said Charles hastily. "Nothing that makes sense, I mean."

For the moment the old lady said nothing more, but later that day, when they were alone together, she returned to the subject.

"I wish you would tell me, Charles, what it was that made you ask me about the picture of your uncle."

Charles looked embarrassed.

"I told you, Aunt Mary. It was nothing but a silly fancy of mine—quite absurd."

"Charles," said Mrs. Harter in her most autocratic voice, "I insist upon knowing."

"Well, my dear aunt, if you will have it, I fancied I saw him—the man in the picture, I mean—looking out of the end window when I was coming up the drive last night. Some effect of the light, I suppose. I wondered who on earth he could be, the face was so—early Victorian, if you know what I mean. And then Elizabeth said there was no one, no visitor or stranger in the house, and later in the evening I happened to drift into the spare room, and there was the picture over the mantelpiece. My man to the life! It is quite easily explained, really, I expect. Subconscious and all that. Must have noticed the picture before without realizing that I had noticed it, and then just fancied the face at the window."

"The end window?" said Mrs. Harter sharply.

"Yes, why?"

"Nothing," said Mrs. Harter.

But she was startled all the same. That room had been her husband's dressing-room.

That same evening, Charles again being absent, Mrs. Harter sat listening to the wireless with feverish impatience. If for the third time she heard the mysterious voice, it would prove to her finally without a shadow of doubt that she was really in communication with some other world.

Although her heart beat faster, she was not surprised when the same break occurred, and after the usual interval of deathly silence the faint faraway Irish voice spoke once more.

*"Mary—you are prepared now. . . . On Friday I shall come for you. . . . Friday at half past nine. . . . Do not be afraid—there will be no pain. . . . Be ready. . . ."*

Then, almost cutting short the last word, the music of the orchestra broke out again, clamorous and discordant.

Mrs. Harter sat very still for a minute or two. Her face had gone white and she looked blue and pinched round the lips.

Presently she got up and sat down at her writing desk. In a somewhat shaky hand she wrote the following lines:

> *Tonight, at 9:15, I have distinctly heard the voice of my dead husband. He told me that he would come for me on Friday night at 9:30. If I should die on that day and at that hour I should like the facts made known so as to prove beyond question the possibility of communicating with the spirit world.*—Mary Harter.

Mrs. Harter read over what she had written, enclosed it in an envelope, and addressed the envelope. Then she rang the bell which was promptly answered by Elizabeth. Mrs. Harter got up from her desk and gave the note she had just written to the old woman.

"Elizabeth," she said, "if I should die on Friday night I should like that note given to Doctor Meynell. No"—as Elizabeth appeared about to protest—"do not argue with me. You have often told me you believe in premonitions. I have a premonition now. There is one thing more. I have left you in my will fifty pounds. I should like you to have a hundred pounds. If I am not able to go to the bank myself before I die, Mr. Charles will see to it."

As before, Mrs. Harter cut short Elizabeth's tearful protests. In pursuance of her determination the old lady spoke to her nephew on the subject the following morning.

"Remember, Charles, that if anything should happen to me, Elizabeth is to have an extra fifty pounds."

"You are very gloomy these days, Aunt Mary," said Charles cheerfully. "What is going to happen to you? According to Doctor Meynell, we shall be celebrating your hundredth birthday in twenty years or so!"

Mrs. Harter smiled affectionately at him but did not answer. After a minute or two she said, "What are you doing on Friday evening, Charles?"

Charles looked a trifle surprised.

"As a matter of fact, the Ewings asked me to go in and play bridge, but if you would rather I stayed at home—"

"No," said Mrs. Harter with determination. "Certainly not. I mean it, Charles. On that night of all nights I should much rather be alone."

Charles looked at her curiously, but Mrs. Harter vouchsafed no further information. She was an old lady of courage and determination. She felt that she must go through with her strange experience singlehanded.

Friday evening found the house very silent. Mrs. Harter sat as usual in her straight-backed chair drawn up to the fireplace. All her preparations were made. That morning she had been to the bank, had drawn out £50 in notes, and had handed them over to Elizabeth despite the latter's tearful protests. She had sorted and arranged all her personal belongings and had labeled one or two pieces of jewelry with the names of friends or relatives. She had also written out a list of instructions for Charles. The Worcester tea service was to go to Cousin Emma, the Sèvres jars to young William, and so on.

Now she looked at the long envelope she held in her hand and drew from it a folded document. This was her will sent to her by Mr. Hopkinson in accordance with her instructions. She had already read it carefully, but now she looked over it once more to refresh her memory. It was a short, concise document. A bequest of £50 to Elizabeth Marshall in consideration of faithful service; two bequests of £500 to a sister and a first cousin, and the remainder to her beloved nephew Charles Ridgeway.

Mrs. Harter nodded her head several times. Charles would be a very rich man when she was dead. Well, he had been a dear good boy to her. Always kind, always affectionate, and with a merry tongue which never failed to please her.

She looked at the clock. Three minutes to the half-hour. Well, she was ready. And she was calm—quite calm. Although she repeated these last words to herself several times, her heart beat strangely and unevenly. She hardly realized it herself, but she was strung up to a fine point of overwrought nerves.

Half past nine. The wireless was switched on. What would she hear? A familiar voice announcing the weather forecast or that faraway voice belonging to a man who died twenty-five years before?

But she heard neither. Instead there came a familiar sound, a sound she knew well but which tonight made her feel as though an icy hand were laid on her heart. A fumbling at the front door—

It came again. And then a cold blast seemed to sweep through the room. Mrs. Harter had now no doubt what her sensations were. She was afraid. She was more than afraid —she was terrified—

And suddenly there came to her the thought: *Twenty-five years is a long time. Patrick is a stranger to me now.*

Terror! That was what was invading her.

A soft step outside the door—a soft, halting footstep. Then the door swung silently open—

Mrs. Harter staggered to her feet, swaying slightly from side to side, her eyes fixed on the open doorway. Something slipped from her fingers into the grate.

She gave a strangled cry which died in her throat. In the

AGATHA CHRISTIE

dim light of the doorway stood a familiar figure with chestnut beard and whiskers and an old-fashioned Victorian
coat.

*Patrick had come for her!*

Her heart gave one terrified leap and stood still. She
slipped to the ground in a crumpled heap.

There Elizabeth found her, an hour later.

Dr. Meynell was called at once and Charles Ridgeway
was hastily summoned from his bridge party. But nothing
could be done. Mrs. Harter was beyond human aid.

It was not until two days later that Elizabeth remembered the note given to her by her mistress. Dr. Meynell
read it with great interest and showed it to Charles
Ridgeway.

"A very curious coincidence," he said. "It seems clear
that your aunt had been having hallucinations about her
dead husband's voice. She must have strung herself up to
such a point that the excitement was fatal, and when the
time actually came she died of the shock."

"Auto-suggestion?" asked Charles.

"Something of the sort. I will let you know the result of
the autopsy as soon as possible, though I have no doubt of
it myself. In the circumstance an autopsy is desirable,
though purely as a matter of form."

Charles nodded comprehendingly.

On the preceding night, when the household was in bed,
he had removed a certain wire which ran from the back of
the radio cabinet to his bedroom on the floor above. Also,
since the evening had been a chilly one, he had asked
Elizabeth to light a fire in his room, and in that fire he had
burned a chestnut beard and whiskers. Some Victorian
clothing belonging to his late uncle he replaced in the cam-
phor-scented chest in the attic.

As far as he could see, he was perfectly safe. His plan,
the shadowy outline of which had first formed in his brain
when Doctor Meynell had told him that his aunt might
with due care live for many years, had succeeded admira-
bly. A sudden shock, Dr. Meynell had said. Charles, that

affectionate young man, beloved of old ladies, smiled to himself.

When the doctor had departed, Charles went about his duties mechanically. Certain funeral arrangements had to be finally settled. Relatives coming from a distance had to have trains looked up for them. In one or two cases they would have to stay the night. Charles went about it all efficiently and methodically, to the accompaniment of an undercurrent of his own thoughts.

*A very good stroke of business!* That was the burden of them. Nobody, least of all his dead aunt, had known in what perilous straits Charles stood. His activities, carefully concealed from the world, had landed him where the shadow of a prison loomed ahead.

Exposure and ruin had stared him in the face unless he could in a few short months raise a considerable sum of money. Well—that was all right now. Charles smiled to himself. Thanks to—yes, call it a practical joke—nothing criminal about *that*—he was saved. He was now a very rich man. He had no anxieties on the subject, for Mrs. Harter had never made any secret of her intentions.

Chiming in very appositely with these thoughts, Elizabeth put her head round the door and informed him that Mr. Hopkinson was here and would like to see him.

About time, too, Charles thought. Repressing a tendency to whistle, he composed his face to one of suitable gravity and went to the library. There he greeted the precise old gentleman who had been for over a quarter of a century the late Mrs. Harter's legal adviser.

The lawyer seated himself at Charles's invitation and with a dry little cough entered upon business matters.

"I did not quite understand your letter to me, Mr. Ridgeway. You seemed to be under the impression that the late Mrs. Harter's will was in our keeping."

Charles stared at him.

"But surely—I've heard my aunt say as much."

"Oh! quite so, quite so. It *was* in our keeping."

*"Was?"*

"That is what I said. Mrs. Harter wrote to us, asking that it might be forwarded to her on Tuesday last."

An uneasy feeling crept over Charles. He felt a far-off premonition of unpleasantness.

"Doubtless it will come to light among her papers," continued the lawyer smoothly.

Charles said nothing. He was afraid to trust his tongue. He had already been through Mrs. Harter's papers pretty thoroughly, well enough to be quite certain that no will was among them. In a minute or two, when he had regained control of himself, he said so. His voice sounded unreal to himself, and he had a sensation as of cold water trickling down his back.

"Has anyone been through her personal effects?" asked the lawyer.

Charles replied that the maid, Elizabeth, had done so. At Mr. Hopkinson's suggestion Elizabeth was sent for. She came promptly, grim and upright, and answered the questions put to her.

She had been through all her mistress's clothes and personal belongings. She was quite sure that there had been no legal document such as a will among them. She knew what the will looked like—her poor mistress had had it in her hand only the morning of her death.

"You are sure of that?" asked the lawyer sharply.

"Yes, sir. She told me so. And she made me take fifty pounds in notes. The will was in a long blue envelope."

"Quite right," said Mr. Hopkinson.

"Now I come to think of it," continued Elizabeth, "that same blue envelope was lying on this table the morning after—but empty. I laid it on the desk."

"I remember seeing it there," said Charles.

He got up and went over to the desk. In a minute or two he turned round with an envelope in his hand which he handed to Mr. Hopkinson. The latter examined it and nodded his head.

"That is the envelope in which I dispatched the will on Tuesday last."

Both men looked hard at Elizabeth.

"Is there anything more, sir?" she inquired respectfully.

"Not at present, thank you."

Elizabeth went toward the door.

"One minute," said the lawyer. "Was there a fire in the grate that evening?"

"Yes, sir, there was always a fire."

"Thank you, that will do."

Elizabeth went out. Charles leaned forward, resting a shaking hand on the table.

"What do you think? What are you driving at?" Mr. Hopkinson shook his head.

"We must still hope the will may turn up. If it does not—"

"Well, if it does not?"

"I am afraid there is only one conclusion possible. Your aunt sent for that will in order to destroy it. Not wishing Elizabeth to lose by that, she gave her the amount of her legacy in cash."

"But why?" cried Charles wildly. "Why?"

Mr. Hopkinson coughed. A dry cough.

"You have had no—er—disagreement with your aunt, Mr. Ridgeway?" he murmured.

Charles gasped.

"No, indeed," he cried warmly. "We were on the kindliest, most affectionate terms, right up to the end."

"Ah!" said Mr. Hopkinson, not looking at him.

It came to Charles with a shock that the lawyer did not believe him. Who knew what this dry old stick might not have heard? Rumors of Charles's doings might have come round to him. What more natural than that he should suppose that these same rumors had come to Mrs. Harter, and that aunt and nephew should have had an altercation on the subject?

But it wasn't so! Charles knew one of the bitterest moments of his career. His lies had been believed. Now that he spoke the truth, belief was withheld. The irony of it!

Of course his aunt had never burned the will! Of course—

His thoughts came to a sudden check. What was that picture rising before his eyes? An old lady with one hand clasped to her heart—something slipped—a paper—falling on the red-hot embers—

Charles's face grew livid. He heard a hoarse voice—his own—asking, "If that will's never found?"

"There is a former will of Mrs. Harter's still extant. Dated September, 1950. By it Mrs. Harter leaves everything to her niece, Miriam Harter, now Miriam Robinson."

What was the old fool saying? Miriam? Miriam with her nondescript husband, and her four whining brats. All his cleverness—for Miriam!

The telephone rang sharply at his elbow. He took up the receiver. It was the doctor's voice, hearty and kindly.

"That you, Ridgeway? Thought you'd like to know. The autopsy's just concluded. Cause of death as I surmised. But as a matter of fact the cardiac trouble was much more serious than I suspected when she was alive. With the utmost care she couldn't have lived longer than two months at the outside. Thought you'd like to know. Might console you more or less."

"Excuse me," said Charles, "would you mind saying that again?"

"She couldn't have lived longer than two months," said the doctor in a slightly louder tone. "All things work out for the best, you know, my dear fellow—"

But Charles had slammed back the receiver on its hook. He was conscious of the lawyer's voice speaking from a long way off.

"Dear me, Mr. Ridgeway, are you ill?"

Curse them all! The smug-faced lawyer. That poisonous old ass Meynell. No hope in front of him—only the shadow of the prison wall.

He felt that Somebody had been playing with him—playing with him like a cat with a mouse. Somebody must be laughing. . . .

# GREENSHAW'S FOLLY

THE TWO MEN rounded the corner of the shrubbery.

"Well, there you are," said Raymond West. "That's it."

Horace Bindler took a deep, appreciative breath.

"But my dear," he cried, "how wonderful." His voice rose in a high screech of esthetic delight, then deepened in reverent awe. "It's unbelievable. Out of this world! A period piece of the best."

"I thought you'd like it," said Raymond West, complacently.

"Like it? My dear—" Words failed Horace. He unbuckled the strap of his camera and got busy. "This will be one of the gems of my collection," he said happily. "I do think, don't you, that it's rather amusing to have a collection of monstrosities? The idea came to me one night seven years ago in my bath. My last real gem was in the Campo Santo at Genoa, but I really think this beats it. What's it called?"

"I haven't the least idea," said Raymond.

"I suppose it's got a name?"

"It must have. But the fact is that it's never referred to round here as anything but Greenshaw's Folly."

"Greenshaw being the man who built it?"

"Yes. In 1860 or '70 or thereabouts. The local success story of the time. Barefoot boy who had risen to immense prosperity. Local opinion is divided as to why he built this house, whether it was sheer exuberance of wealth or whether it was done to impress his creditors. If the latter, it didn't impress them. He either went bankrupt or the next thing to it. Hence the name, Greenshaw's Folly."

Horace's camera clicked. "There," he said in a satisfied voice. "Remind me to show you Number 310 in my collection. A really incredible marble mantelpiece in the Italian manner." He added, looking at the house, "I can't conceive of how Mr. Greenshaw thought of it all."

"Rather obvious in some ways," said Raymond. "He had visited the *châteaux* of the Loire, don't you think? Those turrets. And then, rather unfortunately, he seems to have traveled in the Orient. The influence of the Taj Mahal is unmistakable. I rather like the Moorish wing," he added, "and the traces of a Venetian palace."

"One wonders how he ever got hold of an architect to carry out these ideas."

Raymond shrugged his shoulders.

"No difficulty about that, I expect," he said. "Probably the architect retired with a good income for life while poor old Greenshaw went bankrupt."

"Could we look at it from the other side?" asked Horace, "or are we trespassing?"

"We're trespassing all right," said Raymond, "but I don't think it will matter."

He turned toward the corner of the house and Horace skipped after him.

"But who lives here? Orphans or holiday visitors? It can't be a school. No playing fields or brisk efficiency."

"Oh, a Greenshaw lives here still," said Raymond over his shoulder. "The house itself didn't go in the crash. Old Greenshaw's son inherited it. He was a bit of a miser and lived here in a corner of it. Never spent a penny. Probably never had a penny to spend. His daughter lives here now. Old Lady—very eccentric."

As he spoke Raymond was congratulating himself on having thought of Greenshaw's Folly as a means of entertaining his guest. These literary critics always professed themselves as longing for a weekend in the country, and were wont to find the country extremely boring when they got there. Tomorrow there would be the Sunday papers, and for today Raymond West congratulated himself on suggesting a visit to Greenshaw's Folly to enrich Horace Bindler's well-known collection of monstrosities.

They turned the corner of the house and came out on a neglected lawn. In one corner of it was a large artificial rockery, and bending over it was a figure at the sight of which Horace clutched Raymond delightedly by the arm.

"My dear," he exclaimed, "do you see what she's got on? A sprigged print dress. Just like a housemaid—when there were housemaids. One of my most cherished memories is staying at a house in the country when I was quite a boy where a real housemaid called you in the morning, all crackling in a print dress and a cap. Yes, my boy, *really*—a cap. Muslin with streamers. No, perhaps it was the parlormaid who had the streamers. But anyway she was a real housemaid and she brought in an enormous brass can of hot water. What an exciting day we're having."

The figure in the print dress had straightened up and turned toward them, trowel in hand. She was a sufficiently startling figure. Unkempt locks of iron-grey fell wispily on her shoulders and a straw hat, rather like the hats that horses wear in Italy, was crammed down on her head. The colored print dress she wore fell nearly to her ankles. Out of a weather-beaten, not too clean face, shrewd eyes surveyed them appraisingly.

"I must apologize for trespassing, Miss Greenshaw," said Raymond West, as he advanced toward her, "but Mr. Horace Bindler who is staying with me—"

Horace bowed and removed his hat.

"—is most interested in—er—ancient history and—er— fine buildings."

Raymond West spoke with the ease of a famous author who knows that he is a celebrity, that he can venture where other people may not.

Miss Greenshaw looked up at the sprawling exuberance behind her.

"It *is* a fine house," she said appreciatively. "My grandfather built it—before my time, of course. He is reported as having said that he wished to astonish the natives."

"I'll say he did that, ma'am," said Horace Bindler.

"Mr. Bindler is the well-known literary critic," said Raymond West.

Miss Greenshaw had clearly no reverence for literary critics. She remained unimpressed.

"I consider it," said Miss Greenshaw, referring to the

house, "as a monument to my grandfather's genius. Silly fools come here and ask me why I don't sell it and go and live in a flat. What would *I* do in a flat? It's my home and I live in it," said Miss Greenshaw. "Always have lived here." She considered, brooding over the past. "There were three of us. Laura married the curate. Papa wouldn't give her any money, said clergymen ought to be unworldly. She died, having a baby. Baby died, too. Nettie ran away with the riding master. Papa cut her out of his will, of course. Handsome fellow, Harry Fletcher, but no good. Don't think Nettie was happy with him. Anyway, she didn't live long. They had a son. He writes to me sometimes, but of course he isn't a Greenshaw. I'm the last of the Greenshaws." She drew up her bent shoulders with a certain pride, and readjusted the rakish angle of the straw hat. Then, turning, she said sharply:

"Yes, Mrs. Cresswell, what is it?"

Approaching them from the house was a figure that, seen side by side with Miss Greenshaw, seemed ludicrously dissimilar. Mrs. Cresswell had a marvelously dressed head of well-blued hair towering upward in meticulously arranged curls and rolls. It was as though she had dressed her head to go as a French marquise to a fancy dress party. The rest of her middle-aged person was dressed in what ought to have been rustling black silk but was actually one of the shinier varieties of black rayon. Although she was not a large woman, she had a well-developed and sumptuous bosom. Her voice, when she spoke, was unexpectedly deep. She spoke with exquisite diction—only a slight hesitation over words beginning with "h" and the final pronunciation of them with an exaggerated aspirate gave rise to a suspicion that at some remote period in her youth she might have had trouble over dropping her h's.

"The fish, madam," said Mrs. Cresswell, "the slice of cod. It has not arrived. I have asked Alfred to go down for it and he refuses."

Rather unexpectedly, Miss Greenshaw gave a cackle of laughter.

"Refuses, does he?"

"Alfred, madam, has been most disobliging."

Miss Greenshaw raised two earth-stained fingers to her lips, suddenly produced an ear-splitting whistle and at the same time yelled, "Alfred. Alfred, come here."

Round the corner of the house a young man appeared in answer to the summons, carrying a spade in his hand. He had a bold, handsome face and as he drew near he cast an unmistakably malevolent glance toward Mrs. Cresswell.

"You want me, miss?" he said.

"Yes, Alfred. I hear you've refused to go down for the fish. What about it, eh?"

Alfred spoke in a surly voice.

"I'll go down for it if you wants it, miss. You've only got to say."

"I do want it. I want it for my supper."

"Right you are, miss. I'll go right away."

He threw an insolent glance at Mrs. Cresswell, who flushed and murmured below her breath.

"Now that I think of it," said Miss Greenshaw, "a couple of strange visitors are just what we need, aren't they, Mrs. Cresswell?"

Mrs. Cresswell looked puzzled.

"I'm sorry, madam—"

"For you-know-what," said Miss Greenshaw, nodding her head. "Beneficiary to a will mustn't witness it. That's right, isn't it?" She appealed to Raymond West.

"Quite correct," said Raymond.

"I know enough law to know that," said Miss Greenshaw, "and you two are men of standing."

She flung down the trowel on her weeding basket.

"Would you mind coming up to the library with me?"

"Delighted," said Horace eagerly.

She led the way through French windows and through a vast yellow and gold drawing-room with faded brocade on the walls and dust covers arranged over the furniture, then through a large dim hall, up a staircase, and into a room on the second floor.

"My grandfather's library," she announced.

Horace looked round with acute pleasure. It was a room from his point of view quite full of monstrosities. The heads of sphinxes appeared on the most unlikely pieces of furniture, there was a colossal bronze representing, he thought, Paul and Virginia, and a vast bronze clock with classical motifs of which he longed to take a photograph.

"A fine lot of books," said Miss Greenshaw.

Raymond was already looking at the books. From what he could see from a cursory glance there was no book here of any real interest or, indeed, any book which appeared to have been read. They were all superbly bound sets of the classics as supplied ninety years ago for furnishing a gentleman's library. Some novels of a bygone period were included. But they too showed little signs of having been read.

Miss Greenshaw was fumbling in the drawers of a vast desk. Finally she pulled out a parchment document.

"My will," she explained. "Got to leave your money to someone—or so they say. If I died without a will, I suppose that son of a horse coper would get it. Handsome fellow, Harry Fletcher, but a rogue if ever there was one. Don't see why *his* son should inherit this place. No," she went on, as though answering some unspoken objection, "I've made up my mind. I'm leaving it to Cresswell."

"Your housekeeper?"

"Yes. I've explained it to her. I make a will leaving her all I've got and then I don't need to pay her any wages. Saves me a lot in current expenses, and it keeps her up to the mark. No giving me notice and walking off at any minute. Very la-di-dah and all that, isn't she? But her father was a working plumber in a very small way. *She's* nothing to give herself airs about."

By now Miss Greenshaw had unfolded the parchment. Picking up a pen, she dipped it in the inkstand and wrote her signature, *Katherine Dorothy Greenshaw*.

"That's right," she said. "You've seen me sign it, and then you two sign it, and that makes it legal."

She handed the pen to Raymond West. He hesitated a moment, feeling an unexpected repulsion to what he was asked to do. Then he quickly scrawled his well-known autograph, for which his morning's mail usually brought at least six requests.

Horace took the pen from him and added his own minute signature.

"That's done," said Miss Greenshaw.

She moved across to the bookcases and stood looking at them uncertainly, then she opened a glass door, took out a book, and slipped the folded parchment inside.

"I've my own places for keeping things," she said.

"*Lady Audley's Secret*," Raymond West remarked, catching sight of the title as she replaced the book.

Miss Greenshaw gave another cackle of laughter.

"Best-seller in its day," she remarked. "But not like your books, eh?"

She gave Raymond a sudden friendly nudge in the ribs. Raymond was rather surprised that she even knew he wrote books. Although Raymond West was a "big name" in literature, he could hardly be described as a best-seller. Though softening a little with the advent of middle-age, his books dealt bleakly with the sordid side of life.

"I wonder," Horace demanded breathlessly, "if I might just take a photograph of the clock."

"By all means," said Miss Greenshaw. "It came, I believe, from the Paris Exhibition."

"Very probably," said Horace. He took his picture.

"This room's not been used much since my grandfather's time," said Miss Greenshaw. "This desk's full of old diaries of his. Interesting, I should think. I haven't the eyesight to read them myself. I'd like to get them published, but I suppose one would have to work on them a good deal."

"You could engage someone to do that," said Raymond West.

"Could I really? It's an idea, you know. I'll think about it."

Raymond West glanced at his watch.

"We mustn't trespass on your kindness any longer," he said.

"Pleased to have seen you," said Miss Greenshaw graciously. "Thought you were the policeman when I heard you coming round the corner of the house."

"Why a policeman?" demanded Horace, who never minded asking questions.

Miss Greenshaw responded unexpectedly.

"If you want to know the time, ask a policeman," she carolled, and with this example of Victorian wit she nudged Horace in the ribs and roared with laughter.

"It's been a wonderful afternoon," sighed Horace as they walked home. "Really, that place has *everything*. The only thing the library needs is a body. Those old-fashioned detective stories about murder in the library—that's just the kind of library I'm sure the authors had in mind."

"If you want to discuss murder," said Raymond, "you must talk to my Aunt Jane."

"Your Aunt Jane? Do you mean Miss Marple?" Horace felt a little at a loss.

The charming old-world lady to whom he had been introduced the night before seemed the last person to be mentioned in connection with murder.

"Oh, yes," said Raymond. "Murder is a specialty of hers."

"But my dear, how intriguing! What do you really mean?"

"I mean just that," said Raymond. He paraphrased: "Some commit murder, some get mixed up in murders, others have murder thrust upon them. My Aunt Jane comes into the third category."

"You are joking."

"Not in the least. I can refer you to the former Commissioner of Scotland Yard, several Chief Constables, and one or two hard-working inspectors of the C.I.D."

Horace said happily that wonders would never cease. Over the tea table they gave Joan West, Raymond's wife, Louise Oxley, her niece, and old Miss Marple, a résumé of the afternoon's happenings, recounting in detail everything that Miss Greenshaw had said to them.

"But I do think," said Horace, "that there is something a little *sinister* about the whole setup. That duchess-like creature, the housekeeper—arsensic, perhaps, in the teapot, now that she knows her mistress has made the will in her favor?"

"Tell us, Aunt Jane," said Raymond. "Will there be murder or won't there? What do *you* think?"

"I think," said Miss Marple, winding up her wool with a rather severe air, "that you shouldn't joke about these things as much as you do, Raymond. Arsenic is, of course, *quite* a possibility. So easy to obtain. Probably present in the tool shed already in the form of weed killer."

"Oh, really, darling," said Joan West, affectionately. "Wouldn't that be rather too obvious?"

"It's all very well to make a will," said Raymond. "I don't suppose the poor old thing has anything to leave except that awful white elephant of a house, and who would want that?"

"A film company possibly," said Horace, "or a hotel or an institution?"

"They'd expect to buy it for a song," said Raymond, but Miss Marple was shaking her head.

"You know, dear Raymond, I cannot agree with you there. About the money, I mean. The grandfather was evidently one of those lavish spenders who make money easily but can't keep it. He may have gone broke, as you say, but hardly bankrupt or else his son would not have had the house. Now the son, as is so often the case, was of an entirely different character from his father. A miser. A man who saved every penny. I should say that in the course of his lifetime he probably put by a very good sum. This Miss Greenshaw appears to have taken after him—to dislike spending money, that is. Yes, I should think it quite likely that she has quite a substantial sum tucked away."

"In that case," said Joan West, "I wonder now—what about Louise?"

They looked at Louise as she sat, silent, by the fire.

Louise was Joan West's niece. Her marriage had recently, as she herself put it, come unstuck, leaving her with two young children and bare sufficiency of money to keep them on.

"I mean," said Joan, "if this Miss Greenshaw really wants someone to go through diaries and get a book ready for publication . . ."

"It's an idea," said Raymond.

Louise said in a low voice, "It's work I could do—and I think I'd enjoy it."

"I'll write to her," said Raymond.

"I wonder," said Miss Marple thoughtfully, "what the old lady meant by that remark about a policeman?"

"Oh, it was just a joke."

"It reminded me," said Miss Marple, nodding her head vigorously, "yes, it reminded me very much of Mr. Naysmith."

"Who was Mr. Naysmith?" asked Raymond, curiously.

"He kept bees," said Miss Marple, "and was very good at doing the acrostics in the Sunday papers. And he liked giving people false impressions just for fun. But sometimes it led to trouble."

Everybody was silent for a moment, considering Mr. Naysmith, but as there did not seem to be any points of resemblance between him and Miss Greenshaw, they decided that dear Aunt Jane was perhaps a *little* bit disconnected in her old age.

Horace Bindler went back to London without having collected any more monstrosities and Raymond West wrote a letter to Miss Greenshaw telling her that he knew of a Mrs. Louise Oxley who would be competent to undertake work on the diaries. After a lapse of some days a letter arrived, written in spidery old-fashioned handwriting, in which Miss Greenshaw declared herself anxious to avail herself of the services of Mrs. Oxley, and making an appointment for Mrs. Oxley to come and see her.

Louise duly kept the appointment, generous terms were arranged, and she started work the following day.

"I'm awfully grateful to you," she said to Raymond. "It will fit in beautifully. I can take the children to school, go on to Greenshaw's Folly, and pick them up on my way back. How fantastic the whole setup is! That old woman has to be seen to be believed."

On the evening of her first day at work she returned and described her day.

"I've hardly seen the housekeeper," she said. "She came in with coffee and biscuits at half-past eleven with her mouth pursed up very prunes and prisms, and would hardly speak to me. I think she disapproves deeply of my hav-

ing been engaged." She went on, "It seems there's quite a
feud between her and the gardener, Alfred. He's a local boy
and fairly lazy, I should imagine, and he and the housekeeper won't speak to each other. Miss Greenshaw said in
her rather grand way, 'There have always been feuds as far
as I can remember between the garden and the house staff.
It was so in my grandfather's time. There were three men
and a boy in the garden then, and eight maids in the house,
but there was always friction.' "

On the next day Louise returned with another piece of
news.

"Just fancy," she said, "I was asked to ring up the nephew today."

"Miss Greenshaw's nephew?"

"Yes. It seems he's an actor playing in the stock company that's doing a summer season at Boreham-on-Sea. I
rang up the theater and left a message asking him to lunch
tomorrow. Rather fun, really. The old girl didn't want the
housekeeper to know. I think Mrs. Cresswell has done
something that's annoyed her."

"Tomorrow another installment of this thrilling serial,"
murmured Raymond.

"It's exactly like a serial, isn't it? Reconciliation with the
nephew, blood is thicker than water—another will to be
made and the old will destroyed."

"Aunt Jane, you're looking very serious."

"Was I, my dear? Have you heard any more about the
policeman?"

Louise looked bewildered. "I don't know anything about
a policeman."

"That remark of hers, my dear," said Miss Marple,
"must have meant something."

Louise arrived at her work the following day in a cheerful mood. She passed through the open front door—the
doors and windows of the house were always open. Miss
Greenshaw appeared to have no fear of burglars, and was
probably justified, as most things in the house weighed several tons and were of no marketable value.

Louise had passed Alfred in the drive. When she first
noticed him he had been leaning against a tree smoking a

cigarette, but as soon as he had caught sight of her he had seized a broom and begun diligently to sweep leaves. An idle young man, she thought, but good-looking. His features reminded her of someone. As she passed through the hall on her way upstairs to the library, she glanced at the large picture of Nathaniel Greenshaw which presided over the mantelpiece, showing him in the acme of Victorian prosperity, leaning back in a large armchair, his hands resting on the gold Albert across his capacious stomach. As her glance swept up from the stomach to the face with its heavy jowls, its bushy eyebrows and its flourishing black mustache, the thought occurred to her that Nathaniel Greenshaw must have been handsome as a young man. He had looked, perhaps, a little like Alfred . . .

She went into the library on the second floor, shut the door behind her, opened her typewriter, and got out the diaries from the drawer at the side of her desk. Through the open window she caught a glimpse of Miss Greenshaw below, in a puce-colored sprigged print, bending over the rockery, weeding assiduously. They had had two wet days, of which the weeds had taken full advantage.

Louise, a town-bred girl, decided that if she ever had a garden it would never contain a rockery which needed weeding by hand. Then she settled down to her work.

When Mrs. Cresswell entered the library with the coffee tray at half-past eleven, she was clearly in a very bad temper. She banged the tray down on the table and observed to the universe:

"Company for lunch—and nothing in the house! What am *I* supposed to do, I should like to know? And no sign of Alfred."

"He was sweeping in the drive when I got here," Louise offered.

"I daresay. A nice soft job."

Mrs. Cresswell swept out of the room, slamming the door behind her. Louise grinned to herself. She wondered what "the nephew" would be like.

She finished her coffee and settled down to her work again. It was so absorbing that time passed quickly. Nathaniel Greenshaw, when he started to keep a diary, had succumbed to the pleasures of frankness. Typing out a passage relating to the personal charms of a barmaid in the neighboring town, Louise reflected that a good deal of editing would be necessary.

As she was thinking this, she was startled by a scream from the garden. Jumping up, she ran to the open window. Below her Miss Greenshaw was staggering away from the rockery toward the house. Her hands were clasped to her breast and between her hands there protruded a feathered shaft that Louise recognized with stupefaction to be the shaft of an arrow.

Miss Greenshaw's head, in its battered straw hat, fell forward on her breast. She called up to Louise in a failing voice: ". . . shot . . . he shot me . . . with an arrow . . . get help . . ."

Louise rushed to the door. She turned the handle, but the door would not open. It took a moment or two of futile endeavor to realize that she was locked in. She ran back to the window and called down.

"I'm locked in!"

Miss Greenshaw, her back toward Louise and swaying a little on her feet, was calling up to the housekeeper at a window farther along.

"Ring police . . . telephone . . ."

Then, lurching from side to side like a drunkard, Miss Greenshaw disappeared from Louise's view through the window and staggered into the drawing-room on the ground floor. A moment later Louise heard a crash of broken china, a heavy fall, and then silence. Her imagination reconstructed the scene. Miss Greenshaw must have stumbled blindly into a small table with a Sèvres tea set on it.

Desperately Louise pounded on the library door, calling and shouting. There was no creeper or drainpipe outside the window that could help her to get out that way.

Tired at last of beating on the door, Louise returned to the window. From the window of her sitting-room farther along, the housekeeper's head appeared.

"Come and let me out, Mrs. Oxley. I'm locked in."

"So am I."

"Oh, dear, isn't it awful? I've telephoned the police. There's an extension in this room, but what I can't understand, Mrs. Oxley, is our being locked in. *I* never heard a key turn, did you?"

"No. I didn't hear anything at all. Oh, dear, what shall we do? Perhaps Alfred might hear us." Louise shouted at the top of her voice, "Alfred, Alfred."

"Gone to his dinner as likely as not. What time is it?"

Louise glanced at her watch.

"Twenty-five past twelve."

"He's not supposed to go until half-past, but he sneaks off earlier whenever he can."

"Do you think—do you think—"

Louise meant to ask "Do you think she's dead?"—but the words stuck in her throat.

There was nothing to do but wait. She sat down on the window sill. It seemed an eternity before the stolid helmeted figure of a police constable came round the corner of the house. She leaned out of the window and he looked up at her, shading his eyes with his hand.

"What's going on here?" he demanded.

From their respective windows, Louise and Mrs. Cresswell poured a flood of excited information down on him.

The constable produced a notebook and a pencil. "You ladies ran upstairs and locked yourselves in? Can I have your names, please?"

"Somebody locked us in. Come and let us out."

The constable said reprovingly, "All in good time," and disappeared through the French window below.

Once again time seemed infinite. Louise heard the sound of a car arriving, and, after what seemed an hour, but was actually only three minutes, first Mrs. Cresswell and then Louise were released by a police sergeant more alert than the original constable.

"Miss Greenshaw?" Louise's voice faltered. "What— what's happened?"

The sergeant cleared his throat.

"I'm sorry to have to tell you, madam," he said, "what

I've already told Mrs. Cresswell here. Miss Greenshaw is dead."

"Murdered," said Mrs. Cresswell. "That's what it is—murder."

The sergeant said dubiously, "Could have been an accident—some country lads shooting arrows."

Again there was the sound of a car arriving.

The sergeant said, "That'll be the M.O." and he started downstairs.

But it was not the M.O. As Louise and Mrs. Cresswell came down the stairs, a young man stepped hesitatingly through the front door and paused, looking round him with a somewhat bewildered air.

Then, speaking in a pleasant voice that in some way seemed familiar to Louise—perhaps it reminded her of Miss Greenshaw's—he asked, "Excuse me, does—er—does Miss Greenshaw live here?"

"May I have your name if you please," said the sergeant, advancing upon him.

"Fletcher," said the young man. "Nat Fletcher. I'm Miss Greenshaw's nephew, as a matter of fact."

"Indeed, sir, well—I'm sorry—"

"Has anything happened?" asked Nat Fletcher.

"There's been an—accident. Your aunt was shot with an arrow—penetrated the jugular vein—"

Mrs. Cresswell spoke hysterically and without her usual refinement: "Your h'aunt's been murdered, that's what's 'appened. Your h'aunt's been murdered."

Inspector Welch drew his chair a little nearer to the table and let his gaze wander from one to the other of the four people in the room. It was evening of the same day. He had called at Wests' house to take Louise Oxley once more over her statement.

"You are sure of the exact words? *Shot—he shot me—with an arrow—get help?*"

Louise nodded.

"And the time?"

"I looked at my watch a minute or two later—it was then 12:25—"

"Your watch keeps good time?"

"I looked at the clock as well." Louise left no doubt of her accuracy.

The Inspector turned to Raymond West.

"It appears, sir, that about a week ago you and a Mr. Horace Bindler were witnesses to Miss Greenshaw's will?"

Briefly, Raymond recounted the events of the afternoon visit he and Horace Bindler had paid to Greenshaw's Folly.

"This testimony of yours may be important," said Welch. "Miss Greenshaw distinctly told you, did she, that her will was being made in favor of Mrs. Cresswell, the housekeeper, and that she was not paying Mrs. Cresswell any wages in view of the expectations Mrs. Cresswell had of profiting by her death?"

"That is what she told me—yes."

"Would you say that Mrs. Cresswell was definitely aware of these facts?"

"I should say undoubtedly. Miss Greenshaw made a reference in my presence to beneficiaries not being able to witness a will and Mrs. Cresswell clearly understood what she meant by it. Moreover, Miss Greenshaw herself told me that she had come to this arrangement with Mrs. Cresswell."

"So Mrs. Cresswell had reason to believe she was an interested party. Motive clear enough in her case, and I daresay she'd be our chief suspect now if it wasn't for the fact that she was securely locked in her room like Mrs. Oxley here, and also that Miss Greenshaw definitely said a *man* shot her—"

"She definitely *was* locked in her room?"

"Oh, yes. Sergeant Cayley let her out. It's a big old-fashioned lock with a big old-fashioned key. The key was in the lock and there's not a chance that it could have been turned from inside or any hanky-panky of that kind. No, you can *take* it definitely that Mrs. Cresswell was locked inside that room and couldn't get out. And there were no bows and arrows in the room and Miss Greenshaw couldn't in any case have been shot from her window—the angle forbids it. No, Mrs. Cresswell's out."

He paused, then went on: "Would you say that Miss Greenshaw, in your opinion, was a practical joker?"

Miss Marple looked up sharply from her corner.

"So the will wasn't in Mrs. Cresswell's favor after all?" she said.

Inspector Welch looked over at her in a rather surprised fashion.

"That's a very clever guess of yours, madam," he said. "No. Mrs. Cresswell isn't named as beneficiary."

"Just like Mr. Naysmith," said Miss Marple, nodding her head. "Miss Greenshaw told Mrs. Cresswell she was going to leave her everything and so got out of paying her wages; and then she left her money to somebody else. No doubt she was vastly pleased with herself. No wonder she chortled when she put the will away in *Lady Audley's Secret*."

"It was lucky Mrs. Oxley was able to tell us about the will and where it was put," said the Inspector. "We might have had a long hunt for it otherwise."

"A Victorian sense of humor," murmured Raymond West.

"So she left her money to her nephew after all," said Louise.

The Inspector shook his head.

"No," he said, "she didn't leave it to Nat Fletcher. The story goes around here—of course I'm new to the place and I only get the gossip that's second-hand—but it seems that in the old days both Miss Greenshaw and her sister were set on the handsome young riding master, and the sister got him. No, she didn't leave the money to her nephew—" Inspector Welch paused, rubbing his chin. "She left it to Alfred," he said.

"Alfred—the gardener?" Joan spoke in a surprised voice.

"Yes, Mrs. West. Alfred Pollock."

"But why?" cried Louise.

Miss Marple coughed and murmured, "I would imagine, though perhaps I am wrong, that there may have been— what we might call *family* reasons."

"You could call them that in a way," agreed the Inspector. "It's quite well-known in the village, it seems, that

Thomas Pollock, Alfred's grandfather, was one of old Mr. Greenshaw's by-blows."

"Of course," cried Louise, "the resemblance!"

She remembered how after passing Alfred she had come into the house and looked up at old Greenshaw's portrait.

"I daresay," said Miss Marple, "that she thought Alfred Pollock might have a pride in the house, might even want to live in it, whereas her nephew would almost certainly have no use for it whatever and would sell it as soon as he could possibly do so. He's an actor, isn't he? What play exactly is he acting in at present?"

Trust an old lady to wander from the point, thought Inspector Welch; but he replied civilly, "I believe madam, they are doing a season of Sir James M. Barrie's plays."

"Barrie," said Miss Marple thoughtfully.

"*What Every Woman Knows,*" said Inspector Welch, and then blushed. "Name of a play," he said quickly. "I'm not much of a theater-goer myself," he added, "but the wife went along and saw it last week. Quite well done, she said it was."

"Barrie wrote some very charming plays," said Miss Marple, "though I must say that when I went with an old friend of mine, General Easterly, to see Barrie's *Little Mary*—" she shook her head sadly "—neither of us knew where to look."

The Inspector, unacquainted with the play *Little Mary*, seemed completely fogged.

Miss Marple explained: "When I was a girl, Inspector, nobody ever mentioned the word *stomach*."

The Inspector looked even more at sea. Miss Marple was murmuring titles under her breath.

"*The Admirable Chrichton.* Very clever, *Mary Rose*—a charming play. I cried, I remember. *Quality Street* I didn't care for so much. Then there was *A Kiss for Cinderella*. Oh, of course!"

Inspector Welch had no time to waste on theatrical discussion. He returned to the matter at hand.

"The question is," he said, "did Alfred Pollock know the old lady had made a will in his favor? Did she tell him?" He added, "You see—there's an Archery Club over at Bore-

ham—and *Alfred Pollock's a member*. He's a good shot indeed with a bow and arrow."

"Then isn't your case quite clear?" asked Raymond
West. "It would fit in with the doors being locked on the
two women—he'd know just where they were in the
house."

The Inspector looked at him. He spoke with deep
melancholy.

"He's got an alibi," said the Inspector.

"I always think alibis are definitely suspicious," Raymond remarked.

"Maybe, sir," said Inspector Welch. "You're talking as a
writer."

"I don't write detective stories," said Raymond West,
horrified at the mere idea.

"Easy enough to say that alibis are suspicious," went on
Inspector Welch, "but unfortunately we've got to deal with
facts." He sighed. "We've got three good suspects," he
went on. "Three people who, as it happened, were very
close upon the scene at the time. Yet the odd thing is that
it looks as though none of the three could have done it.
The housekeeper I've already dealt with; the nephew, Nat
Fletcher, at the moment Miss Greenshaw was shot, was a
couple of miles away filling up his car at a garage and asking his way; as for Alfred Pollock, six people will swear
that he entered the Dog and Duck at twenty past twelve and
was there for an hour having his usual bread and cheese
and beer."

"Deliberately establishing an alibi," said Raymond West
hopefully.

"Maybe," said Inspector Welch, "but if so, he *did* establish it."

There was a long silence. Then Raymond turned his
head to where Miss Marple sat upright and thoughtful.

"It's up to you, Aunt Jane," he said. "The Inspector's
baffled, the Sergeant's baffled, I'm baffled, Joan's baffled,
Louise is baffled. But to you, Aunt Jane, it is crystal clear.
Am I right?"

"I wouldn't say that," said Miss Marple, "not *crystal*
clear. And murder, dear Raymond, isn't a game. I don't sup-

pose poor Miss Greenshaw wanted to die, and it was a particularly brutal murder. Very well-planned and quite cold-
blooded. It's not a thing to make *jokes* about."

"I'm sorry," said Raymond. "I'm not really as callous as
I sound. One treats a thing lightly to take away from the—
well, the horror of it."

"That is, I believe, the modern tendency," said Miss
Marple. "All these wars, and having to joke about funerals.
Yes, perhaps I was thoughtless when I implied that you
were callous."

"It isn't," said Joan, "as though we'd known her at all
well."

"That is *very* true," said Miss Marple. "You, dear Joan,
did not know her at all. I did not know her at all. Raymond gathered an impression of her from one afternoon's
conversation. Louise knew her for only two days."

"Come now, Aunt Jane," said Raymond, "tell us your
views. You don't mind, Inspector?"

"Not at all," said the Inspector politely.

"Well, my dear, it would seem that we have three people
who had—or might have thought they had—a motive to
kill the old lady. And three quite simple reasons why none
of the three could have done so. The housekeeper could
not have killed Miss Greenshaw because she was locked in
her room and because her mistress definitely stated that a
*man* shot her. The gardener was inside the Dog and Duck
at the time, the nephew at the garage."

"Very clearly put, madam," said the Inspector.

"And since it seems most unlikely that any outsider
should have done it, where, then, are we?"

"That's what the Inspector wants to know," said Raymond West.

"One so often looks at a thing the wrong way round,"
said Miss Marple apologetically. "If we can't alter the
movements or the positions of those three people, then
couldn't we perhaps alter the time of the murder?"

"You mean that both my watch and the clock were
wrong?" asked Louise.

"No, dear," said Miss Marple, "I didn't mean that at all.

I mean that the murder didn't occur when you thought it occurred."

"But I *saw* it," cried Louise.

"Well, what I have been wondering, my dear, was whether you weren't *meant* to see it. I've been asking myself, you know, whether that wasn't the real reason why you were engaged for this job."

"What *do* you mean, Aunt Jane?"

"Well, dear, it seems odd. Miss Greenshaw did not like spending money—yet she engaged you and agreed quite willingly to the terms you asked. It seems to me that perhaps you were meant to be there in that library on the second floor, looking out of the window so that you could be the key witness—someone from outside of irreproachably good character—to fix a definite time and place for the murder."

"But you can't mean," said Louise, incredulously, "that Miss Greenshaw *intended* to be murdered."

"What I mean, dear," said Miss Marple, "is that you didn't really know Miss Greenshaw. There's no real reason, is there, why the Miss Greenshaw you saw when you went up to the house should be the same Miss Greenshaw that Raymond saw a few days earlier? Oh, yes, I know," she went on, to prevent Louise's reply, "she was wearing the peculiar old-fashioned print dress and the strange straw hat, and had unkempt hair. She corresponded exactly to the description Raymond gave us last weekend. But those two women, you know, were much the same age, height, and size. The housekeeper, I mean, and Miss Greenshaw."

"But the housekeeper is fat!" Louise exclaimed. "She's got an enormous bosom."

Miss Marple coughed.

"But my dear, surely, nowadays I have seen—er—them myself in shops most indelicately displayed. It is very easy for anyone to have a—a bosom—of *any* size and dimension."

"What are you trying to say?" demanded Raymond.

"I was just thinking that during the two days Louise was working there, one woman could have played both parts. You said yourself, Louise, that you hardly saw the housekeeper, except for the one minute in the morning when she brought you the tray with coffee. One sees those clever artists on the stage coming in as different characters with only a moment or two to spare, and I am sure the change could have been effected quite easily. That marquise head-dress could be just a wig slipped on and off."

"Aunt Jane! Do you mean that Miss Greenshaw was dead before I started work there?"

"Not dead. Kept under drugs, I should say. A very easy job for an unscrupulous woman like the housekeeper to do. Then she made the arrangements with you and got you to telephone to the nephew to ask him to lunch at a definite time. The only person who would have known that this Miss Greenshaw was *not* Miss Greenshaw would have been Alfred. And if you remember, the first two days you were working there it was wet, and Miss Greenshaw stayed in the house. Alfred never came into the house because of his feud with the housekeeper. And on the last morning Alfred was in the drive, while Miss Greenshaw was working on the rockery—I'd like to have a look at that rockery."

"Do you mean it was Mrs. Cresswell who killed Miss Greenshaw?"

"I think that after bringing you your coffee, the house-keeper locked the door on you as she went out, then car-ried the unconscious Miss Greenshaw down to the draw-ing-room, then assumed her 'Miss Greenshaw' disguise and went out to work on the rockery where you could see her from the upstairs window. In due course she screamed and came staggering to the house clutching an arrow as though it had penetrated her throat. She called for help and was careful to say '*he* shot me' so as to remove suspicion from the housekeeper—from herself. She also called up to the housekeeper's window as though she saw her there. Then, once inside the drawing-room, she threw over a table with porcelain on it, ran quickly upstairs, put on her marquise wig, and was able a few moments later to lean her head out of the window and tell you that she, too, was locked in."

"But she *was* locked in," said Louise.

"I know. That is where the policeman comes in."

"What policeman?"

"Exactly—what policeman? I wonder, Inspector, if you would mind telling me how and when *you* arrived on the scene?"

The Inspector looked a little puzzled.

"At 12:29 we received a telephone call from Mrs. Cresswell, housekeeper to Miss Greenshaw, stating that her mistress had been shot. Sergeant Cayley and myself went out there at once in a car and arrived at the house at 12:35. We found Miss Greenshaw dead and the two ladies locked in their rooms."

"So, you see, my dear," said Miss Marple to Louise. "The police constable *you* saw wasn't a real police constable at all. You never thought of him again—one doesn't—one just accepts one more uniform as part of the Law."

"But who—why?"

"As to who—well, if they are playing *A Kiss for Cinderella,* a policeman is the principal character. Nat Fletcher would only have to help himself to the costume he wears on the stage. He'd ask his way at a garage, being careful to call attention to the time—12:25; then he would drive on quickly, leave his car round a corner, slip on his police uniform, and do his 'act.' "

"But why—why?"

"*Someone* had to lock the housekeeper's door on the outside, and someone had to drive the arrow through Miss Greenshaw's throat. You can stab anyone with an arrow just as well as by shooting it—but it needs force."

"You mean they were both in it?"

"Oh, yes, I think so. Mother and son as likely as not."

"But Miss Greenshaw's sister died long ago."

"Yes, but I've no doubt Mr. Fletcher married again—he sounds like the sort of man who would. I think it possible that the child died too, and that this so-called nephew was the second wife's child, and not really a relation at all. The woman got the post as housekeeper and spied out the land. Then he wrote to Miss Greenshaw as her nephew and proposed to call on her—he may have even made some joking reference to coming in his policeman's uniform—remember, she said she was expecting a policeman. But I think Miss Greenshaw suspected the truth and refused to see him. He would have been her heir if she had died without making a will—but of course once she had made a will in the housekeeper's favor, as they thought, then it was clear sailing."

"But why use an arrow?" objected Joan. "So very far-fetched."

"Not far-fetched at all, dear. Alfred belonged to an Archery Club—Alfred was meant to take the blame. The fact that he was in the pub as early as 12:20 was most unfortunate from their point of view. He always left a little before his proper time and that would have been just right." She shook her head. "It really seems all wrong—morally, I mean, that Alfred's laziness should have saved his life."

The Inspector cleared his throat.

"Well, madam, these suggestions of yours are very interesting. I shall, of course, have to investigate—"

Miss Marple and Raymond West stood by the rockery and looked down at a gardening basket full of dying vegetation.

Miss Marple murmured:

"Alyssum, saxifrage, cystis, thimble campanula . . . Yes, that's all the proof *I* need. Whoever was weeding here yesterday morning was no gardener—she pulled up plants as well as weeds. So now I *know* I'm right. Thank you, dear Raymond, for bringing me here. I wanted to see the place for myself."

She and Raymond both looked up at the outrageous pile of Greenshaw's Folly.

A cough made them turn. A handsome young man was also looking at the monstrous house.

"Plaguey big place," he said. "Too big for nowadays—or so they say. I dunno about that. If I won a football pool and made a lot of money, that's the kind of house I'd like to build."

He smiled bashfully at them, then rumpled his hair.

"Reckon I can say so now—that there house was built by my great-grandfather," said Alfred Pollock. "And a fine house it is, for all they call it Greenshaw's Folly!"

# THE CASE OF THE PERFECT MAID

"OH, IF YOU PLEASE, Madam, could I speak to you a moment?"

It might be thought that this request was in the nature of an absurdity, since Edna, Miss Marple's little maid, was actually speaking to her mistress at the moment.

Recognizing the idiom, however, Miss Marple said promptly: "Certainly, Edna, come in and shut the door. What is it?"

Obediently shutting the door, Edna advanced into the room, pleated the corner of her apron between her fingers and swallowed once or twice.

"Yes, Edna?" said Miss Marple encouragingly.

"Oh please, M'am, it's my cousin Gladdie. You see, she's lost her place."

"Dear me, I am sorry to hear that. She was at Old Hall, wasn't she, with the Miss—Misses—Skinners?"

"Yes, M'am, that's right, M'am. And Gladdie's very upset about it—very upset indeed."

"Gladys has changed places rather often before, though, hasn't she?"

"Oh yes, M'am. She's always one for a change. Gladdie is. She never seems to get really settled, if you know what I mean. But she's always been the one to give the notice, you see!"

"And this time it's the other way round?" asked Miss Marple drily.

"Yes, M'am, and it's upset Gladdie something awful."

Miss Marple looked slightly surprised. Her recollection of Gladys, who had occasionally come to drink tea in the kitchen on her 'days out,' was a stout, giggling girl of unshakably equable temperament.

Edna went on: "You see, M'am, it's the way it happened —the way Miss Skinner looked."

"How," inquired Miss Marple patiently, "did Miss Skinner look?"

This time Edna got well away with her news bulletin.

"Oh M'am, it was ever such a shock to Gladdie. You see, one of Miss Emily's brooches was missing and such a hue and cry for it as never was, and of course, nobody likes a thing like that to happen; it's upsetting, M'am, if you know what I mean. And Gladdie's helped search everywhere and there was Miss Lavinia saying she was going to the police about it, and then it turned up again, pushed right to the back of a drawer in the dressing table, and very thankful Gladdie was.

"And the very next day as ever was a plate got broken, and Miss Lavinia she bounced out right away and told Gladdie to take a month's notice. And what Gladdie feels is it couldn't have been the plate and that Miss Lavinia was just making an excuse of that, and that it must be because of the brooch and they think as she took it and put it back when the police was mentioned, and Gladdie wouldn't do such a thing, not never she wouldn't, and what she feels is as it will get around and tell against her and it's a very serious thing for a girl as you know, M'am."

Miss Marple nodded. Though having no particular liking for the bouncing, self-opinioned Gladys, she was quite sure of the girl's intrinsic honesty and could well imagine that the affair must have upset her.

Edna said wistfully: "I suppose, M'am, there isn't anything you could do about it? Gladdie's in ever such a taking."

"Tell her not to be silly," said Miss Marple crisply. "If she didn't take the brooch—which I'm sure she didn't— then she has no cause to be upset."

"It'll get about," said Edna dismally.

Miss Marple said. "I—er—am going up that way this afternoon. I'll have word with the Misses Skinners."

"Oh, thank you, Madam," said Edna.

Old Hall was a big Victorian house surrounded by woods and parkland. Since it had been proved unlettable and unsalable as it was, an enterprising speculator had divided it into four flats with a central hot water system, and the use of 'the grounds' to be held in common by the tenants. The experiment had been satisfactory. A rich and eccentric old lady and her maid occupied one flat. The old lady had a passion for birds and entertained a feathered gathering to meals every day. A retired Indian judge and his wife rented a second. A very young couple, recently married, occupied the third, and the fourth had been taken only two months ago by two maiden ladies of the name of Skinner. The four sets of tenants were only on the most distant terms with each other, since none of them had anything in common. The landlord had been heard to say that this was an excellent thing. What he dreaded were friendships followed by estrangements and subsequent complaints to him.

Miss Marple was acquainted with all the tenants, though she knew none of them well. The elder Miss Skinner, Miss Lavinia, was what might be termed the working member of the firm. Miss Emily, the younger, spent most of her time in bed suffering from various complaints which, in the opinion of St. Mary Mead, were largely imaginary. Only Miss Lavinia believed devoutly in her sister's martyrdom and patience under affliction, and willingly ran errands and trotted up and down to the village for things that "my sister had suddenly fancied."

It was the view of St. Mary Mead that if Miss Emily suffered half as much as she said she did, she would have sent for Doctor Haydock long ago. But Miss Emily, when this was hinted to her, shut her eyes in a superior way and murmured that her case was not a simple one—the best specialists in London had been baffled by it—and that a wonderful new man had put her on a most revolutionary course of treatment and that she really hoped her health would improve under it. No humdrum G.P. could possibly understand her case.

"And it's my opinion," said the outspoken Miss Hartnell, "that she's very wise not to send for him. Dear Doctor

Haydock, in that breezy manner of his, would tell her that there was nothing the matter with her and to get up and not make a fuss! Do her a lot of good!"

Failing such arbitrary treatment, however, Miss Emily continued to lie on sofas, to surround herself with strange little pill boxes, and to reject nearly everything that had been cooked for her and ask for something else—usually something difficult and inconvenient to get.

The door was opened to Miss Marple by "Gladdie," looking more depressed than Miss Marple had ever thought possible. In the sitting room (a quarter of the late drawing room, which had been partitioned into a dining room, drawing room, bathroom and housemaid's cupboard), Miss Lavinia rose to greet Miss Marple.

Lavinia Skinner was a tall, gaunt, bony female of fifty. She had a gruff voice and an abrupt manner.

"Nice to see you," she said. "Emily's lying down— feeling low today, poor dear. Hope she'll see you, it would cheer her up, but there are times when she doesn't feel up to seeing anybody. Poor dear, she's wonderfully patient."

Miss Marple responded politely. Servants were the main topic of conversation in St. Mary Mead so it was not difficult to lead the conversation in that direction. Miss Marple said she had heard that that nice girl, Gladys Holmes, was leaving?

Miss Lavinia nodded.

"Wednesday week. Broke things, you know. Can't have that."

Miss Marple sighed and said we all had to put up with things nowadays. It was so difficult to get girls to come to the country. Did Miss Skinner really think it was wise to part with Gladys?

"Know it's difficult to get servants," admitted Miss Lavinia. "The Devereuxs haven't got anybody—but then I don't wonder—always quarreling, jazz on all night—meals any time—that girl knows nothing of housekeeping, I pity her husband! Then the Larkins have just lost their maid. Of course, what with the judge's Indian temper and his wanting Chota Hazri, as he calls it, at 6 in the morning

and Mrs. Larkin always fussing, I don't wonder at that
ther. Mrs. Carmichael's Janet is a fixture, of course
though in my opinion she's the most disagreeable woman,
and absolutely bullies the old lady."

"Then don't you think you might reconsider your deci-
sion about Gladys. She really is a nice girl. I know all her
family; very honest and superior."

Miss Lavinia shook her head.

"I've got my reasons," she said importantly.

Miss Marple murmured: "You missed a brooch, I understand—"

"Now who has been talking? I suppose the girl has.
Quite frankly, I'm almost certain she took it. And then
got frightened and put it back—but of course one can't say
anything unless one is sure." She changed the subject. "Do
come and see Miss Emily, Miss Marple. I'm sure it would
do her good."

Miss Marple followed meekly to where Miss Lavinia
knocked on a door; was bidden enter and ushered her
guest into the best room in the flat, most of the light of
which was excluded by half-drawn blinds. Miss Emily was
lying in bed, apparently enjoying the half gloom and her
own indefinite sufferings.

The dim light showed her to be a thin, indecisive looking
creature, with a good deal of grayish yellow hair untidily
wound around her head and erupting into curls, the whole
thing looking like a bird's nest of which no self-respecting
bird could be proud. There was a smell in the room of eau-
de-cologne, stale biscuits and camphor.

With half-closed eyes and in a thin, weak voice, Emily
Skinner explained that this was "one of her bad days."

"The worst of ill-health is," said Miss Emily in a melancholy tone, "that one knows what burden one is to everyone around one.

"Lavinia is very good to me. Lavvie dear, I do so hate
giving trouble but if my hot water bottle could only be
filled in the way I like it—too full it weighs on me so—on
the other hand, if it is not sufficiently filled, it gets cold
immediately!"

"I'm sorry, dear. Give it to me. I will empty a little out."

"Perhaps, if you're doing that, it might be refilled. There are no rusks in the house, I suppose—no, no, it doesn't matter. I can do without. Some weak tea and a slice of lemon—no lemons? No, really, I couldn't drink tea without lemon. I think the milk was slightly turned this morning. It has put me right against milk in my tea. It doesn't matter. I can do without my tea. Only I do feel so weak. Oysters, they say, are nourishing. I wonder if I could fancy a few. No, no, too much bother to get hold of them so late in the day. I can fast until tomorrow."

Lavinia left the room murmuring something incoherent about bicycling down to the village.

Miss Emily smiled feebly at her guest and remarked that she did hate giving anyone any trouble.

Miss Marple told Edna that evening that she was afraid her embassy had met with no succcess.

She was rather troubled to find that rumors as to Gladys' dishonesty were already going around the village.

In the Post Office, Miss Wetherby tackled her: "My dear Jane, they gave her a written reference saying she was willing and sober and respectable, but saying nothing about honesty. That seems to me most significant! I hear there was some trouble about a brooch. I think there must be something in it, you know, because one doesn't let a servant go nowadays unless it's something rather grave. They'll find it most difficult to get anyone else. Girls simply will not go to Old Hall. They're nervous coming home on their days out. You'll see, the Skinners won't find anyone else, and then, perhaps that dreadful hypochondriac sister will have to get up and do something!"

Great was the chagrin of the village when it was made known that the Misses Skinners had engaged, from an agency, a new maid who, by all accounts, was a perfect paragon.

"A three years' reference recommending her most warmly, she prefers the country, and actually asks less wages than Gladys. I really feel we have been most fortunate."

"Well, really," said Miss Marple, to whom these details

were imparted by Miss Lavinia in the fishmonger's shop. "It does seem too good to be true."

It then became the opinion of St. Mary Mead that the paragon would cry off at the last minute and fail to arrive.

None of these prognostications came true however, and the village was able to observe the domestic treasure, by name, Mary Higgins, driving through the village in Reed's taxi to Old Hall. It had to be admitted that her appearance was good. A most respectable looking woman, very neatly dressed.

When Miss Marple next visited Old Hall, on the occasion of recruiting stall-holders for the Vicarage Fete, Mary Higgins opened the door. She was certainly a most superior looking maid, at a guess forty years of age, with neat black hair, rosy cheeks, a plump figure discreetly arrayed in black with a white apron and cap—"quite the good, old-fashioned type of servant," as Miss Marple explained afterwards, and with the proper, inaudible, respectful voice, so different from the loud but adenoidal accents of Gladys.

Miss Lavinia was looking far less harassed than usual and, although she regretted that she could not take a stall owing to her preoccupation with her sister, she nevertheless tendered a handsome monetary contribution, and promised to produce a consignment of penwipers and babies' socks.

Miss Marple commented on her air of well-being.

"I really feel I owe a great deal to Mary. I am so thankful I had the resolution to get rid of that other girl. Mary is really invaluable. Cooks nicely and waits beautifully and keeps our little flat scrupulously clean—mattresses turned over every day. And she is really wonderful with Emily!"

Miss Marple hastily inquired after Emily.

"Oh, poor dear, she has been very much under the weather lately. She can't help it, of course, but it really makes things a little difficult, sometimes. Wanting certain things cooked and then, when they come, saying she can't eat now—and then wanting them again half an hour later and everything spoilt and having to be done again. It makes, of course, a lot of work—but fortunately Mary

seem to mind at all. She's used to waiting on in-
~~~e~~ says, and understands them. It is such a

~~Dear~~ me," said Miss Marple. "You are fortunate."

"Yes, indeed. I really feel Mary has been sent to us as
an answer to prayer."

"She sounds to me," said Miss Marple, "almost too good
to be true. I should—well, I should be a little careful if I
were you."

Lavinia Skinner failed to perceive the point of this remark. She said: "Oh! I assure you I do all I can to make
her comfortable. I don't know what I should do if she
left."

"I don't expect she'll leave until she's ready to leave,"
said Miss Marple and stared very hard at her hostess.

Miss Lavinia said: "If one has no domestic worries, it
takes such a load off one's mind, doesn't it? How is your
little Edna shaping?"

"She's doing quite nicely. Not much ahead, of course.
Not like your Mary. Still I do know all about Edna, because she's a village girl."

As she went out into the hall she heard the invalid's
voice fretfully raised: "This compress has been allowed to
get quite dry—Doctor Allerton particularly said moisture
continually renewed. There, there, leave it. I want a cup of
tea and a boiled egg—boiled only three minutes and a half,
remember, and send Miss Lavinia to me."

The efficient Mary emerged from the bedroom and, saying to Lavinia, "Miss Emily is asking for you, Madam,"
proceeded to open the door for Miss Marple, helping her
into her coat and handing her her umbrella in the most irreproachable fashion.

Miss Marple took the umbrella, dropped it, tried to pick
it up and dropped her bag which flew open. Mary politely
retrieved various odds and ends—a handkerchief, an engagement book, an old-fashioned leather purse, two
shillings, three pennies and a striped piece of peppermint
rock.

Miss Marple received the last with some signs of
confusion.

"Oh dear, that must have been Mrs. Clement's little boy. He was sucking it, I remember, and he took my bag to play with. He must have put it inside. It's terribly sticky, isn't it?"

"Shall I take it, Madam?"

"Oh, would you? Thank you so much."

Mary stooped to retrieve the last item, a small mirror upon recovering which Miss Marple exclaimed fervently: "How lucky now that that isn't broken."

She thereupon departed, Mary standing politely by the door holding a piece of striped rock with a completely expressionless face.

For ten days longer St. Mary Mead had to endure hearing of the excellencies of Miss Lavinia's and Miss Emily's treasure.

On the eleventh day, the village awoke to its big thrill.

Mary, the paragon, was missing! Her bed had not been slept in and the front door was found ajar. She had slipped out quietly during the night.

And not Mary alone was missing! Two brooches and five rings of Miss Lavinia's; three rings, a pendant, a bracelet and four brooches of Miss Emily's were missing also!

It was the beginning of a chapter of catastrophe.

Young Mrs. Devereux had lost her diamonds which she kept in an unlocked drawer and also some valuable furs given to her as a wedding present. The judge and his wife also had had jewelry taken and a certain amount of money. Mrs. Carmichael was the greatest sufferer. Not only had she some very valuable jewels but she also kept a large sum of money in the flat which had gone. It had been Janet's evening out and her mistress was in the habit of walking round the gardens at dusk calling to the birds and scattering crumbs. It seemed clear that Mary, the perfect maid, had had keys to fit all the flats!

There was, it must be confessed, a certain amount of ill-natured pleasure in St. Mary Mead. Miss Lavinia had boasted so much of her marvelous Mary.

"And all the time, my dear, just a common thief!"

Interesting revelation followed. Not only had Mary dis-

appeared into the blue, but the agency who had provided
her and vouched for her credentials was alarmed to find
that the Mary Higgins who had applied to them and whose
references they had taken up had, to all intents and pur-
poses, never existed. It was the name of a bonafide servant
who had lived with the bonafide sister of a dean, but the
real Mary Higgins was existing peacefully in a place in
Cornwall.

"Clever, the whole thing," Inspector Slack was forced to
admit. "And, if you ask me, that woman works in with a
gang. There was a case of much the same kind in North-
umberland a year ago. Stuff was never traced and they
never caught her. However, we'll do better than that in
Much Benham!"

Inspector Slack was always a confident man.

Nevertheless, weeks passed and Mary Higgins remained
triumphantly at large. In vain Inspector Slack redoubled
that energy that so belied his name.

Miss Lavinia remained tearful. Miss Emily was so upset,
and felt so alarmed by her condition that she actually sent
for Doctor Haydock.

The whole of the village was terribly anxious to know
what he thought of Miss Emily's claims to ill health, but
naturally could not ask him. Satisfactory data came to
hand on the subject, however, through Mr. Meek, the chem-
ist's assistant, who was walking out with Clara, Mrs.
Price-Ridley's maid. It was then known that Doctor
Haydock had prescribed a mixture of assafoetida and
valerian which, according to Mr. Meek, was the stock rem-
edy for malingerers in the Army!

Soon afterwards it was learned that Miss Emily, not rel-
ishing the medical attention she had had, was declaring
that in the state of her health she felt it her duty to be near
the specialist in London who understood her case. It was,
she said, only fair to Lavinia.

The flat was put up for subletting.

It was a few days after that that Miss Marple, rather
pink and flustered, called at the police station in Much
Benham and asked for Inspector Slack.

Inspector Slack did not like Miss Marple. But he was aware that the Chief Constable, Colonel Melchett, did not share that opinion. Rather grudgingly, therefore, he received her.

"Good afternoon, Miss Marple, what can I do for you?"

"Oh dear," said Miss Marple, "I'm afraid you're in a hurry."

"Lot of work on," said Inspector Slack, "but I can spare a few moments."

"Oh dear," said Miss Marple. "I hope I shall be able to put what I say properly. So difficult, you know, to explain oneself, don't you think? No, perhaps you don't. But you see, not having been educated in the modern style—just a governess, you know, who taught one the dates on the Kings of England and General Knowledge—Doctor Brewer —three kinds of diseases of wheat—bright, mildew—now what was the third—was it smut?"

"Do you want to talk about smut?" asked Inspector Slack and then blushed.

"Oh, no, no," Miss Marple hastily disclaimed any wish to talk about smut. "Just an illustration, you know. And how needles are made and all that. Discursive, you know, but not teaching one to keep to the point. Which is what I want to do. It's about Miss Skinner's maid, Gladys, you know."

"Mary Higgins," said Inspector Slack.

"Oh yes, the second maid. But it's Gladys Holmes I mean—rather an impertinent girl and far too pleased with herself but really strictly honest, and it's so important that that should be recognized."

"No charge against her so far as I know," said the inspector.

"No, I know there isn't a charge—but that makes it worse. Because, you see, people go on thinking things. Oh dear—I knew I should explain badly. What I really mean is that the important thing is to find Mary Higgins."

"Certainly," said Inspector Slack. "Have you any ideas on the subject?"

"Well, as a matter of fact, I have," said Miss Marple.

"May I ask you a question? Are fingerprints of no use to you?"

"Ah," said Inspector Slack, "that's where she was a bit too artful for us. Did most of her work in rubber gloves or housemaid's gloves, it seems. And she'd been careful—wiped off everything in her bedroom and on the sink. Couldn't find a single fingerprint in the place!"

"If you did have her fingerprints, would it help?"

"It might, Madam. They may be known at the Yard. This isn't her first job, I'd say!"

Miss Marple nodded brightly. She opened her bag and extracted a small cardboard box. Inside it, wedged in cotton wool, was a small mirror.

"From my handbag," said Miss Marple. "The maid's prints are on it. I think they should be satisfactory—she touched an extremely sticky substance a moment previously."

Inspector Slack stared.

"Did you get her fingerprints on purpose?"

"Of course."

"You suspected her then?"

"Well, you know it did strike me that she was a little too good to be true. I practically told Miss Lavinia so. But she simply wouldn't take the hint! I'm afraid, you know, Inspector, that I don't believe in paragons. Most of us have our faults—and domestic service shows them up very quickly!"

"Well," said Inspector Slack, recovering his balance, "I'm obliged to you, I'm sure. We'll send these up to the Yard and see what they have to say."

He stopped. Miss Marple had put her head a little on one side and was regarding him with a good deal of meaning.

"You wouldn't consider, I suppose, Inspector, looking a little nearer home?"

"What do you mean, Miss Marple?"

"It's very difficult to explain, but when you come across a peculiar thing you notice it. Although, often, peculiar things may be the merest trifles. I've felt that all along, you know; I mean about Gladys and the brooch. She's an honest girl; she didn't take that brooch. Then why did Miss

Skinner think she did? Miss Skinner's not a fool; far from it! Why was she so anxious to let a girl go who was a good servant when servants are hard to get? It was peculiar, you know. So I wondered. I wondered a good deal. And I noticed another peculiar thing! Miss Emily's a hypochondriac, but she's the first hypochondriac who hasn't sent for some doctor or other at once. Hypochondriacs love doctors. Miss Emily didn't!"

"What are you suggesting, Miss Marple?"

"Well, I'm suggesting, you know, that Miss Lavinia and Miss Emily are peculiar people. Miss Emily spends nearly all her time in a dark room. And if that hair of hers isn't a wig I—I'll eat my own back switch! And what I say is this —it's perfectly possible for a thin, pale, gray-haired, whining woman to be the same as a black-haired, rosy-cheeked, plump woman. And nobody that I can find ever saw Miss Emily and Mary Higgins at one and the same time.

"Plenty of time to get impressions of all the keys, plenty of time to find out all about the other tenants, and then— get rid of the local girl. Miss Emily takes a brisk walk across country one night and arrives at the station as Mary Higgins next day. And then, at the right moment, Mary Higgins disappears, and off goes the hue and cry after her. I'll tell you where you'll find her, Inspector. On Miss Emily Skinner's sofa! Get her fingerprints if you don't believe me, but you'll find I'm right! A couple of clever thieves, that's what the Skinners are—and no doubt in league with a clever post and rails or fence or whatever you call it. But they won't get away with it this time! I'm not going to have one of our village girl's character for honesty taken away like that! Gladys Holmes is as honest as the day and everybody's going to know it! Good afternoon!"

Miss Marple had stalked out before Inspector Slack had recovered.

"Whew!" he muttered. "I wonder if she's right?"

He soon found out that Miss Marple was right again.

Colonel Melchett congratulated Slack on his efficiency and Miss Marple had Gladys come to tea with Edna and spoke to her seriously on settling down in a good situation when she got one.

# AT THE BELLS AND MOTLEY

MR. SATTERTHWAITE was annoyed. Altogether it had been an unfortunate day. They had started late; they had taken the wrong turning and lost themselves amid the wilds of Salisbury Plain. Now it was close on eight o'clock; they were still a matter of forty miles from Marswick Manor, whither they were bound, and a blowout had supervened to render matters still more trying.

Mr. Satterthwaite, looking like some small bird whose plumage had been ruffled, walked up and down in front of the village garage while his chauffeur conversed in hoarse undertones with the local expert.

"Half an hour *at* least," said that worthy, pronouncing judgment.

"And lucky at that," supplemented Masters, the chauffeur. "More like three quarters if you ask me."

"What is that—place, anyway?" demanded Mr. Satterthwaite fretfully. Being a little gentleman considerate of the feelings of others, he substituted the word "place" for "Godforsaken hole" which had first risen to his lips.

"Kirtlington Mallet."

Mr. Satterthwaite was not much wiser, and yet a faint familiarity seemed to linger round the name. He looked about him disparagingly. Kirtlington Mallet seemed to consist of one straggling street, the garage and the post office on one side of it balanced by three indeterminate shops on the other side. Farther down the road, however, Mr. Satterthwaite perceived something that creaked and swung in the wind, and his spirits rose ever so slightly.

"There's an inn here, I see," he remarked.

"Bells and Motley," said the garage man. "That's it—yonder."

"If I might make a suggestion, sir," said Masters. "Why not try it? They would be able to give you some sort of a meal, no doubt—not of course, what you are accustomed to—" He paused apologetically, for Mr. Satterthwaite was accustomed to the best cooking of continental chefs, and had in his own service a *cordon bleu* to whom he paid a fabulous salary.

"We shan't be able to take the road again for another three quarters of an hour, sir. I'm sure of that. And it's already past eight o'clock. You could ring up Sir George Foster, sir, from the inn, and acquaint him with the cause of our delay."

"You seem to think you can arrange everything, Masters," said Mr. Satterthwaite snappily.

Masters, who did think so, maintained a respectful silence.

Mr. Satterthwaite, in spite of his earnest wish to discountenance any suggestion that might possibly be made to him—he was in that mood—nevertheless looked down the road toward the creaking inn sign with faint inward approval. He was a man of birdlike appetite, an epicure; but even such men can be hungry.

"The Bells and Motley," he said thoughtfully. "That's an odd name for an inn. I don't know that I ever heard it before."

"There's odd folks come to it by all account," said the local man.

He was bending over the wheel, and his voice came muffled and indistinct.

"Odd folks?" queried Mr. Satterthwaite. "Now what do you mean by that?"

The other hardly seemed to know what he meant.

"Folks that come and go. That kind," he said vaguely.

Mr. Satterthwaite reflected that people who come to an inn are almost of necessity those who "come and go." The definition seemed to him to lack precision. But nevertheless his curiosity was stimulated. Somehow or other he had got to put in three quarters of an hour. The Bells and Motley would be as good as anywhere else.

With his usual small, mincing steps he walked away down the road. From afar there came a rumble of thunder. The mechanic looked up and spoke to Masters: "There's a storm coming over. Thought I could feel it in the air."

"Crikey," said Masters. "And forty miles to go."

"Ah!" said the other. "There's no need to be hurrying over this job. That little boss of yours doesn't look as though he'd relish being out in thunder and lightning."

"Hope they'll do him well at that place," muttered the chauffeur. "I'll be pushing along there for a bite myself presently."

"Billy Jones is all right," said the garage man. "Keeps a good table."

Mr. William Jones, a big burly man of fifty, and land-lord of the Bells and Motley, was at this minute beaming ingratiatingly down on little Mr. Satterthwaite.

"Can do you a nice steak, sir—and fried potatoes, and as good a cheese as any gentleman could wish for. This way, sir, in the coffee room. We're not very full at present, the last of the fishing gentlemen just gone. A little later we'll be full again for the hunting. Only one gentleman here at present, name of Quin—"

Mr. Satterthwaite stopped dead.

"Quin?" he said excitedly. "Did you say Quin?"

"That's the name, sir. Friend of yours, perhaps?"

"Yes, indeed. Oh! yes, most certainly." Twittering with excitement, Mr. Satterthwaite hardly realized that the world might contain more than one man of that name. He had no doubts at all. In an odd way, the information fitted in with what the man at the garage had said. "Folks that come and go." A very apt description of Mr. Quin. And the name of the inn too seemed a peculiarly fitting and appropriate one.

"Dear me, dear me," said Mr. Satterthwaite. "What a *very* odd thing. That we should meet like this! Mr. Harley Quin, is it not?"

"That's right, sir. This is the coffee room, sir. Ah! here is the gentleman."

Tall, dark, smiling, the familiar figure of Mr. Quin rose from the table at which he was sitting, and the well-remembered voice spoke.

"Ah! Mr. Satterthwaite, we meet again. An unexpected meeting!"

Mr. Satterthwaite was shaking him warmly by the hand.

"Delighted. Delighted, I'm sure. A lucky breakdown for me. My car, you know. And you are staying here? For long?"

"One night only."

"Then I am indeed fortunate."

Mr. Satterthwaite sat down opposite his friend with a little sigh of satisfaction, and regarded the dark, smiling face opposite him with a pleasurable expectancy.

The other man shook his head gently.

"I assure you," he said, "that I have not a bowl of goldfish or a rabbit to produce from my sleeve."

"Too bad," cried Mr. Satterthwaite, a little taken aback. "Yes, I must confess—I do rather adopt that attitude toward you. A man of magic. Ha, ha. That is how I regard you. A man of magic."

"And yet," said Mr. Quin, "it is you who do the conjuring tricks, not I."

"Ah!" said Mr. Satterthwaite eagerly. "But I cannot do them without you. I lack—shall we say—inspiration?"

Mr. Quin smilingly shook his head. "That is too big a word. I speak the cue, that is all."

The landlord came in at that minute with bread and a slab of yellow butter. As he set the things on the table there was a vivid flash of lightning, and a clap of thunder almost overhead.

"A wild night, gentlemen."

"Oh such a night—" began Mr. Satterthwaite, and stopped.

"Funny now," said the landlord, "if those weren't just the words I was going to use myself. It was just such a night as this when Captain Harwell brought his bride home, the very day before he disappeared forever."

"Ah!" cried Mr. Satterthwaite, suddenly. "Of course!"

He had got the clue. He knew now why the name Kirt-

lington Mallet was familiar. Three months before he had
read every detail of the astonishing disappearance of Captain Richard Harwell. Like other newspaper readers all
over Great Britain, he had puzzled over the details of the
disappearance, and, also like every other Briton, had
evolved his own theories.

"Of course," he repeated. "It was at Kirtlington Mallet it
happened."

"It was at this house he stayed for the hunting last
winter," said the landlord. "Oh! I knew him well. A main
handsome young gentleman and not one that you'd think
had a care on his mind. He was done away with—that's
my belief. Many's the time I've seen them come riding
home together—he and Miss Le Couteau, and all the village saying there'd be a match come of it—and sure
enough, so it did. A very beautiful young lady, and well
thought of, for all she was a Canadian and a stranger. Ah!
there's some dark mystery there. We'll never know the
rights of it. It broke her heart. It did, sure enough. You've
heard as she's sold the place up and gone abroad; couldn't
abear to go on here with everyone staring and pointing after her—through no fault of her own, poor young dear? A
black mystery, that's what it is."

He shook his head, then, suddenly recollecting his duties, hurried from the room.

"A black mystery," said Mr. Quin softly.

His voice was provocative in Mr. Satterthwaite's ears.

"Are you pretending that we can solve the mystery
where Scotland Yard failed?" he asked sharply.

The other made a characteristic gesture.

"Why not? Time has passed. Three months. That makes
a difference."

"That is a curious idea of yours," said Mr. Satterthwaite
slowly. "That one sees things better afterward than at the
time."

"The longer the time that has elapsed, the more things
fall into proportion. One sees them in their true relation-
ship to one another."

There was a silence which lasted for some minutes.

"I am not sure," said Mr. Satterthwaite, in a h
voice, "that I remember the facts clearly by now."

"I think you do," said Mr. Quin quietly.

It was all the encouragement Mr. Satterthwaite needed.
His general role in life was that of listener and looker on.
Only in the company of Mr. Quin was the position re-
versed. There Mr. Quin was the appreciative listener, and
Mr. Satterthwaite took the center of the stage.

"It was just over a year ago," he said, "that Ashley
Grange passed into the possession of Miss Eleanor Le
Couteau. It is a beautiful old house, but it had been neglected and allowed to remain empty for many years. It
could not have found a better chatelaine. Miss Le Couteau
was a French Canadian, her forebears were *émigrés* from
the French Revolution, and had handed down to her a collection of almost priceless French relics and antiques. She
was a buyer and a collector also, with a very fine and
discriminating taste, so much so that, when she decided to
sell Ashley Grange and everything it contained after the
tragedy, Mr. Cyrus G. Bradburn, the American millionaire,
made no bones about paying the fancy price of sixty thousand pounds for the Grange as it stood."

Mr. Satterthwaite paused.

"I mention these things," he said apologetically, "not because they are relevant to the story—strictly speaking, they
are not—but to convey an atmosphere, the atmosphere of
young Mrs. Harwell."

Mr. Quin nodded. "Atmosphere is always valuable," he
said gravely.

"So we get a picture of this girl," continued the other.

"Just twenty-three, dark, beautiful, accomplished, nothing
crude and unfinished about her. And rich—we must not
forget that. She was an orphan. A Mrs. St. Clair, a lady of
unimpeachable breeding and social standing, lived with her
as duenna. But Eleanor Le Couteau had complete control
of her own fortune. And fortune hunters are never hard
to seek. At least a dozen impecunious young men were to
be found dangling around her on all occasions, in the hunting-
field, in the ballroom, wherever she went. Young Lord Lec-

ɑn, the most eligible party in the country, is reported to have asked her to marry him, but she remained heart-free. That is, until the coming of Captain Richard Harwell.

"Captain Harwell had put up at the local inn for the hunting. He was a dashing rider to hounds, a handsome laughing daredevil of a fellow. You remember the old saying, Mr. Quin? 'Happy the wooing that's not long doing.' The adage was carried out at least in part. At the end of two months, Richard Harwell and Eleanor Le Couteau were engaged.

"The marriage followed three months afterward. The happy pair went abroad for a two weeks' honeymoon, and then returned to take up their residence at Ashley Grange. The landlord has just told us that it was on a night of storm such as this that they returned to their home. An omen, I wonder? Who can tell. Be that as it may, the following morning very early—about half-past seven—Captain Harwell was seen walking in the garden by one of the gardeners, John Mathias. He was bareheaded, and was whistling. We have a picture there, a picture of lightheartedness, of careless happiness. And yet from that minute, as far as we know, no one ever set eyes on Captain Richard Harwell again."

Mr. Satterthwaite paused, pleasantly conscious of a dramatic moment. The admiring glance of Mr. Quin gave him the tribute he needed, and he went on.

"The disappearance was remarkable—unaccountable. It was not till the following day that the distracted wife called in the police. As you know, they have not succeeded in solving the mystery."

"There have, I suppose, been theories?" asked Mr. Quin.

"Oh! theories, I grant you. Theory No. 1, that Captain Harwell had been murdered, done away with. But if so, where was the body? It could hardly have been spirited away. And besides, what motive was there? As far as was known, Captain Harwell had not an enemy in the world."

He paused abruptly, as though uncertain. Mr. Quin leaned forward. "You are thinking," he said softly, "of young Stephen Grant."

"I am," admitted Mr. Satterthwaite. "Stephen Grant, if I remember rightly, had been in charge of Captain Harwell's horses, and had been discharged by his master for some trifling offence. On the morning after the homecoming, very early, Stephen Grant was seen in the vicinity of Ashley Grange, and could give no good account of his presence there. He was detained by the police as being concerned in the disappearance of Captain Harwell, but nothing could be proved against him, and he was eventually discharged. It is true that he might be supposed to bear a grudge against Captain Harwell for his summary dismissal, but the motive was undeniably of the flimsiest. I suppose the police felt they must do something. You see, as I said just now, Captain Harwell had not an enemy in the world."

"As far as was known," said Mr. Quin reflectively.

Mr. Satterthwaite nodded appreciatively.

"We are coming to that. What, after all, *was* known of Captain Harwell? When the police came to look into his antecedents they were confronted with a singular paucity of material. Who was Richard Harwell? Where did he come from? He had appeared literally out of the blue, as it seemed. He was a magnificent rider, and apparently well off. Nobody in Kirtlington Mallet had bothered to inquire further. Miss Le Couteau had had no parents or guardians to make inquiries into the prospects and standing of her fiancé. She was her own mistress. The police theory at this point was clear enough. A rich girl and an impudent impostor. The old story!

"But it was not quite that. True, Miss Le Couteau had no parents or guardians, but she had an excellent firm of solicitors in London who acted for her. Their evidence made the mystery deeper. Eleanor Le Couteau had wished to settle a sum outright upon her prospective husband, but he had refused. He himself was well off, he declared. It was proved conclusively that Harwell never had a penny of his wife's money. Her fortune was absolutely intact.

"He was, therefore, no common swindler; but was his object a refinement of the art? Did he propose blackmail at some future date if Eleanor Harwell should wish to marry

some other man? I will admit that something of that kind
seemed to me the most likely solution. It has always
seemed so to me—until tonight."

Mr. Quin leaned forward, prompting him.

"Tonight?"

"Tonight—I am not satisfied with that. How did he
manage to disappear so suddenly and completely—at that
hour in the morning, with every laborer bestirring himself
and tramping to work? Bareheaded, too."

"There is no doubt about that latter point—since the
gardener saw him?"

"Yes—the gardener—John Mathias. Was there anything
there, I wonder?"

"The police would not overlook him," said Mr. Quin.

"They questioned him closely. He never wavered in his
statement. His wife bore him out. He left his cottage at
seven to attend to the greenhouses; he returned at twenty
minutes to eight. The servants in the house heard the front
door slam at about a quarter after seven. That fixes the
time when Captain Harwell left the house. Ah! yes, I know
what you are thinking."

"Do you, I wonder?" said Mr. Quin.

"I fancy so. Time enough for Mathias to have made
away with his master. But why, man, why? And if so,
where did he hide the body?"

The landlord came in bearing a tray.

"Sorry to have kept you so long, gentlemen."

The odor from the dishes was pleasant to Mr. Satterthwaite's nostrils. He felt gracious. "This looks excellent," he
said. "Most excellent. We have been discussing the disappearance of Captain Harwell. What became of the gardener Mathias?"

"Took a place in Essex, I believe. Didn't care to stay
hereabouts. There were some as looked askance at him,
you understand. Not that I ever believed he had anything
to do with it."

Mr. Satterthwaite helped himself. Mr. Quin followed
suit. The landlord seemed disposed to linger and chat. Mr.
Satterthwaite had no objection; on the contrary. "This
Mathias now," he said. "What kind of a man was he?"

"Middle-aged chap, must have been a powerful fellow once, but bent and crippled with rheumatism. He had that mortal bad, was laid up many a time with it, unable to do any work. For my part, I think it was sheer kindness on Miss Eleanor's part to keep him on. He'd outgrown his usefulness as a gardener, though his wife managed to make herself useful up at the house. Been a cook, she had, and always willing to lend a hand."

"What sort of a woman was she?" asked Mr. Satterthwaite, quickly.

The landlord's answer disappointed him. "A plain body. Middle-aged, and dour-like in manner. Deaf, too. Not that I ever knew much of them. They'd only been here a month, you understand, when the thing happened. They say he'd been a rare good gardener in his time, though. Wonderful testimonials Miss Eleanor had with him."

"Was she interested in gardening?" asked Mr. Quin softly.

"No, sir, I couldn't say that she was, not like some of the ladies round here who pay good money to gardeners and spend the whole of their time grubbing about on their knees as well. Foolishness I call it. You see, Miss Le Couteau wasn't here very much except in the winter for the hunting. The rest of the time she was up in London and away in those foreign seaside places where they say the French ladies don't so much as put a toe into the water for fear of spoiling their costumes, or so I've heard."

Mr. Satterthwaite smiled. "There was no—er—woman of any kind mixed up with Captain Harwell?" he asked. Though his first theory was disposed of, he nevertheless clung to his idea.

Mr. William Jones shook his head. "Nothing of that sort. Never a whisper of it. No, it's a dark mystery, that's what it is."

"And your theory? What do you yourself think?" persisted Mr. Satterthwaite.

"What do I think?"

"Yes."

"Don't know what to think. It's my belief as how he was

done in, but who by I can't say. I'll fetch you gentlemen the cheese."

He stumped from the room bearing empty dishes. The storm, which had been quieting down, suddenly broke out with redoubled vigor. A flash of forked lightning and a great clap of thunder close upon each other made little Mr. Satterthwaite jump, and before the last echoes of the thunder had died away, a girl came into the room carrying the advertised cheese.

She was tall and dark, and handsome in a sullen fashion of her own. Her likeness to the landlord of the Bells and Motley was apparent enough to proclaim her his daughter.

"Good evening, Mary," said Mr. Quin. "A stormy night."

She nodded. "I hate these stormy nights," she muttered.

"You are afraid of thunder, perhaps?" said Mr. Satterthwaite kindly.

"Afraid of thunder? Not me! There's little that I'm afraid of. No, but the storm sets them off. Talking, talking, the same thing over and over again, like a lot of parrots. Father begins it: 'It reminds me, this does, of the night poor Captain Harwell—' And so on, and so on." She turned on Mr. Quin. "You've heard how he goes on. What's the sense of it? Can't anyone let past things be?"

"A thing is only past when it is done with," said Mr. Quin.

"Isn't this done with? Suppose he wanted to disappear? These fine gentlemen do sometimes."

"You think he disappeared of his own free will?"

"Why not? It would make better sense than to suppose a kindhearted creature like Stephen Grant murdered him. What should he murder him for, I should like to know? Stephen had had a drop too much one day and spoke to him saucy like, and got the sack for it. But what of it? He got another place just as good. Is that a reason to murder a man in cold blood?"

"But surely," said Mr. Satterthwaite, "the police were quite satisfied of his innocence."

"The police! What do the police matter? When Stephen comes into the bar of an evening, every man looks at him queer like. They don't really believe he murdered Harwell, but they're not sure, and so they look at him sideways and edge away. Nice life for a man, to see people shrink away from you, as though you were something different from the rest of the folks. Why won't Father hear of our getting married, Stephen and I? 'You can take your pigs to a better market, my girl. I've nothing against Stephen, but—well, we don't know, do we?' "

She stopped, her breast heaving with the violence of her resentment.

"It's cruel, cruel, that's what it is," she burst out. "Stephen, that wouldn't hurt a fly! And all through life there'll be people who'll think he did it. It's turning him queer and bitter like. I don't wonder, I'm sure. And the more he's like that, the more people think there must have been something in it."

Again she stopped. Her eyes were fixed on Mr. Quin's face, as though something in it was drawing this outburst from her.

"Can nothing be done?" said Mr. Satterthwaite.

He was genuinely distressed. The thing was, he saw, inevitable. The very vagueness and unsatisfactoriness of the evidence against Stephen Grant made it the more difficult for him to disprove the accusation.

The girl whirled round on him. "Nothing but the truth can help him," she cried. "If Captain Harwell were to be found, if he was to come back. If the true rights of it were only known—"

She broke off with something very like a sob, and hurried quickly fom the room.

"A fine-looking girl," said Mr. Satterthwaite. "A sad case altogether. I wish—I very much wish that something could be done about it."

His kind heart was troubled.

"We are doing what we can," said Mr. Quin. "There is still nearly half an hour before your car can be ready."

Mr. Satterthwaite stared at him. "You think we can come at the truth by—talking it over like this?"

"You have seen much of life," said Mr. Quin gravely. "More than most people."

"Life has passed me by," said Mr. Satterthwaite bitterly.

"But in so doing has sharpened your vision. Where others are blind you can see."

"It is true," said Mr. Satterthwaite. "I am a great observer."

He plumed himself complacently. The moment of bitterness was past. "I look at it like this," he said after a minute or two. "To get at the cause for a thing, we must study the effect."

"Very good," said Mr. Quin approvingly.

"The effect in this case is that Miss Le Couteau—Mrs. Harwell, I mean—is a wife and yet not a wife. She is not free—she cannot marry again. And look at it as we will, we see Richard Harwell as a sinister figure, a man from nowhere with a mysterious past."

"I agree," said Mr. Quin. "You see what all are bound to see, what cannot be missed, Captain Harwell in the limelight, a suspicious figure."

Mr. Satterthwaite looked at him doubtfully. The words seemed somehow to suggest a faintly different picture to his mind. "We have studied the effect," he said. "Or call it the *result*. We can now pass—"

Mr. Quin interrupted him. "You have not touched on the result on the strictly material side."

"You are right," said Mr. Satterthwaite, after a moment or two for consideration. "One should do the thing thoroughly. Let us say then that the result of the tragedy is that Mrs. Harwell is a wife and not a wife, unable to marry again, that Mr. Cyrus Bradburn has been able to buy Ashley Grange and its contents for—sixty thousand pounds, was it?—and that somebody in Essex has been able to secure John Mathias as a gardener! For all that, we do not suspect 'somebody in Essex' or Mr. Cyrus Bradburn of having engineered the disappearance of Captain Harwell."

"You are sarcastic," said Mr. Quin.

Mr. Satterthwaite looked sharply at him. "But surely you agree—"

"Oh! I agree," said Mr. Quin. "The idea is absurd. What next?"

"Let us imagine ourselves back on the fatal day. The disappearance has taken place, let us say, this very morning."

"No, no," said Mr. Quin, smiling. "Since, in our imagination at least, we have power over time, let us turn it the other way. Let us say the disappearance of Captain Harwell took place a hundred years ago. That we, in the twenty-first century, are looking back."

"You are a strange man," said Mr. Satterthwaite slowly. "You believe in the past, not the present. Why?"

"You used, not long ago, the word atmosphere. There is no atmosphere in the present."

"That is true, perhaps," said Mr. Satterthwaite thoughtfully. "Yes, it is true. The present is apt to be—parochial."

"A good word," said Mr. Quin.

Mr. Satterthwaite gave a funny little bow. "You are too kind," he said.

"Let us take—not this present year, that would be too difficult, but say—last year," continued the other. "Sum it up for me, you, who have the gift of the neat phrase."

Mr. Satterthwaite thought for a minute. He was jealous of his reputation.

"A hundred years ago we have the age of powder and patches," he said. "Shall we say that today is the age of crossword puzzles and cat burglars?"

"Very good," approved Mr. Quin. "You mean that nationally, not internationally, I presume?"

"As to crossword puzzles, I must confess that I do not know," said Mr. Satterthwaite. "But the cat burglar had a great inning on the Continent. You remember that series of famous thefts from French châteaux? It is surmised that one man alone could not have done it. The most miraculous feats were performed to gain admission. There was a theory that a troupe of acrobats were concerned—the Clondinis. I once saw their performance—truly masterly. A mother, son, and daughter. They vanished from the stage in a rather mysterious fashion. But we are wandering from our subject."

"Not very far," said Mr. Quin. "Only across the Channel."

"Where the French ladies will not wet their toes according to our worthy host," said Mr. Satterthwaite laughing.

There was a pause. It seemed somehow significant.

"Why did he disappear?" cried Mr. Satterthwaite. "Why? Why? It is incredible, a kind of conjuring trick."

"Yes," said Mr. Quin. "A conjuring trick. That describes it exactly. Atmosphere again, you see. And wherein does the essence of a conjuring trick lie?"

" 'The quickness of the hand deceives the eye,' " quoted Mr. Satterthwaite glibly.

"That is everything, is it not? To deceive the eye? Sometimes by the quickness of the hand, sometimes—by other means. There are many devices, the pistol shot, the waving of a red handkerchief, something that seems important, but in reality is not. The eye is diverted from the real business, it is caught by the spectacular action that means nothing—nothing at all."

Mr. Satterthwaite leaned forward, his eyes shining. "There is something in that. It is an idea."

He drew in his breath sharply. "The disappearance," breathed Mr. Satterthwaite. "Take that away, and it leaves nothing."

"Nothing? Suppose things took the same course without that dramatic gesture."

"You mean—supposing Miss Le Couteau were still to sell Ashley Grange to Mr. Bradburn and leave—for no reason?"

"Well."

"Well, why not? It would have aroused talk, I suppose; there would have been a lot of interest displayed in the value of the contents, in— Ah! wait!"

He was silent a minute, then burst out. "You are right, there is too much limelight, the limelight on Captain Harwell. And because of that, *she* has been in shadow. *Miss Le Couteau!* Everyone asking 'Who was Captain Harwell? Where did he come from?' But because she is the injured party, no one makes inquiries about her. Was she really a French Canadian? Were those wonderful heirlooms really handed down to her? You were right when you said just now that we had not wandered far from our subject—*only across the Channel.* Those so-called heirlooms were stolen from the French châteaux, most of them valuable *objets d'art*, and in consequence difficult to dispose of. She buys the house—for a mere song, probably—settles down there and pays a good sum to an irreproachable Englishwoman to chaperon her. Then *he* comes. The plot is laid beforehand. The marriage, the disappearance, and the nine days' wonder! What more natural than that a broken-hearted woman should want to sell everything that reminds her of past happiness? The American is a connoisseur, the things are genuine and beautiful, some of them beyond price. He makes an offer, she accepts. She leaves the neighborhood, a sad and tragic figure. The great *coup* has come off. The eye of the public has been deceived by the quickness of the hand and the spectacular nature of the trick."

Mr. Satterthwaite paused, flushed with triumph.

"But for you, I should never have seen it," he said with sudden humility. "You have a most curious effect upon me. One says things so often without even seeing what they really mean. You have the knack of showing one. But it is still not quite clear to me. It must have been most difficult for Harwell to disappear as he did. After all, the police all over England were looking for him."

"They were probably looking," said Mr. Quin, "all over England."

"It would have been simplest to remain hidden at the Grange," mused Mr. Satterthwaite. "If it could be managed."

"He was, I think, very near the Grange," said Mr. Quin.

His look of significance was not lost on Mr. Satterthwaite. "Mathias's cottage?" he exclaimed. "But the police must have searched it?"

"Repeatedly, I should imagine," said Mr. Quin.

"Mathias," said Mr. Satterthwaite, frowning.

"And Mrs. Mathias," said Mr. Quin.

Mr. Satterthwaite stared hard at him. "If that gang was really the Clondinis," he said dreamily, "there are three of them in it. The two young ones were Harwell and Eleanor Le Couteau. The mother now, was she Mrs. Mathias? But in that case."

"Mathias suffered from rheumatism, did he not?" said Mr. Quin innocently.

"Oh!" cried Mr. Satterthwaite. "I have it. But could it be done? I believe it could. Listen. Mathias was there a month. During that time, Harwell and Eleanor were away for a fortnight on a honeymoon. For the fortnight before the wedding, they were supposedly in town. A clever man could have doubled the parts of Harwell and Mathias. When Harwell was at Kirtlington Mallet, Mathias was conveniently laid up with rheumatism, with Mrs. Mathias to sustain the fiction. Her part was very necessary. Without her, someone might have suspected the truth. As you say, Harwell was hidden in Mathias's cottage. He *was* Mathias. When at last the plans matured, and Ashley Grange was sold, he and his wife gave out that they were taking a place in Essex. Exit John Mathias and his wife—forever."

There was a knock at the coffee-room door, and Masters entered.

"The car is at the door, sir," he said.

Mr. Satterthwaite rose. So did Mr. Quin, who went across to the window, pulling the curtains. A beam of moonlight streamed into the room.

"The storm is over," he said.

Mr. Satterthwaite was pulling on his gloves. "The Commissioner is dining with me next week," he said importantly. "I shall put my theory—ah!—before him."

"It will be easily proved or disproved," said Mr. Quin. "A comparison of the objects at Ashley Grange with a list supplied by the French police—!"

"Just so," said Mr. Satterthwaite. "Rather hard luck on Mr. Bradburn, but—well—"

"He can, I believe, stand the loss," said Mr. Quin.

Mr. Satterthwaite held out his hand. "Good-by," he said. "I cannot tell you how much I have appreciated this unexpected meeting. You are leaving here tomorrow, I think you said?"

"Possibly tonight. My business here is done. I come and go, you know."

Mr. Satterthwaite remembered hearing those same words earlier in the evening. Rather curious.

He went out to the car and the waiting Masters. From

the open door into the bar the landlord's voice floated out, rich and complacent.

"A dark mystery," he was saying. "A dark mystery, that's what it is."

But he did not use the word "dark." The word he used suggested quite a different color. Mr. William Jones was a man of discrimination who suited his adjectives to his company. The company in the bar liked their adjectives full flavored.

Mr. Satterthwaite reclined luxuriously in the comfortable limousine. His breast was swelled with triumph. He saw the girl Mary come out on the steps and stand under the creaking inn sign.

"She little knows," said Mr. Satterthwaite to himself. "She little knows what *I* am going to do!"

The sign of the Bells and Motley swayed gently in the wind.

# THE CASE OF THE DISTRESSED LADY

THE BUZZER on Mr. Parker Pyne's desk purred discreetly. "Yes?" said the great man.

"A young lady wishes to see you," announced his secretary. "She has no appointment."

"You may send her in, Miss Lemon." A moment later he was shaking hands with his visitor. "Good morning," he said. "Do sit down."

The girl sat down and looked at Mr. Parker Pyne. She was a pretty girl and quite young. Her hair was dark and wavy with a row of curls at the nape of the neck. She was beautifully turned out from the white knitted cap on her head to the cobweb stockings and dainty shoes. Clearly she was nervous.

"You are Mr. Parker Pyne?" she asked.

"I am."

"The one who—who—advertises?"

"The one who advertises."

"You say that if people aren't—aren't happy—to—to come to you."

"Yes."

She took the plunge. "Well, I'm frightfully unhappy. So I thought I'd come along and just—and just see."

Mr. Parker Pyne waited. He felt there was more to come.

"I—I'm in frightful trouble." She clenched her hands nervously.

"So I see," said Mr. Parker Pyne. "Do you think you could tell me about it?"

That, it seemed, was what the girl was by no means sure

of. She stared at Mr. Parker Pyne with a desperate intentness. Suddenly she spoke with a rush.

"Yes, I will tell you.—I've made up my mind now. I've been nearly crazy with worry. I didn't know what to do or whom to go to. And then I saw your advertisement. I thought it was probably just a ramp, but it stayed in my mind. It sounded so comforting, somehow. And then I thought—well, it would do no harm to come and see. I could always make an excuse and get away again if I didn't —well, if I didn't—"

"Quite so; quite so," said Mr. Pyne.

"You see," said the girl, "it means—well, trusting somebody."

"And you feel you can trust me?" he said, smiling.

"It's odd," said the girl with unconscious rudeness, "but I do. Without knowing anything about you! I'm *sure* I can trust you."

"I can assure you," said Mr. Pyne, "that your trust will not be misplaced."

"Then," said the girl, "I'll tell you about it. My name is Daphne St. John."

"Yes, Miss St. John."

"Mrs. I'm—I'm married."

"Pshaw!" muttered Mr. Pyne, annoyed with himself as he noted the platinum circlet on the third finger of her left hand. "Stupid of me."

"If I weren't married," said the girl, "I shouldn't mind so much. I mean, it wouldn't matter so much. It's the thought of Gerald— Well, here—here's what all the trouble's about!"

She dived in her bag, took something out, and flung it down on the desk where, gleaming and flashing, it rolled over to Mr. Parker Pyne.

It was a platinum ring with a large solitaire diamond.

Mr. Pyne picked it up, took it to the window, tested it on the pane, applied a jeweler's lens to his eye and examined it closely.

"An exceedingly fine diamond," he remarked, coming back to the table; "worth, I should say, about two thousand pounds at least."

"Yes. And it's stolen! I stole it! And I don't know what to do."

"Dear me!" said Mr. Parker Pyne. "This is very interesting."

His client broke down and sobbed into an inadequate handkerchief.

"Now, now," said Mr. Pyne. "Everything's going to be all right."

The girl dried her eyes and sniffed. "Is it?" she said. "Oh, *is* it?"

"Of course it is. Now, just tell me the whole story."

"Well, it began by my being hard up. You see, I'm frightfully extravagant. And Gerald gets so annoyed about it. Gerald's my husband. He's a lot older than I am, and he's got very—well, very austere ideas. He thinks running into debt is dreadful. So I didn't tell him. And I went over to Le Touquet with some friends and I thought perhaps I might be lucky at chemmy and get straight again. I did win at first. And then I lost, and then I thought I must go on. And I went on. And—and—"

"Yes, yes," said Mr. Parker Pyne. "You need not go into details. You were in a worse plight than ever. That is right, is it not?"

Daphne St. John nodded. "And by then, you see, I simply couldn't tell Gerald. Because he hates gambling. Oh, I was in an awful mess. Well, we went down to stay with the Dortheimers near Cobham. He's frightfully rich, of course. His wife, Naomi, was at school with me. She's pretty and a dear. While we were there, the setting of this ring got loose. On the morning we were leaving, she asked me to take it up to town and drop it at her jeweler's in Bond Street." She paused.

"And now we come to the difficult part," said Mr. Pyne helpfully. "Go on, Mrs. St. John."

"You won't ever tell, will you?" demanded the girl pleadingly.

"My clients' confidences are sacred. And anyway, Mrs. St. John, you have told me so much already that I could probably finish the story for myself."

"That's true. All right. But I hate saying it—it sounds so

awful. I went to Bond Street. There's another shop there—
Viro's. They—copy jewelry. Suddenly I lost my head. I
took the ring in and said I wanted an exact copy; I said I
was going abroad and didn't want to take real jewelry with
me. They seemed to think it quite natural.

"Well I got the paste replica—it was so good you
couldn't have told it from the original—and I sent it off by
registered post to Lady Dortheimer. I had a box with the
jeweler's name on it, so that was all right, and I made a
professional-looking parcel. And then I—I—pawned the
real one." She hid her face in her hands. "How could I?
How could I? I was just a low, mean, common thief."

Mr. Parker Pyne coughed. "I do not think you have
quite finished," he said.

"No, I haven't. This, you understand, was about six
weeks ago. I paid off all my debts and got square again,
but of course I was miserable all the time. And then an old
cousin of mine died and I came into some money. The first
thing I did was to redeem the wretched ring. Well, that's all
right; here it is. But something terribly difficult has happened."

"Yes?"

"We've had a quarrel with the Dortheimers. It's over
some shares that Sir Reuben persuaded Gerald to buy. He
was terribly let in over them and he told Sir Reuben what
he thought of him—and oh, it's all dreadful! And now, you
see, I can't get the ring back."

"Couldn't you send it to Lady Dortheimer
anonymously?"

"That gives the whole thing away. She'll examine her
own ring, find it's a fake, and guess at once what I've
done."

"You say she is a friend of yours. What about telling her
the whole truth—throwing yourself on her mercy?"

Mrs. St. John shook her head. "We're not such friends
as that. Where money or jewelry is concerned, Naomi's as
hard as nails. Perhaps she couldn't prosecute me if I gave
the ring back, but she could tell everyone what I've done
and I'd be ruined. Gerald would know and he would never
forgive me. Oh, how awful everything is!" She began to

cry again. "I've thought and I've thought, and I can't see *what* to do! Oh, Mr. Pyne, can't you do anything?"

"Several things," said Mr. Parker Pyne.

"You can? Really?"

"Certainly. I suggested the simplest way because in my long experience I have always found it the best. It avoids unlooked-for complications. Still, I see the force of your objections. At present no one knows of this unfortunate occurrence but yourself?"

"And you," said Mrs. St. John.

"Oh, I do not count. Well, then, your secret is safe at present. All that is needed is to exchange the rings in some unsuspicious manner."

"That's it," the girl said eagerly.

"That should not be difficult. We must take a little time to consider the best method—"

She interrupted him. "But there is no time! That's what's driving me nearly crazy. She's going to have the ring reset."

"How do you know?"

"Just by chance. I was lunching with a woman the other day and I admired a ring she had on—a big emerald. She said it was the newest thing—and that Naomi Dortheimer was going to have her diamond reset that way."

"Which means that we shall have to act quickly," said Mr. Pyne thoughtfully.

"Yes, yes."

"It means gaining admission to the house—and if possible not in a menial capacity. Servants have little chance of handling valuable rings. Have you any ideas yourself, Mrs. St. John?"

"Well, Naomi is giving a big party on Wednesday. And this friend of mine mentioned that she had been looking for some exhibition dancers. I don't know if anything has been settled—"

"I think that can be managed," said Mr. Parker Pyne. "If the matter is already settled it will be more expensive, that is all. One thing more, do you happen to know where the main light switch is situated?"

"As it happens I *do* know that, because a fuse blew out

late one night when the servants had all gone to bed.
box at the back of the hall—inside a little cupboard."

At Mr. Parker Pyne's request she drew him a sketch.

"And now," said Mr. Parker Pyne, "everything is going
to be all right, so don't worry, Mrs. St. John. What about
the ring? Shall I take it now, or would you rather keep it
till Wednesday?"

"Well, perhaps I'd better keep it."

"Now, no more worry, mind you," Mr. Parker Pyne admonished her.

"And your—fee?" she asked timidly.

"That can stand over for the moment. I will let you
know on Wednesday what expenses have been necessary.
The fee will be nominal, I assure you."

He conducted her to the door, then rang the buzzer on
his desk.

"Send Claude and Madeleine here."

Claude Luttrell was one of the handsomest specimens of
lounge lizard to be found in England. Madeleine de Sara
was the most seductive of vamps.

Mr. Parker Pyne surveyed them with approval. "My
children," he said, "I have a job for you. You are going to
be internationally famous exhibition dancers. Now, attend
to this carefully, Claude, and mind you get it right . . ."


Lady Dortheimer was fully satisfied with the arrangements for her ball. She surveyed the floral decorations and
approved, gave a few last orders to the butler, and remarked to her husband that so far nothing had gone wrong!

It was a slight disappointment that Michael and Juanita,
the dancers from the Red Admiral, had been unable to
fulfill their contract at the last moment, owing to Juanita's
spraining her ankle, but instead, two new dancers were
being sent (so ran the story over the telephone) who had
created a furor in Paris.

The dancers duly arrived and Lady Dortheimer approved. The evening went splendidly. Jules and Sanchia
did their turn, and most sensational it was. A wild Spanish
Revolution dance. Then a dance called the Degenerate's
Dream. Then an exquisite exhibition of modern dancing.

The "cabaret" over, normal dancing was resumed. The handsome Jules requested a dance with Lady Dortheimer. They floated away. Never had Lady Dortheimer had such a perfect partner.

Sir Reuben was searching for the seductive Sanchia—in vain. She was not in the ballroom.

She was, as a matter of fact, out in the deserted hall near a small box, with her eyes fixed on the jeweled watch which she wore round her wrist.

"You are not English—you cannot be English—to dance as you do," murmured Jules into Lady Dortheimer's ear. "You are the sprite, the spirit of the wind. *Droushcka petrovka navarouchi.*"

"What is that language?"

"Russian," said Jules mendaciously. "I say something in Russian that I dare not say in English."

Lady Dortheimer closed her eyes. Jules pressed her closer to him.

Suddenly the lights went out. In the darkness Jules bent and kissed the hand that lay on his shoulder. As she made to draw it away, he caught it, raised it to his lips again. Somehow, a ring slipped from her finger into his hand.

To Lady Dortheimer it seemed only a second before the lights went on again. Jules was smiling at her.

"Your ring," he said. "It slipped off. You permit?" He replaced it on her finger. His eyes said a number of things while he was doing it.

Sir Reuben was talking about the main switch. "Some idiot. Practical joke, I suppose."

Lady Dortheimer was not interested. Those few minutes of darkness had been very pleasant.

Mr. Parker Pyne arrived at his office on Thursday morning to find Mrs. St. John already awaiting him.

"Show her in," said Mr. Pyne.

"Well?" She was all eagerness.

"You look pale," he said accusingly.

She shook her head. "I couldn't sleep last night. I was wondering—"

"Now, here is the little bill for expenses. Train fares,

costumes, and fifty pounds to Michael and Juanita. Sixty-five pounds, seventeen shillings."

"Yes, yes! But about last night—was it all right? Did it happen?"

Mr. Parker Pyne looked at her in suprise. "My dear young lady, naturally it is all right. I took it for granted that you understood that."

"What a relief! I was afraid—"

Mr. Parker Pyne shook his head reproachfully. "Failure is a word not tolerated in this establishment. If I do not think I can succeed I refuse to undertake a case. If I do take a case, its success is practically a foregone conclusion."

"She's really got her ring back and suspects nothing?"

"Nothing whatever. The operation was most delicately conducted."

Daphne St. John sighed. "You don't know the load off my mind. What were you saying about expenses?"

"Sixty-five pounds, seventeen shillings."

Mrs. St. John opened her bag and counted out the money. Mr. Parker Pyne thanked her and wrote out a receipt.

"But your fee?" murmured Daphne. "This is only for expenses."

"In this case there is no fee."

"Oh, Mr. Pyne! I couldn't, really!"

"My dear young lady, I insist. I will not touch a penny. It would be against my principles. Here is your receipt. And now—"

With the smile of a happy conjurer bringing off a successful trick, he drew a small box from his pocket and pushed it across the table. Daphne opened it. Inside, to all appearances, lay the identical diamond ring.

"Brute!" said Mrs. St. John, making a face at it. "How I hate you! I've a good mind to throw you out of the window."

"I shouldn't do that," said Mr. Pyne. "It might surprise people."

"You're quite sure it isn't the real one?" said Daphne.

"No, no! The one you showed me the other day is safely on Lady Dortheimer's finger."

"Then that's all right." Daphne rose with a happy laugh.

"Curious your asking me that," said Mr. Parker Pyne. "Of course Claude, poor fellow, hasn't many brains. He might easily have got muddled. So, to make sure, I had an expert look at this thing this morning."

Mrs. St. John sat down again rather suddenly. "Oh! And he said?"

"That it was an extraordinarily good imitation," said Mr. Parker Pyne, beaming. "First-class work. So that sets your mind at rest, doesn't it?"

Mrs. St. John started to say something, then stopped. She was starring at Mr. Parker Pyne.

The latter resumed his seat behind the desk and looked at her benevolently. "The cat who pulled the chestnuts out of the fire," he said dreamily. "Not a pleasant role. Not a role I should care to have any of my staff undertake. Excuse me. Did you say anything?"

"I—no, nothing."

"Good. I want to tell you a little story, Mrs. St. John. It concerns a young lady. A fair-haired young lady, I think. She is not married. Her name is not St. John. Her Christian name is not Daphne. On the contrary, her name is Ernestine Richards, and until recently she was secretary to Lady Dortheimer.

"Well, one day the setting of Lady Dortheimer's diamond ring became loose and Miss Richards brought it up to town to have it fixed. Quite like your story here, is it not? The same idea occurred to Miss Richards that occurred to you. She had the ring copied. But she was a far-sighted young lady. She saw a day coming when Lady Dortheimer would discover the substitution. When that happened, she would remember who had taken the ring to town and Miss Richards would be instantly suspected.

"So what happened? First, I fancy, Miss Richards invested in a La Merveilleuse transformation—Number Seven side parting, I think"—his eyes rested innocently on his client's wavy locks—"shade dark brown. Then she called on me. She showed me the ring, allowed me to satisfy myself that it was genuine, thereby disarming suspicion on my part. That done and a plan of substitution arranged, the young lady took the ring to the jeweler, who in due course returned it to Lady Dortheimer.

"Yesterday evening the other ring, the false ring, was hurriedly handed over at the last minute at Waterloo Station. Quite rightly, Miss Richards did not consider that Mr. Luttrell was likely to be an authority on diamonds. But just to satisfy myself that everything was aboveboard I arranged for a friend of mine, a diamond merchant, to be on the train. He looked at the ring and pronounced at once, 'This is not a real diamond; it is an excellent paste replica.'

"You see the point, of course, Mrs. St. John? When Lady Dortheimer discovered her loss, what would she remember? The charming young dancer who slipped the ring off her finger when the lights went out! She would make inquiries and find that the dancers originally engaged were bribed not to come. If matters were traced back to my office, my story of a Mrs. St. John would seem feeble in the extreme. Lady Dortheimer never knew a Mrs. St. John. The story would sound a flimsy fabrication.

"Now you see, don't you, that I could not allow that? And so my friend Claude replaced on Lady Dortheimer's finger the same ring that he took off." Mr. Parker Pyne's smile was less benevolent now.

"You see why I could not take a fee? I guarantee to give happiness. Clearly I have not made *you* happy. I will say just one thing more. You are young; possibly this is your first attempt at anything of the kind. Now I, on the contrary, am comparatively advanced in years, and I have had a long experience in the compilation of statistics. From that experience I can assure you that in eighty-seven percent of cases dishonesty does not pay. Eighty-seven percent. Think of it!"

With a brusque movement the pseudo Mrs. St. John rose. "You oily old brute!" she said. "Leading me on! Making me pay expenses! And all the time——" She choked, and rushed toward the door.

"Your ring," said Mr. Parker Pyne, holding it out to her.

She snatched it from him, looked at it, and flung it out of the open window.

A door banged and she was gone.

# THE THIRD FLOOR FLAT

"BROTHER!" said Pat.

With a deepening frown she rummaged wildly in the silken trifle she called an evening bag. Two young men and another girl watched her anxiously. They were all standing outside the closed door of Patricia Garnett's flat.

"It's no good," said Pat. "It's not there. And now what shall we do?"

"What is life without a latchkey?" murmured Jimmy Faulkener.

He was a short, broad-shouldered young man, with good-tempered blue eyes.

Pat turned on him angrily.

"Don't make jokes, Jimmy. This is serious."

"Look again, Pat," said Donovan Bailey. "It must be there somewhere."

He had a lazy, pleasant voice that matched his lean, dark figure.

"If you ever brought it out," said the other girl, Mildred Hope.

"Of course I brought it out," said Pat. "I believe I gave it to one of you two." She turned on the men accusingly. "I told Donovan to take it for me."

But she was not to find a scapegoat so easily. Donovan put in a firm disclaimer, and Jimmy backed him up.

"I saw you put it in your bag, myself," said Jimmy.

"Well, then, one of you dropped it out when you picked up my bag. I've dropped it once or twice."

"Once or twice!" said Donovan. "You've dropped it a dozen times at least, besides leaving it behind on every possible occasion."

"I can't see why everything on earth doesn't drop out of it the whole time," said Jimmy.

"The point is—how are we going to get in?" said Mildred.

She was a sensible girl, who kept to the point, but she was not nearly so attractive as the impulsive and troublesome Pat.

All four of them regarded the closed door blankly.

"Couldn't the porter help?" suggested Jimmy. "Hasn't he got a master key or something of that kind?"

Pat shook her head. There were only two keys. One was inside the flat, hung up in the kitchen, and the other was—or should be—in the maligned bag.

"If only the flat were on the ground floor," wailed Pat. "We could have broken open a window or something. Donovan, you wouldn't like to be a cat burglar, would you?"

Donovan declined firmly but politely to be a cat burglar.

"A flat on the fourth floor is a bit of an undertaking," said Jimmy.

"How about a fire escape?" suggested Donovan.

"There isn't one."

"There should be," said Jimmy. "A building five storeys high ought to have a fire escape."

"I daresay," said Pat. "But what should be doesn't help us. How am I ever to get into my flat?"

"Isn't there a sort of thingummybob?" said Donovan. "A thing the tradesmen send up chops and Brussels sprouts in?"

"The service lift," said Pat. "Oh, yes, but it's only a sort of wire-basket thing. Oh! wait—I know. What about the coal lift?"

"Now that," said Donovan, "is an idea."

Mildred made a discouraging suggestion.

"It'll be bolted," she said. "In Pat's kitchen, I mean, on the inside."

But the idea was instantly negatived.

"Don't you believe it," said Donovan.

"Not in *Pat's* kitchen," said Jimmy. "Pat never locks and bolts things."

"I don't think it's bolted," said Pat. "I took the dustbin off this morning, and I'm sure I never bolted it afterwards, and I don't think I've been near it since."

"Well," said Donovan, "that fact's going to be very useful to us to-night, but, all the same, young Pat, let me point out to you that these slack habits are leaving you at the mercy of burglars (non-feline) every night."

Pat disregarded these admonitions.

"Come on," she cried, and began racing down the four flights of stairs. The others followed her. Pat led them through a dark recess, apparently full to overflowing of perambulators, and through another door into the well of the flats, and guided them to the right lift. There was, at the moment, a dust-bin on it. Donovan lifted it off and stepped gingerly onto the platform in its place. He wrinkled up his nose.

"A little noisome," he remarked. "But what of that? Do I go alone on this venture or is anyone coming with me?"

"I'll come, too," said Jimmy.

He stepped on by Donovan's side.

"I suppose the lift will bear me," he added, doubtfully.

"You can't weigh much more than a ton of coal," said Pat, who had never been particularly strong on her weights-and-measures table.

"And anyway, we shall soon find out," said Donovan cheerfully, as he hauled on the rope.

With a grinding noise they disappeared from sight.

"This thing makes an awful noise," remarked Jimmy, as they passed up through blackness. "What will the people in the other flats think?"

"Ghosts or burglars, I expect," said Donovan. "Hauling this rope is quite heavy work. The porter of Friars Mansions does more work than I ever suspected. I say, Jimmy, old son, are you counting the floors?"

"Oh, Lord! no. I forgot about it."

"Well, I have, which is just as well. That's the third we're passing now. The next is ours."

"And now, I suppose," grumbled Jimmy, "we shall find that Pat did bolt the door after all."

But these fears were unfounded. The wooden door swung back at a touch and Donovan and Jimmy stepped out into inky blackness.

"We ought to have a torch for this wild night work," explained Donovan. "If I know Pat, everything's on the floor, and we shall smash endless crockery before I can get to the light switch. Don't move about, Jimmy, till I get the light on."

He felt his way cautiously over the floor, uttering one fervent "Ouch!" as a corner of the kitchen table took him unawares in the ribs. He reached the switch, and in another moment another "Ouch!" floated out of the darkness.

"What's the matter?" asked Jimmy.

"Light won't come on. Dud bulb, I suppose. Wait a minute. I'll turn the sitting-room light on."

The sitting-room was immediately across the passage. Jimmy heard Donovan go out of the door, and presently fresh muffled cries reached him. He himself edged his way cautiously across the kitchen.

"What's the matter?"

"I don't know. Rooms get bewitched at night, I believe. Everything seems to be in a different place. Chairs and tables where you least expected it. Oh, hell! here's another!"

But at this moment Jimmy fortunately connected with the electric-light switch and pressed it down. In another minute two young men were looking at each other in silent horror.

This room was not Pat's sitting-room. They were in the wrong flat.

To begin with, the room was about ten times more crowded than Pat's, which explained Donovan's pathetic bewilderment at repeatedly cannoning into chairs and tables. There was a large round table in the centre of the room covered with a baize cloth, and there was an aspidistra in the window. It was, in fact, the kind of room whose owner, the young man felt sure, would be difficult to explain to. With silent horror they gazed down at the table, on which lay a little pile of letters.

"Mrs. Ernestine Grant," breathed Donovan, picking

them up and reading the name. "Oh! help. Do you think she's heard us?"

"It's a miracle she hasn't heard you," said Jimmy. "What with the way you've been crashing into the furniture. Come on, let's get out of here quickly."

They hastily switched off the light and retraced their steps on tip-toe to the lift. Jimmy breathed a sigh of relief as they regained the fastness of its depths without further incident.

"I do like a woman to be a good, sound sleeper," he said approvingly. "Mrs. Ernestine Grant has her points."

"I see it now," said Donovan; "why we made the mistake in the floor, I mean. Out in that well we started up from the basement." He heaved on the rope, and the lift shot up. "We're right this time."

"I devoutly trust we are," said Jimmy, as he stepped out into another inky void. "My nerves won't stand many more shocks of this kind."

But no further nerve strain was imposed. The first click of the light showed them Pat's kitchen, and in another minute they were opening the front door and admitting the two girls who were waiting outside.

"You have been a long time," grumbled Pat. "Mildred and I have been waiting here ages."

"We've had an adventure," said Donovan. "We might have been hauled off to the police station as dangerous malefactors."

Pat had passed on into the sitting-room, where she switched on the light and dropped her wrap on the sofa. She listened with lively interest to Donovan's account of his adventures.

"I'm glad she didn't catch you," she commented. "I'm sure she's an old curmudgeon. I got a note from her this morning—wanted to see me sometime—something she had to complain about—my piano, I suppose. People who don't like pianos over their heads shouldn't come and live in flats. I say, Donovan, you've hurt your hand. It's all over blood. Go and wash it under the tap."

Donovan looked down at his hand in surprise. He went

out of the room obediently and presently his voice called to Jimmy.

"Hullo," said the other, "what's up? you haven't hurt yourself badly, have you?"

"I haven't hurt myself at all."

There was something so queer in Donovan's voice that Jimmy stared at him in surprise. Donovan held out his washed hand and Jimmy saw that there was no mark or cut of any kind on it.

"That's odd," he said, frowning. "There was quite a lot of blood. Where did it come from?"

And then, suddenly, he realised what his quicker-witted friend had already seen.

"By Jove," he said. "It must have come from that flat."

He stopped, thinking over the possibilities his words implied.

"You're sure it was—er—blood?" he said. "Not paint?" Donovan shook his head.

"It was blood, all right," he said, and shivered.

They looked at each other. The same thought was clearly in both of their minds. It was Jimmy who voiced it first.

"I say," he said awkwardly. "Do you think we ought to —well—go down again—and have—a—a look around? See it's all right, you know?"

"What about the girls?"

"We won't say anything to them. Pat's going to put on an apron and make us an omelet. We'll be back by the time they wonder where we are."

"Oh, well, come on," said Donovan. "I suppose we've got to go through with it. I daresay there isn't anything really wrong."

But his tone lacked conviction. They got into the lift and descended to the floor below. They found their way across the kitchen without much difficulty and once more switched on the sitting-room light.

"It must have been in here," said Donovan, "that—that I got the stuff on me. I never touched anything in the kitchen."

He looked round him. Jimmy did the same, and they both frowned. Everything looked neat and commonplace and miles removed from any suggestion of violence or gore.

Suddenly Jimmy started and caught his companion's arm.

"Look!"

Donovan followed the pointing finger, and in his turn uttered an exclamation. From beneath the heavy rep curtains there protruded a foot—a woman's foot in a gaping patent-leather shoe.

Jimmy went to the curtains and drew them sharply apart. In the recess of the window a woman's huddled body lay on the floor, a sticky dark pool beside it. She was dead, there was no doubt of that. Jimmy was attempting to raise her up when Donovan stopped him.

"You'd better not do that. She oughtn't to be touched till the police come."

"The police. Oh! of course. I say, Donovan, what a ghastly business. Who do you think she is? Mrs. Ernestine Grant?"

"Looks like it. At any rate, if there's anyone else in the flat they're keeping jolly quiet."

"What do we do next?" asked Jimmy. "Run out and get a policeman or ring up from Pat's flat?"

"I should think ringing up would be best. Come on, we might as well go out the front door. We can't spend the whole night going up and down in that evil-smelling lift."

Jimmy agreed. Just as they were passing through the door he hesitated.

"Look here; do you think one of us ought to stay—just to keep an eye on things—till the police come?"

"Yes, I think you're right. If you'll stay, I'll run up and telephone."

He ran quickly up the stairs and rang the bell of the flat above. Pat came to open it, a very pretty Pat with a flushed face and a cooking apron on. Her eyes widened in surprise.

"You? But how—Donovan, what is it? Is anything the matter?"

He took both her hands in his.

"It's all right, Pat—only we've made rather an unpleasant discovery in the flat below. A woman—dead."

"Oh!" She gave a little gasp. "How horrible. Has she had a fit or something?"

"No. It looks—well—it looks rather as though she had been murdered."

"Oh! Donovan."

"I know. It's pretty beastly."

Her hands were still in his. She had left them there—was even clinging to him. Darling Pat—how he loved her. Did she care at all for him! Sometimes he thought she did. Sometimes he was afraid that Jimmy Faulkener—remembrances of Jimmy waiting patiently below made him start guiltily.

"Pat, dear, we must telephone to the police."

"Monsieur is right," said a voice behind him. "And in the meantime, while we are waiting their arrival, perhaps I can be of some slight assistance."

They had been standing in the doorway of the flat, and now they peered out on to the landing. A figure was standing on the stairs a little way above them. It moved down and into their range of vision.

They stood staring at a little man with very fierce moustaches and an egg-shaped head. He wore a resplendent dressing-gown and embroidered slippers. He bowed gallantly to Patricia.

"Mademoiselle!" he said. "I am, as perhaps you know, the tenant of the flat above. I like to be up high—the air—the view over London. I take the flat in the name of Mr. O'-Connor. But I am not an Irishman. I have another name. That is why I venture to put myself at your service. Permit me."

With a flourish he pulled out a card and handed it to Pat. She read it.

"M. Hercule Poirot. Oh!" She caught her breath. *"The* M. Poirot? The great detective? And you will really help?"

"That is my intention, Mademoiselle. I nearly offered my help earlier in the evening."

Pat looked puzzled.

"I heard you discussing how to gain admission to your flat. Me, I am very clever at picking locks. I could without doubt have opened your door for you, but I hesitated to suggest it. You would have had the grave suspicions of me."

Pat laughed.

"Now, Monsieur," said Poirot to Donovan. "Go in, I pray of you, and telephone to the police. I will descend to the flat below."

Pat came down the stairs with him. They found Jimmy on guard and Pat explained Poirot's presence. Jimmy, in his turn, explained to Poirot his and Donovan's adventures. The detective listened attentively.

"The lift door was unbolted, you say? You emerged into the kitchen, but the light it would not turn on."

He directed his footsteps to the kitchen as he spoke. His fingers pressed the switch.

"*Tiens! Voilà ce qui est curieux!*" he said as the light flashed on. "It functions perfectly now, I wonder—"

He held up a finger to ensure silence and listened. A faint sound broke the stillness—the sound of an unmistakable snore.

"Ah!" said Poirot. "*La chambre de domestique.*"

He tiptoed across the kitchen into a little pantry, out of which led a door. He opened the door and switched on the light. The room was the kind of dog-kennel designed by the builders of flats to accommodate a human being. The floor space was almost entirely occupied by the bed. In the bed was a rosy-cheeked girl lying on her back with her mouth wide open snoring placidly.

Poirot switched off the light and beat a retreat.

"She will not wake," he said. "We will let her sleep till the police come."

He went back to the sitting room. Donovan had joined them.

"The police will be here almost immediately, they say," he said breathlessly. "We are to touch nothing."

Poirot nodded.

"We will not touch," he said. "We will look, that is all."

He moved into the room. Mildred had come down with Donovan, and all four young people stood in the doorway and watched him with breathless interest.

"What I can't understand, sir, is this," said Donovan. "I never went near the window—how did the blood come on my hand?"

"My young friend, the answer to that stares you in the face. Of what colour is the tablecloth? Red, is it not? and doubtless you did put your hand on the table."

"Yes, I did. Is that—" He stopped.

Poirot nodded. He was bending over the table. He indicated with his hand a dark patch on the red.

"It was here that the crime was committed," he said solemnly. "The body was moved afterwards."

Then he stood upright and looked slowly round the room. He did not move, he handled nothing, but nevertheless the four watching felt as though every object in that rather frowsty place gave up its secret to his observant eye.

Hercule Poirot nodded his head as though satisfied. A little sigh escaped him.

"I see," he said.

"You see what?" asked Donovan curiously.

"I see," said Poirot, "what you doubtless felt—that the room is overfull of furniture."

Donovan smiled ruefully.

"I did go barging about a bit," he confessed. "Of course, everything was in a different place to Pat's room, and I couldn't make it out."

"Not everything," said Poirot.

Donovan looked at him inquiringly.

"I mean," said Poirot apologetically, "that certain things are always fixed. In a block of flats the door, the window, the fireplace—they are in the same place in the rooms which are below each other."

"Isn't that rather splitting hairs?" asked Mildred. She was looking at Poirot with faint disapproval.

"One should always speak with absolute accuracy. That is a little—how do you say?—fad of mine."

There was the noise of footsteps on the stairs, and three men came in. They were a police inspector, a constable, and the divisional surgeon. The Inspector recognised Poirot and greeted him in an almost reverential manner. Then he turned to the others.

"I shall want statements from everyone," he began, "but in the first place—"

Poirot interrupted.

"A little suggestion. We will go back to the flat upstairs and Mademoiselle here shall do what she was planning to do—make us an omelet. Me, I have a passion for the omelets. Then, M. l'Inspecteur, when you have finished here, you will mount to us and ask questions at your leisure."

It was arranged accordingly, and Poirot went up with them.

"M. Poirot," said Pat, "I think you're a perfect dear. And you shall have a lovely omelet. I really make omelets frightfully well."

"That is good. Once, Mademoiselle, I loved a beautiful young English girl, who resembled you greatly—but alas! she could not cook. So perhaps everything was for the best."

There was a faint sadness in his voice, and Jimmy Faulkener looked at him curiously.

Once in the flat, however, he exerted himself to please and amuse. The grim tragedy below was almost forgotten.

The omelet had been consumed and duly praised by the time that Inspector Rice's footsteps were heard. He came in accompanied by the doctor, having left the constable below.

"Well, Monsieur Poirot," he said. "It all seems clear and above-board—not much in your line, though we may find it hard to catch the man. I'd just like to hear how the discovery came to be made."

Donovan and Jimmy between them recounted the happenings of the evening. The Inspector turned reproachfully to Pat.

"You shouldn't leave your lift door unbolted, Miss. You really shouldn't."

"I shan't again," said Pat, with a shiver. "Somebody might come in and murder me like that poor woman below."

"Ah! but they didn't come in that way, though," said the Inspector.

"You will recount to us what you have discovered, yes?" said Poirot.

"I don't know as I ought to—but seeing it's you, M. Poirot. . . ."

*"Précisément,"* said Poirot. "And these young people—they will be discreet."

"The newspapers will get hold of it, anyway, soon enough," said the Inspector. "There's no real secret about the matter. Well, the dead woman's Mrs. Grant, all right. I had the porter up to identify her. Woman of about thirty-five. She was sitting at the table, and she was shot with an automatic pistol of small calibre, probably by someone sitting opposite her at table. She fell forward, and that's how the bloodstain came on the table."

"But wouldn't someone have heard the shot?" asked Mildred.

"The pistol was fitted with a silencer. No, you wouldn't hear anything. By the way, did you hear the screech the maid let out when we told her her mistress was dead? No. Well, that just shows how unlikely it was that anyone would hear the other."

"Has the maid no story to tell?" asked Poirot.

"It was her evening out. She's got her own key. She came in about ten o'clock. Everything was quiet. She thought her mistress had gone to bed."

"She did not look in the sitting room, then?"

"Yes, she took the letters in there which had come by the evening post, but she saw nothing unusual—any more than Mr. Faulkener and Mr. Bailey did. You see, the murderer had concealed the body rather neatly behind the curtains."

"But it was a curious thing to do, don't you think?"

Poirot's voice was very gentle, yet it held something that made the Inspector look up quickly.

"Didn't want the crime discovered till he'd had time to make his getaway."

"Perhaps—perhaps—but continue with what you were saying."

"The maid went out at five o'clock. The doctor here puts the time of death as—roughly—about four to five hours ago. That's right, isn't it?"

The doctor, who was a man of few words, contented himself with jerking his head affirmatively.

"It's a quarter to twelve now. The actual time can, I think, be narrowed down to a fairly definite hour."

He took out a crumpled sheet of paper.

"We found this in the pocket of the dead woman's dress. You needn't be afraid of handling it. There are no finger-prints on it."

Poirot smoothed out the sheet. Across it some words were printed in small prim capitals.

"I will come to see you this evening at half-past seven.— J. F."

"A compromising document to leave behind," comment-ed Poirot, as he handed it back.

"Well, he didn't know she'd got it in her pocket," said the Inspector. "He probably thought she'd destroyed it. We've evidence that he was a careful man, though. The pistol she was shot with we found under the body—and there again no fingerprints. They'd been wiped off very carefully with a silk handkerchief."

"How do you know," said Poirot, "that it was a silk handkerchief?"

"Because we found it," said the Inspector triumphantly. "At the last, as he was drawing the curtains, he must have let it fall unnoticed."

He handed across a big white silk handkerchief—a good-quality handkerchief. It did not need the Inspector's finger to draw Poirot's attention to the mark on it in the centre. It was neatly marked and quite legible. Poirot read the name out.

"John Fraser."

"That's it," said the Inspector. "John Fraser—J. F. in the note. We know the name of the man we have to look for, and I daresay when we find out a little about the dead woman, and her relations come forward, we shall soon get a line on him."

"I wonder," said Poirot. "No, *mon cher*, somehow I do

not think he will be easy to find, your John Fraser. He is a strange man—careful, since he marks his handkerchiefs and wipes the pistol with which he has committed the crime—yet careless since he loses his handkerchief and does not search for a letter that might incriminate him."

"Flurried, that's what he was," said the Inspector.

"It is possible," said Poirot. "Yes, it is possible. And he was not seen entering the building?"

"There are all sorts of people going in and out at that time. These are big blocks. I suppose none of you"—he addressed the four collectively—"saw anyone coming out of the flat?"

Pat shook her head.

"We went out earlier—about seven o'clock."

"I see." The Inspector rose. Poirot accompanied him to the door.

"As a little favour, may I examine the flat below?"

"Why, certainly, M. Poirot. I know what they think of you at headquarters. I'll leave you a key. I've got two. It will be empty. The maid cleared out to some relatives, too scared to stay there alone."

"I thank you," said M. Poirot. He went back into the flat thoughtful.

"You're not satisfied, M. Poirot?" said Jimmy.

"No," said Poirot. "I am not satisfied."

Donovan looked at him curiously. "What is it that— well, worries you?"

Poirot did not answer. He remained silent for a minute or two, frowning, as though in thought, then he made a sudden impatient movement of shoulders.

"I will say good-night to you, Mademoiselle. You must be tired. You have had much cooking to do—eh?"

Pat laughed.

"Only the omelet. I didn't do dinner. Donovan and Jimmy came and called for us, and we went out to a little place in Soho."

"And then without doubt, you went to a theatre?"

"Yes. 'The Brown Eyes of Caroline.' "

"Ah!" said Poirot. "It should have been blue eyes—the blue eyes of Mademoiselle."

He made a sentimental gesture, and then once more wished Pat good-night, also Mildred, who was staying the night by special request, as Pat admitted frankly that she would get the horrors if left alone on this particular night.

The two young men accompanied Poirot. When the door was shut, and they were preparing to say good-bye to him on the landing, Poirot forestalled them.

"My young friends, you heard me say that I was not satisfied? *Eh bien*, it is true—I am not. I go now to make some little investigations of my own. You would like to accompany me—yes?"

An eager assent greeted his proposal. Poirot led the way to the flat below and inserted the key the Inspector had given him in the lock. On entering, he did not, as the others had expected, enter the sitting-room. Instead he went straight to the kitchen. In a little recess which served as a scullery a big iron bin was standing. Poirot uncovered this, and doubling himself up, began to rootle in it with the energy of a ferocious terrier.

Both Jimmy and Donovan stared at him in amazement.

Suddenly with a cry of triumph he emerged. In his hand he held aloft a small stoppered bottle.

"*Voilà!*" he said. "I find what I seek."

He sniffed at it delicately.

"Alas! I am *enrhumé*—I have the cold in the head."

Donovan took the bottle from him and sniffed in his turn, but could smell nothing. He took out the stopper and held the bottle to his nose before Poirot's warning cry could stop him.

Immediately he fell like a log. Poirot, by springing forward, partly broke his fall.

"Imbecile!" he cried. "The idea. To remove the stopper in that foolhardy manner! Did he not observe how delicately I handled it? Monsieur—Faulkener—is it not? Will you be so good as to get me a little brandy? I observed a decanter in the sitting-room."

Jimmy hurried off, but by the time he returned, Donovan was sitting up and declaring himself quite all right again. He had to listen to a short lecture from Poirot on the necessity of caution in sniffing at possibly poisonous substances.

"I think I'll be off home," said Donovan, rising shakily to his feet. "That is, if I can't be any more use here. I feel a bit wonky still."

"Assuredly," said Poirot. "That is the best thing you can do. M. Faulkener, attend me here a little minute. I will return on the instant."

He accompanied Donovan to the door and beyond. They remained outside on the landing talking for some minutes. When Poirot at last re-entered the flat he found Jimmy standing in the sitting-room gazing round him with puzzled eyes.

"Well, M. Poirot," he said, "what next?"

"There is nothing next. The case is finished."

"What?"

"I know everything—now."

Jimmy stared at him.

"That little bottle you found?"

"Exactly. That little bottle."

Jimmy shook his head.

"I can't make head or tail of it. For some reason or other I can see you are dissatisfied with the evidence against this John Fraser, whoever he may be."

"Whoever he may be," repeated Poirot softly. "If he is anyone at all—well, I shall be surprised."

"I don't understand."

"He is a name—that is all—a name carefully marked on a handkerchief!"

"And the letter?"

"Did you notice that it was printed? Now why? I will tell you. Handwriting might be recognised, and a typewritten letter is more easily traced than you would imagine—but if a real John Fraser wrote that letter those two points would not have appealed to him! No, it was written on purpose, and put in the dead woman's pocket for us to find. There is no such person as John Fraser."

Jimmy looked at him inquiringly.

"And so," went on Poirot, "I went back to the point that first struck me. You heard me say that certain things in a room were always in the same place under given circumstances. I gave three instances. I might have mentioned a fourth—the electric-light switch, my friend."

Jimmy still stared uncomprehendingly. Poirot went on.

"Your friend Donovan did not go near the window—it was by resting his hand on this table that he got it covered in blood! But I asked myself at once—why did he rest it there? What was he doing groping about this room in darkness? For remember, my friend, the electric-light switch is always in the same place by the door. Why, when he came to this room, did he not at once feel for the light and turn it on? That was the natural, the normal thing to do. According to him, he tried to turn on the light in the kitchen, but failed. Yet when I tried the switch it was in perfect working order. Did he, then, not wish the light to go on just then? If it had gone on you would both have seen at once that you were in the wrong flat. There would have been no reason to come into this room."

"What are you driving at, M. Poirot? I don't understand. What do you mean?"

"I mean—this."

Poirot held up a Yale door-key.

"The key of this flat?"

"No, *mon ami,* the key of the flat above. Mademoiselle Patricia's key, which M. Donovan Bailey abstracted from her bag some time during the evening."

"But why—why?"

"*Parbleu!* so that he could do what he wanted to do—gain admission to this flat in a perfectly unsuspicious manner. He made sure that the lift door was unbolted earlier in the evening."

"Where did you get the key?"

Poirot's smile broadened.

"I found it just now—where I looked for it—in M. Donovan's pocket. See you, that little bottle I pretended to find was a ruse. M. Donovan is taken in. He does what I knew he would do—unstoppers it and sniffs. And in that little bottle is Ethyl Chloride, a very powerful instant anaesthetic. It gives me just the moment or two of unconsciousness I need. I take from his pocket the two things that I knew would be there. This key was one of them—the other—"

He stopped and then went on:

"I questioned at the time the reason the Inspector gave for the body being concealed behind the curtain. To gain time? No, there was more than that. And so I thought of just one thing—the post, my friend. The evening post that comes at half-past nine or thereabouts. Say the murderer does not find something he expects to find, but that something may be delivered by post later. Clearly, then, he must come back. But the crime must not be discovered by the maid when she comes in, or the police would take possession of the flat, so he hides the body behind the curtain. And the maid suspects nothing and lays the letters on the table as usual."

"The letters?"

"Yes, the letters." Poirot drew something from his pocket.

"This is the second article I took from M. Donovan when he was unconscious." He showed the superscription —a typewritten envelope addressed to Mrs. Ernestine Grant. "But I will ask you one thing first, M. Faulkener, before we look at the contents of this letter. Are you or are you not in love with Mademoiselle Patricia?"

"I care for Pat terribly—but I've never thought I had a chance."

"You thought that she cared for M. Donovan? It may be that she had begun to care for him—but it was only a beginning, my friend. It is for you to make her forget—to stand by her in her trouble."

"Trouble?" said Jimmy sharply.

"Yes, trouble. We will do all we can to keep her name out of it, but it will be impossible to do so entirely. She was, you see, the motive."

He ripped open the envelope that he held. An enclosure fell out. The covering letter was brief, and was from a firm of solicitors.

DEAR MADAM,

The document you enclose is quite in order, and the fact of the marriage having taken place in a foreign country does not invalidate it in any way.

Yours truly, etc.

Poirot spread out the enclosure. It was a certificate of marriage between Donovan Bailey and Ernestine Grant, dated eight years ago.

"Good grief!" said Jimmy. "Pat said she'd had a letter from the woman asking to see her, but she never dreamed it was anything important."

Poirot nodded.

"M. Donovan knew—he went to see his wife this evening before going to the flat above (a strange irony, by the way, that led the unfortunate woman to come to this building where her rival lived)—he murdered her in cold blood—and then went on to his evening's amusement. His wife must have told him that she had sent the marriage certificate to her solicitors, and was expecting to hear from them. Doubtless he himself had tried to make her believe that there was a flaw in the marriage."

"He seemed in quite good spirits, too, all the evening. M. Poirot, you haven't let him escape?" Jimmy shuddered.

"There is no escape for him," said Poirot gravely. "You need not fear."

"It's Pat I'm thinking about mostly," said Jimmy. "You don't think—she really cared."

*"Mon ami*, that is your part," said Poirot gently. "To make her turn to you and forget. I do not think you will find it very difficult!"

# THE PLYMOUTH EXPRESS

ALEC SIMPSON, R.N., stepped from the platform at Newton Abbot into a first-class compartment of the Plymouth
Express. A porter followed him with a heavy suitcase. He
was about to swing it up to the rack, but the young sailor
stopped him.

"No—leave it on the seat. I'll put it up later. Here you
are."

"Thank you, sir." The porter, generously tipped,
withdrew.

Doors banged; a stentorian voice shouted: "Plymouth
only. Change for Torquay. Plymouth next stop." Then a
whistle blew, and the train drew slowly out of the station.

Lieutenant Simpson had the carriage to himself. The De-
cember air was chilly, and he pulled up the window. Then
he sniffed vaguely, and frowned. What a smell there was!
Reminded him of that time in hospital, and the operation
on his leg. Yes, chloroform; that was it!

He let the window down again, changing his seat to one
with its back to the engine. He pulled a pipe out of his
pocket and lit it. For a time he sat inactive, looking out
into the night and smoking.

At last he roused himself, and opening the suitcase, took
out some papers and magazines, then closed the suitcase
again and endeavored to shove it under the opposite seat—
without success. Some hidden obstacle resisted it. He
shoved harder with rising impatience, but it still stuck out
halfway into the carriage.

"Why the devil won't it go in?" he muttered, and hauling
it out completely, he stooped down and peered under the
seat. . . .

A moment later a cry rang out into the night, and the great train came to an unwilling halt in obedience to the imperative jerking of the communication-cord.

*"Mon ami,"* said Poirot, "you have, I know, been deeply interested in this mystery of the Plymouth Express. Read this."

I picked up the note he flicked across the table to me. It was brief and to the point.

Dear Sir:
    I shall be obliged if you will call upon me at your earliest convenience.

                                        Yours faithfully,
                                        EBENEZER HALLIDAY.

The connection was not clear to my mind, and I looked inquiringly at Poirot.

For answer he took up the newspaper and read aloud:

" 'A sensational discovery was made last night. A young naval officer returning to Plymouth found under the seat of his compartment the body of a woman, stabbed through the heart. The officer at once pulled the communication-cord, and the train was brought to a standstill. The woman, who was about thirty years of age, and richly dressed, has not yet been identified.'

"And later we have this: 'The woman found dead in the Plymouth Express has been identified as the Honorable Mrs. Rupert Carrington.' You see now, my friend? Or if you do not, I will add this—Mrs. Rupert Carrington was, before her marriage, Flossie Halliday, daughter of old man Halliday, the steel king of America."

"And he has sent for you? Splendid!"

"I did him a little service in the past—an affair of bearer bonds. And also, when I was in Paris for a royal visit, I had Mademoiselle Flossie pointed out to me. *La jolie petite pensionnaire!* She had the *jolie dot* too! It caused trouble. She nearly made a bad affair."

"How was that?"

"A certain Count de la Rochefour. *Un bien mauvais*

*sujet!* A bad hat, as you would say. An adventurer pure and simple, who knew how to appeal to a romantic young girl. Luckily her father got wind of it in time. He took her back to America in haste. I heard of her marriage some years later, but I know nothing of her husband."

"H'm," I said. "The Honorable Rupert Carrington is no beauty, by all accounts. He'd pretty well run through his own money on the turf, and I should imagine old man Halliday's dollars came along in the nick of time. I should say that for a good-looking, well-mannered, utterly unscrupulous young scoundrel, it would be hard to find his match!"

"Ah, the poor little lady! *Elle n'est pas bien tombée!*"

"I fancy he made it pretty obvious at once that it was her money, and not she, that had attracted him. I believe they drifted apart almost at once. I have heard rumors lately that there was to be a definite legal separation."

"Old man Halliday is no fool. He would tie up her money pretty tight."

"I dare say. Anyway, I know as a fact that the Honorable Rupert is said to be extremely hard up."

"Ah-ha! I wonder—"

"You wonder what?"

"My good friend, do not jump down my throat like that. You are interested, I see. Supposing you accompany me to see Mr. Halliday. There is a taxi stand at the corner."

A few minutes sufficed to whirl us to the superb house in Park Lane rented by the American magnate. We were shown into the library, and almost immediately we were joined by a large, stout man, with piercing eyes and an aggressive chin.

"M. Poirot?" said Mr. Halliday. "I guess I don't need to tell you what I want you for. You've read the papers, and I'm never one to let the grass grow under my feet. I happened to hear you were in London, and I remembered the good work you did over those bonds. Never forget a name. I've got the pick of Scotland Yard, but I'll have my own man as well. Money no object. All the dollars were made for my little girl—and now she's gone, I'll spend my last cent to catch the scoundrel that did it! See? So it's up to you to deliver the goods."

Poirot bowed.

"I accept, monsieur, all the more willingly that I saw your daughter in Paris several times. And now I will ask you to tell me the circumstances of her journey to Plymouth and any other details that seem to you to bear upon the case."

"Well, to begin with," responded Halliday, "she wasn't going to Plymouth. She was going to join a house-party at Avonmead Court, the Duchess of Swansea's place. She left London by the twelve-fourteen from Paddington, arriving at Bristol (where she had to change) at two-fifty. The principal Plymouth expresses, of course, run via Westbury, and do not go near Bristol at all. The twelve-fourteen does a nonstop run to Bristol, afterward stopping at Weston, Taunton, Exeter and Newton Abbot. My daughter traveled alone in her carriage, which was reserved as far as Bristol, her maid being in a third-class carriage in the next coach."

Poirot nodded, and Mr. Halliday went on: "The party at Avonmead Court was to be a very gay one, with several balls, and in consequence my daughter had with her nearly all her jewels—amounting in value, perhaps, to about a hundred thousand dollars."

"*Un moment*," interrupted Poirot. "Who had charge of the jewels? Your daughter, or the maid?"

"My daughter always took charge of them herself, carrying them in a small blue morocco case."

"Continue, monsieur."

"At Bristol the maid, Jane Mason, collected her mistress' dressing-bag and wraps, which were with her, and came to the door of Flossie's compartment. To her intense surprise, my daughter told her that she was not getting out at Bristol, but was going on farther. She directed Mason to get out the luggage and put it in the cloak-room. She could have tea in the refreshment-room, but she was to wait at the station for her mistress, who would return to Bristol by an up-train in the course of the afternoon. The maid, although very much astonished, did as she was told. She put the luggage in the cloak-room and had some tea. But up-train after up-train came in, and her mistress did not appear. After the arrival of the last train, she left the luggage where it was, and went to a hotel near the station for the night. This morning she read of the tragedy, and returned to town by the first available train."

"Is there nothing to account for your daughter's sudden change of plan?"

"Well, there is this: According to Jane Mason, at Bristol, Flossie was no longer alone in her carriage. There was a man in it who stood looking out of the farther window so that she could not see his face."

"The train was a corridor one, of course?"

"Yes."

"Which side was the corridor?"

"On the platform side. My daughter was standing in the corridor as she talked to Mason."

"And there is no doubt in your mind—excuse me!" He got up, and carefully straightened the inkstand which was a little askew. *"Je vous demande pardon,"* he continued, reseating himself. "It affects my nerves to see anything crooked. Strange, is it not? I was saying, monsieur, that there is no doubt in your mind, as to this probably unexpected meeting being the cause of your daughter's sudden change of plan?"

"It seems the only reasonable supposition."

"You have no idea as to who the gentleman in question might be?"

The millionaire hesitated for a moment, and then replied:

"No—I do not know at all."

"Now—as to the discovery of the body?"

"It was discovered by a young naval officer who at once gave the alarm. There was a doctor on the train. He examined the body. She had been first chloroformed, and then stabbed. He gave it as his opinion that she had been dead about four hours, so it must have been done not long after leaving Bristol—probably between there and Weston, possibly between Weston and Taunton."

"And the jewel-case?"

"The jewel-case, M. Poirot, was missing."

"One thing more, monsieur. Your daughter's fortune—to whom does it pass at her death?"

"Flossie made a will soon after her marriage, leaving everything to her husband." He hesitated for a minute, and then went on: "I may as well tell you, Monsieur Poirot, that I regard my son-in-law as an unprincipled scoundrel, and that, by my advice, my daughter was on the eve of freeing herself from him by legal means—no difficult matter. I settled her money upon her in such a way that he could not touch it during her lifetime, but although they have lived entirely apart for some years, she has frequently acceded to his demands for money, rather than face an open scandal. However, I was determined to put an end to this. At last Flossie agreed, and my lawyers were instructed to take proceedings."

"And where is Monsieur Carrington?"

"In town. I believe he was away in the country yesterday, but he returned last night."

Poirot considered a little while. Then he said: "I think that is all, monsieur."

"You would like to see the maid, Jane Mason?"

"If you please."

Halliday rang the bell, and gave a short order to the footman.

A few minutes later Jane Mason entered the room, a respectable, hard-featured woman, as emotionless in the face of tragedy as only a good servant can be.

"You will permit me to put a few questions? Your mistress, she was quite as usual before starting yesterday morning? Not excited or flurried?"

"Oh, no sir!"

"But at Bristol she was quite different?"

"Yes sir, regular upset—so nervous she didn't seem to know what she was saying."

"What did she say exactly?"

"Well, sir, as near as I can remember, she said: 'Mason, I've got to alter my plans. Something has happened—I mean, I'm not getting out here after all. I must go on. Get out the luggage and put it in the cloak-room; then have some tea, and wait for me in the station.'

" 'Wait for you here, ma'am?' I asked.

" 'Yes, yes. Don't leave the station. I shall return by a later train. I don't know when. It mayn't be until quite late.'

" 'Very well, ma'am,' I says. It wasn't my place to ask questions, but I thought it very strange."

"It was unlike your mistress, eh?"

"Very unlike her, sir."

"What do you think?"

"Well, sir, I thought it was to do with the gentleman in the carriage. She didn't speak to him, but she turned round once or twice as though to ask him if she was doing right."

"But you didn't see the gentleman's face?"

"No sir; he stood with his back to me all the time."

"Can you describe him at all?"

"He had on a light fawn overcoat, and a traveling-cap. He was tall and slender, like, and the back of his head was dark."

"You didn't know him?"

"Oh, no, I don't think so, sir."

"It was not your master, Mr. Carrington, by any chance?"

Mason looked rather startled.

"Oh! I don't think so, sir!"

"But you are not *sure?*"

"It was about the master's build, sir—but I never thought of it being him. We so seldom saw him. . . . I couldn't say it *wasn't* him!"

Poirot picked up a pin from the carpet, and frowned at it severely; then he continued: "Would it be possible for the man to have entered the train at Bristol before you reached the carriage?"

Mason considered.

"Yes sir, I think it would. My compartment was very crowded, and it was some minutes before I could get out— and then there was a very large crowd on the platform, and that delayed me too. But he'd only have had a minute or two to speak to the mistress, that way. I took it for granted that he'd come along the corridor."

"That is more probable, certainly."

He paused, still frowning.

"You know how the mistress was dressed, sir?"

"The papers give a few details, but I would like you to confirm them."

"She was wearing a white fox fur toque, sir, with a white spotted veil, and a blue frieze coat and skirt—the shade of blue they call electric."

"H'm, rather striking."

"Yes," remarked Mr. Halliday. "Inspector Japp is in hopes that that may help us to fix the spot where the crime took place. Anyone who saw her would remember her."

"*Précisément!*—Thank you, mademoiselle."

The maid left the room.

"Well!" Poirot got up briskly. "That is all I can do here —except, monsieur, that I would ask you to tell me everything—but *everything!*"

"I have done so."

"You are sure?"

"Absolutely."

"Then there is nothing more to be said. I must decline the case."

"Why?"

"Because you have not been frank with me."

"I assure you—"

"No, you're keeping something back."

There was a moment's pause, and then Halliday drew a paper from his pocket and handed it to my friend.

"I guess that's what you're after, Monsieur Poirot— though how you know about it fairly gets my goat!"

Poirot smiled, and unfolded the paper. It was a letter written in thin sloping handwriting. Poirot read it aloud.

" 'Chère Madame:

" 'It is with infinite pleasure that I look forward to the felicity of meeting you again. After your so amiable reply to my letter, I can hardly restrain my impatience. I have never forgotten those days in Paris. It is most cruel that you should be leaving London tomorrow. However, before very long, and perhaps sooner than you think, I shall have the joy of beholding once more the lady whose image has ever reigned supreme in my heart.

" 'Believe, chère madame, all the assurances of my most devoted and unaltered sentiments—

" 'Armand de la Rochefour.' "

Poirot handed the letter back to Halliday with a bow.

"I fancy, monsieur, that you did not know that your daughter intended renewing her acquaintance with the Count de la Rochefour?"

"It came as a thunderbolt to me! I found this letter in my daughter's handbag. As you probably know, Monsieur Poirot, this so-called count is an adventurer of the worst type."

Poirot nodded.

"But I want to know how you knew of the existence of this letter?"

My friend smiled. "Monsieur, I did not. But to track footmarks, and recognize cigarette-ash is not sufficient for a detective. He must also be a good psychologist! I knew that you disliked and mistrusted your son-in-law. He benefits by your daughter's death; the maid's description of the mysterious man bears a sufficient resemblance to him. Yet you are not keen on his track! Why? Surely because your suspicions lie in another direction. Therefore you were keeping something back."

"You're right, Monsieur Poirot. I was sure of Rupert's guilt until I found this letter. It unsettled me horribly."

"Yes. The Count says: 'Before very long, and perhaps sooner than you think.' Obviously he would not want to wait until you should get wind of his reappearance. Was it he who traveled down from London by the twelve-fourteen, and came along the corridor to your daughter's compartment? The Count de la Rochefour is also, if I remember rightly, tall and dark!"

The millionaire nodded.

"Well, monsieur, I will wish you good day. Yard, has, I presume, a list of the jewels?"

"Yes. I believe Inspector Japp is here now if y like to see him."

Japp was an old friend of ours, and greeted Poirot with a sort of affectionate contempt.

"And how are you, monsieur? No bad feeling between us, though we *have* our different ways of looking at things. How are the 'little gray cells,' eh? Going strong?"

Poirot beamed upon him. "They function, my good Japp; assuredly they do!"

"Then that's all right. Think it was the Honorable Rupert, or a crook? We're keeping an eye on all the regular places, of course. We shall know if the shiners are disposed of, and of course whoever did it isn't going to keep them to admire their sparkle. Not likely! I'm trying to find out where Rupert Carrington was yesterday. Seems a bit of a mystery about it. I've got a man watching him."

"A great precaution, but perhaps a day late," suggested Poirot gently.

"You always will have your joke, Monsieur Poirot. Well, I'm off to Paddington. Bristol, Weston, Taunton, that's my beat. So long."

"You will come round and see me this evening, and tell me the result?"

"Sure thing, if I'm back."

"That good Inspector believes in matter in motion," murmured Poirot as our friend departed. "He travels; he measures footprints; he collects mud and cigarette-ash! He is extremely busy! He is zealous beyond words! And if I mentioned psychology to him, do you know what he would do, my friend? He would smile! He would say to himself: 'Poor old Poirot! He ages! He grows senile!' Japp is the 'younger generation knocking on the door.' And *ma foi!* They are so busy knocking that they do not notice that the door is open!"

"And what are you going to do?"

"As we have *carte blanche,* I shall expend threepence in ringing up the Ritz—where you may have noticed our Count

.s staying. After that, as my feet are a little damp, and I have sneezed twice, I shall return to my rooms and make myself a *tisano* over the spirit lamp!"

I did not see Poirot again until the following morning. I found him placidly finishing his breakfast.

"Well?" I inquired eagerly. "What has happened?"

"Nothing."

"But Japp?"

"I have not seen him."

"The Count?"

"He left the Ritz the day before yesterday."

"The day of the murder?"

"Yes."

"Then that settles it! Rupert Carrington is cleared."

"Because the Count de la Rochefour has left the Ritz? You go too fast, my friend."

"Anyway, he must be followed, arrested! But what could be his motive?"

"One hundred thousand dollars' worth of jewelry is a very good motive for anyone. No, the question to my mind is: why kill her? Why not simply steal the jewels? She would not prosecute."

"Why not?"

"Because she is a woman, *mon ami*. She once loved this man. Therefore she would suffer her loss in silence. And the Count, who is an extremely good psychologist where women are concerned,—hence his successes,—would know that perfectly well! On the other hand, if Rupert Carrington killed her, why take the jewels, which would incriminate him fatally?"

"As a blind."

"Perhaps you are right, my friend. Ah, here is Japp! I recognize his knock."

The Inspector was beaming good-humoredly.

"Morning, Poirot. Only just got back. I've done some good work! And you?"

"Me, I have arranged my ideas," replied Poirot placidly.

Japp laughed heartily.

"Old chap's getting on in years," he observed beneath

his breath to me. "That won't do for us young folk," he said aloud.

*"Quel dommage?"* Poirot inquired.

"Well, do you want to hear what I've done?"

"You permit me to make a guess? You have found the knife with which the crime was committed, by the side of the line between Weston and Taunton, and you have interviewed the paper-boy who spoke to Mrs. Carrington at Weston!"

Japp's jaw fell. "How on earth did you know? Don't tell me it was those almighty 'little gray cells' of yours!"

"I am glad you admit for once that they are *all mighty!* Tell me, did she give the paper-boy a shilling for himself?"

"No, it was half a crown!" Japp had recovered his temper, and grinned. "Pretty extravagant, these rich Americans!"

"And in consequence the boy did not forget her?"

"Not he. Half-crowns don't come his way every day. She hailed him and bought two magazines. One had a picture of a girl in blue on the cover. 'That'll match me,' she said. Oh! He remembered her perfectly. Well, that was enough for me. By the doctor's evidence, the crime *must* have been committed before Taunton. I guessed they'd throw the knife away at once, and I walked down the line looking for it; and sure enough, there it was. I made inquiries at Taunton about our man, but of course it's a big station, and it wasn't likely they'd notice him. He probably got back to London by a later train."

Poirot nodded. "Very likely."

"But I found another bit of news when I got back. They're passing the jewels, all right! That large emerald was pawned last night—by one of the regular lot. Who do you think it was?"

"I don't know—except that he was a short man."

Japp stared. "Well, you're right there. He's short enough. It was Red Narky."

"Who is Red Narky?" I asked.

"A particularly sharp jewel-thief, sir. And not one to stick at murder. Usually works with a woman—Gracie Kidd; but she doesn't seem to be in it this time—unless she's got off to Holland with the rest of the swag."

"You've arrested Narky?"

"Sure thing. But mind you, it's the other man we want—the man who went down with Mrs. Carrington in the train. He was the one who planned the job, right enough. But Narky won't squeal on a pal."

I noticed that Poirot's eyes had become very green.

"I think," he said gently, "that I can find Narky's pal for you, all right."

"One of your little ideas, eh?" Japp eyed Poirot sharply. "Wonderful how you manage to deliver the goods sometimes, at your age and all. Devil's own luck, of course."

"Perhaps, perhaps," murmured my friend. "Hastings, my hat. And the brush. So! My galoshes, if it still rains! We must not undo the good work of that *tisano*. *Au revoir*, Japp!"

"Good luck to you, Poirot."

Poirot hailed the first taxi we met, and directed the driver to Park Lane.

When we drew up before Halliday's house, he skipped out nimbly, paid the driver and rang the bell. To the footman who opened the door he made a request in a low voice, and we were immediately taken upstairs. We went up to the top of the house, and were shown into a small neat bedroom.

Poirot's eyes roved round the room and fastened themselves on a small black trunk. He knelt in front of it, scrutinized the labels on it, and took a small twist of wire from his pocket.

"Ask Mr. Halliday if he will be so kind as to mount to me here," he said over his shoulder to the footman.

*(It is suggested that the reader pause in his perusal of the story at this point, make his own solution of the mystery—and then see how close he comes to that of the author.—The Editors.)*

The man departed, and Poirot gently coaxed the lock of the trunk with a practiced hand. In a few minutes the lock gave, and he raised the lid of the trunk. Swiftly he began rummaging among the clothes it contained, flinging them out on the floor.

There was a heavy step on the stairs, and Halliday entered the room.

"What in hell are you doing here?" he demanded, staring.

"I was looking, monsieur, for *this*." Poirot withdrew from the trunk a coat and skirt of bright blue frieze, and a small toque of white fox fur.

"What are you doing with my trunk?" I turned to see that the maid, Jane Mason, had entered the room.

"If you will just shut the door, Hastings. Thank you. Yes, and stand with your back against it. Now, Mr. Halliday, let me introduce you to Gracie Kidd, otherwise Jane Mason, who will shortly rejoin her accomplice, Red Narky, under the kind escort of Inspector Japp."

Poirot waved a deprecating hand. "It was of the most simple!" He helped himself to more caviar.

"It was the maid's insistence on the clothes that her mistress was wearing that first struck me. Why was she so anxious that our attention should be directed to them? I reflected that we had only the maid's word for the mysterious man in the carriage at Bristol. As far as the doctor's evidence went, Mrs. Carrington might easily have been murdered *before* reaching Bristol. But if so, then the maid must be an accomplice. And if she were an accomplice, she would not wish this point to rest on her evidence alone. The clothes Mrs. Carrington was wearing were of a striking nature. A maid usually has a good deal of choice as to what her mistress shall wear. Now if, after Bristol, anyone saw a lady in a bright blue coat and skirt, and a fur toque, he will be quite ready to swear he has seen Mrs. Carrington.

"I began to reconstruct. The maid would provide herself with duplicate clothes. She and her accomplice chloroform and stab Mrs. Carrington between London and Bristol, probably taking advantage of a tunnel. Her body is rolled under the seat; and the maid takes her place. At Weston she must make herself noticed. How? In all probability, a newspaperboy will be selected. She will insure his remembering her by giving him a large tip. She also drew his attention to the color of her dress by a remark about one of the magazines. After leaving Weston, she throws the knife out of the window to mark the place where the crime presumably occurred, and changes her clothes, or buttons a long mackintosh over them. At Taunton she leaves the tram and returns to Bristol as soon as possible, where her accomplice has duly left the luggage in the cloak-room. He hands over the ticket and himself returns to London. She waits on the platform, carrying out her rôle, goes to a hotel for the night and returns to town in the morning, exactly as she said.

"When Japp returned from his expedition, he confirmed all my deductions. He also told me that a well-known crook was passing the jewels. I knew that whoever it was would be the exact opposite of the man Jane Mason described. When I heard that it was Red Narky, who always worked with Gracie Kidd—well, I knew just where to find her."

"And the Count?"

"The more I thought of it, the more I was convinced that he had nothing to do with it. That gentleman is much too careful of his own skin to risk murder. It would be out of keeping with his character."

"Well, Monsieur Poirot," said Halliday, "I owe you a big debt. And the check I write after lunch won't go near to settling it."

Poirot smiled modestly, and murmured to me: "The good Japp, he shall get the official credit, all right, but though he has got his Gracie Kidd, I think that I, as the Americans say, have got his goat!"

# THE MYSTERY OF THE SPANISH SHAWL

MR. EASTWOOD looked at the ceiling. Then he looked down at the floor. From the floor his gaze traveled slowly up the right-hand wall. Then, with a sudden stern effort, he focused his gaze once more upon the typewriter before him.

The virgin white of the sheet of paper was defaced by a title written in capital letters.

"THE MYSTERY OF THE SECOND CUCUMBER," so it ran. A pleasing title. Anthony Eastwood felt that anyone reading that title would be at once intrigued and arrested by it. "The Mystery of the Second Cucumber," they would say. "What can that be about? A cucumber? The second cucumber? I must certainly read that story." And they would be thrilled and charmed by the consummate ease with which this master of detective fiction had woven an exciting plot round this simple vegetable.

That was all very well. Anthony Eastwood knew as well as anyone what the story ought to be like—the bother was that somehow or other he couldn't get on with it. The two essentials for a story were a title and a plot—the rest was mere spade-work; sometimes the title led to a plot all by itself, as it were, and then all was plain sailing—but in this case the title continued to adorn the top of the page, and not the vestige of a plot was forthcoming.

Again Anthony Eastwood's gaze sought inspiration from the ceiling, the floor, and the wallpaper, and still nothing materialized.

"I shall call the heroine Sonia," said Anthony, to urge himself on. "Sonia or possibly Dolores—she shall have a skin of ivory pallor—the kind that's not due to ill-health,

and eyes like fathomless pools. The hero shall be called
George, or possibly John—something short and British.
Then the gardener—I suppose there will have to be a gardener, we've got to drag that beastly cucumber in somehow
or other—the gardener might be Scottish, and amusingly pes-
simistic about the early frosts."

This method sometimes worked, but it didn't seem to be
going to this morning. Although Anthony could see Sonia
and George and the comic gardener quite clearly, they
didn't show any willingness to be active and do things.

"I could make it a banana, of course," thought Anthony
desperately. "Or a lettuce, or a Brussels sprout—Brussels
sprout, now, how about that? Really a cryptogram for
Brussels—stolen bearer bonds—sinister Belgian baron."

For a moment a gleam of light seemed to show, but it
died down again. The Belgian baron wouldn't materialize,
and Anthony suddenly remembered that early frosts and
cucumbers were incompatible, which seemed to put the lid
on the amusing remarks of the Scottish gardener.

"Blast it!" said Mr. Eastwood.

He rose and seized the *Daily Mail.* It was just possible
that someone or other had been done to death in such a
way as to lend inspiration to a perspiring author. But the
news this morning was mainly political and foreign. Mr.
Eastwood cast down the paper in disgust.

Next seizing a novel from the table, he closed his eyes
and dabbed his finger down on one of the pages. The word
thus indicated by fate was "sheep." Immediately, with startling brilliance, a whole story unrolled itself in Mr. Eastwood's brain. Lovely girl—lover killed in the war, her
brain unhinged—tends sheep on the Scottish mountains—
mystic meeting with dead lover, final effect of sheep and
moonlight like Academy picture, with girl lying dead in the
snow, and two trails of footsteps. . . .

It was a beautiful story. Anthony came out of its con-
ception with a sigh and a sad shake of the head. He knew
only too well that the editor in question did not want that
kind of story—beautiful though it might be. The kind of
story he wanted, and insisted on having (and incidentally
paid handsomely for getting), was all about mysterious

dark women, stabbed to the heart, a young hero unjustly suspected, and the sudden unraveling of the mystery and fixing of the guilt on the least likely person, by means of wholly inadequate clues—in fact, "THE MYSTERY OF THE SECOND CUCUMBER."

"Although," reflected Anthony, "ten to one he'll alter the title and call it something rotten, like 'Murder Most Foul,' without so much as asking me! Oh, curse that telephone."

He strode angrily to it, and took down the receiver. Twice already in the last hour he had been summoned to it —once for a wrong number, and once to be roped in for dinner by a skittish society dame whom he hated bitterly, but who had been too pertinacious to defeat.

"Hallo!" he growled into the receiver.

A woman's voice answered him, a soft, caressing voice with a trace of foreign accent.

"Is that you, beloved?" it said.

"Well—er—I don't know," said Mr. Eastwood cautiously. "Who's speaking?"

"It is I. Carmen. Listen, beloved. I am pursued—in danger—you must come at once. It is life or death now."

"I beg your pardon," said Mr. Eastwood politely. "I'm afraid you've got the wrong—"

She broke in before he could complete the sentence.

"They are coming. If they find out what I am doing, they will kill me. Do not fail me. Come at once. It is death for me if you don't come. You know, 320 Kirk Street. The word is cucumber. . . . Hush. . . ."

He heard the faint click as she hung up the receiver at the other end. Mr. Eastwood, very much astonished, crossed over to his tobacco jar, and filled his pipe carefully.

"I suppose," he mused, "that that was some curious effect of my subconscious self. She can't have said cucumber. The whole thing is very extraordinary. Did she say cucumber, or didn't she?"

He strolled up and down irresolutely.

"320 Kirk Street. I wonder what it's all about? She'll be expecting the other man to turn up. I wish I could have explained. 320 Kirk Street. The word is cucumber—oh, impossible, absurd—hallucination of a busy brain."

He glanced malevolently at the typewriter.

"What good are you, I should like to know? I've been looking at you all the morning, and a lot of good it's done me. An author should get his plots from life—from life, do you hear? I'm going out to get one now."

He clapped a hat on his head, gazed affectionately at his priceless collection of old enamels, and left the flat.

Kirk Street, as most Londoners know, is a long, straggling thoroughfare, chiefly devoted to antique shops, where all kinds of spurious goods are offered at fancy prices. There are also old brass shops, glass shops, decayed second-hand shops, and second-hand clothes dealers.

No. 320 was devoted to the sale of old glass. Glassware of all kinds filled it to overflowing. It was necessary for Anthony to move gingerly as he advanced up a center aisle flanked by wine glasses and with lusters and chandeliers swaying and twinkling over his head.

A very old lady was sitting at the back of the shop. She had a budding mustache that many an undergraduate might have envied, and a truculent manner.

She looked at Anthony and said, "Well?" in a forbidding voice.

Anthony was a young man somewhat easily discomposed. He immediately inquired the price of some hock glasses.

"Forty-five shillings for half a dozen."

"Oh, really," said Anthony. "Rather nice, aren't they? How much are these things?"

"Beautiful they are, old Waterford. Let you have the pair for eighteen guineas."

Mr. Eastwood felt that he was laying up trouble for himself. In another minute he would be buying something, hypnotized by this fierce old woman's eye. And yet he could not bring himself to leave the shop.

"What about that?" he asked, and pointed to a chandelier.

"Thirty-five guineas."

"Ah!" said Mr. Eastwood regretfully. "That's rather more than I can afford."

"What do you want?" asked the old lady. "Something for a wedding present?"

"That's it," said Anthony, snatching at the explanation. "But they're very difficult to suit."

"Ah, well," said the lady, rising with an air of determination. "A nice piece of old glass comes amiss to nobody. I've got a couple of old decanters here—and there's a nice little liqueur set, just the thing for a bride—"

For the next ten minutes Anthony endured agonies. The lady had him firmly in hand. Every conceivable specimen of the glass maker's art was paraded before his eyes. He became desperate.

"Beautiful, beautiful," he exclaimed in a perfunctory manner, as he put down a large goblet that was being forced on his attention. Then blurted out hurriedly, "I say, are you on the telephone here?"

"No, we're not. There's a call office at the post office just opposite. Now, what do you say, the goblet—or these fine old rummers?"

Not being a woman, Anthony was quite unversed in the gentle art of getting out of a shop without buying anything.

"I'd better have the liqueur set," he said gloomily.

It seemed the smallest thing. He was terrified of being landed with the chandelier.

With bitterness in his heart he paid for his purchase. And then, as the old lady was wrapping up the parcel, courage suddenly returned to him. After all, she would only think him eccentric, and, anyway, what the devil did it matter what she thought?

"Cucumber," he said, clearly and firmly.

The old crone paused abruptly in her wrapping operations.

"Eh? What did you say?"

"Nothing," lied Anthony hastily.

"Oh! I thought you said cucumber."

"So I did," said Anthony defiantly.

"Well," said the old lady. "Why ever didn't you say that

before? Wasting my time. Through that door there and upstairs. She's waiting for you."

As though in a dream, Anthony passed through the door
indicated, and climbed some extremely dirty stairs. At the
top of them a door stood ajar displaying a tiny sitting-
room.

Sitting on a chair, her eyes fixed on the door, and an
expression of eager expectancy on her face, was a girl.

Such a girl! She really had the ivory pallor that Anthony
had so often written about. And her eyes! Such eyes! She
was not English, that could be seen at a glance. She had a
foreign exotic quality which showed itself even in the
costly simplicity of her dress.

Anthony paused in the doorway, somewhat abashed.
The moment of explanations seemed to have arrived. But
with a cry of delight the girl rose and flew into his arms.

"You have come," she cried. "You have come. Oh, the
saints be praised."

Anthony, never one to miss opportunities, echoed her
fervently. She drew away at last, and looked up in his face
with a charming shyness.

"I should never have known you," she declared. "Indeed
I should not."

"Wouldn't you?" said Anthony feebly.

"No, even your eyes seem different—and you are ten
times handsomer than I ever thought you would be."

"Am I?"

To himself Anthony was saying, "Keep calm, my boy,
keep calm. The situation is developing very nicely, but
don't lose your head."

"I may kiss you again, yes?"

"Of course you can," said Anthony heartily. "As often
as you like."

There was a very pleasant interlude.

"I wonder who the devil I am?" thought Anthony. "I
hope to goodness the real fellow won't turn up. What a
perfect darling she is."

Suddenly the girl drew away from him, and terror
showed in her face.

"You were not followed here?"

"No."

"Ah, but they are very cunning. You do not know them as I do. Boris, he is a fiend."

"I'll soon settle Boris for you."

"You are a lion—yes, but a lion. As for them, they are *canaille*—all of them. Listen, I have *it!* They would have killed me had they known. I was afraid—I did not know what to do, and then I thought of you. . . . Hush, what was that?"

It was a sound in the shop below. Motioning to him to remain where he was, she tiptoed out on to the stairs. She returned with a white face and staring eyes.

"It is the police. They are coming up here. You have a knife? A revolver? Which?"

"My dear girl, you don't seriously expect me to murder a policeman?"

"Oh, but you are mad—mad! They will take you away and hang you by the neck until you're dead."

"They'll what?" said Mr. Eastwood, with a very unpleasant feeling going up and down his spine.

Steps sounded on the stair.

"Here they come," whispered the girl. "Deny everything. It is the only hope."

"That's easy enough," muttered Mr. Eastwood, *sotto voce*.

In another minute two men had entered the room. They were in plain clothes, but they had an official bearing that spoke of long training. The smaller of the two, a little dark man with quiet gray eyes, was the spokesman.

"I arrest you, Conrad Fleckman," he said, "for the murder of Anna Rosenborg. Anything you say will be used in evidence against you. Here is my warrant and you will do well to come quietly."

A half-strangled scream burst from the girl's lips. Anthony stepped forward with a composed smile.

"You are making a mistake, officer," he said pleasantly. "My name is Anthony Eastwood."

The two detectives seemed completely unimpressed by his statement.

"We'll see about that later," said one of them, the one

who had not spoken before. "In the meantime, you come along with us."

"Conrad," wailed the girl. "Conrad, do not let them take you."

Anthony looked at the detectives.

"You will permit me, I am sure, to say good-bye to this young lady?"

With more decency of feeling than he had expected, the two men moved towards the door. Anthony drew the girl into the corner by the window, and spoke to her in a rapid undertone.

"Listen to me. What I said was true. I am not Conrad Fleckman. When you rang up this morning, they must have given you the wrong number. My name is Anthony Eastwood. I came in answer to your appeal because—well, I came."

She stared at him incredulously.

"You are not Conrad Fleckman?"

"No."

"Oh!" she cried, with a deep accent of distress. "And I kissed you!"

"That's all right," Mr. Eastwood assured her. "The early Christians made a practice of that sort of thing. Jolly sensible. Now, look here. I'll tool off these people. I shall soon prove my identity. In the meantime, they won't worry you, and you can warn this precious Conrad of yours. Afterwards—"

"Yes?"

"Well—just this. My telephone number is Northwestern 1743—and mind they don't give you the wrong one."

She gave him an enchanting glance, half-tears, half a smile.

"I shall not forget—indeed, I shall not forget."

"That's all right then. Good-bye. I say—"

"Yes?"

"Talking of the early Christians—once more wouldn't matter, would it?"

She flung her arms round his neck. Her lips just touched his.

"I do like you—yes, I do like you. You will remember that, whatever happens, won't you?"

Anthony disengaged himself reluctantly and approached his captors.

"I am ready to come with you. You don't want to detain this young lady, I suppose?"

"No, sir, that will be quite all right," said the small man civilly.

"Decent fellows, these Scotland Yard men," thought Anthony to himself, as he followed them down the narrow stairway.

There was no sign of the old woman in the shop, but Anthony caught a heavy breathing from a door at the rear, and guessed that she stood behind it, cautiously observing events.

Once out in the dinginess of Kirk Street, Anthony drew a long breath, and addressed the smaller of the two men.

"Now, then, Inspector—you are an inspector, I suppose?"

"Yes, sir. Detective-Inspector Verrall. This is Detective-Sergeant Carter."

"Well, Inspector Verrall, the time has come to talk sense—and to listen to it, too. I'm not Conrad What's-his-name. My name is Anthony Eastwood, as I told you, and I am a writer by profession. If you will accompany me to my flat, I think that I shall be able to satisfy you of my identity."

Something in the matter-of-fact way Anthony spoke seemed to impress the detectives. For the first time an expression of doubt passed over Verrall's face.

Carter, apparently, was harder to convince.

"I dare say," he sneered. "But you'll remember the young lady was calling you 'Conrad' all right."

"Ah! that's another matter. I don't mind admitting to you both that for—er—reasons of my own, I was passing myself off upon that lady as a person called Conrad. A private matter, you understand."

"Likely story, isn't it?" observed Carter. "No, sir, you come along with us. Hail that taxi, Joe."

A passing taxi was stopped, and the three men got inside. Anthony made a last attempt, addressing himself to Verrall as the more easily convinced of the two.

"Look here, my dear Inspector, what harm is it going to do you to come along to my flat and see if I'm speaking the truth? You can keep the taxi if you like—there's a generous offer! It won't make five minutes difference either way."

Verrall looked at him searchingly.

"I'll do it," he said suddenly. "Strange as it appears, I believe you're speaking the truth. We don't want to make fools of ourselves at the station by arresting the wrong man. What's the address?"

"Forty-eight Brandenburg Mansions."

Verrall leaned out and shouted the address to the taxi driver. All three sat in silence until they arrived at their destination, when Carter sprang out, and Verrall motioned to Anthony to follow him.

"No need for any unpleasantness," he explained, as he too descended. "We'll go in friendly like, as though Mr. Eastwood was bringing a couple of pals home."

Anthony felt extremely grateful for the suggestion and his opinion of the Criminal Investigation Department rose every minute.

In the hallway they were fortunate enough to meet Rogers, the porter. Anthony stopped.

"Ah! Good evening, Rogers," he remarked casually.

"Good evening, Mr. Eastwood," replied the porter respectfully.

He was attached to Anthony, who set an example of liberality not always followed by his neighbors.

Anthony paused with his foot on the bottom step on the stairs.

"By the way, Rogers," he said casually, "how long have I been living here? I was just having a little discussion about it with these friends of mine."

"Let me see, sir, it must be getting on for close on four years now."

"Just what I thought."

Anthony flung a glance of triumph at the two detectives.

Carter grunted, but Verrall was smiling broadly.

"Good, but not good enough, sir," he remarked. "Shall we go up?"

Anthony opened the door of the flat with his latchkey. He was thankful to remember that Seamark, his man, was out. The fewer witnesses of this catastrophe the better.

The typewriter was as he had left it. Carter strode across to the table and read the headline on the paper.

"THE MYSTERY OF THE SECOND CUCUMBER?" he announced in a gloomy voice.

"A story of mine," exclaimed Anthony nonchalantly.

"That's another good point, sir," said Verrall nodding his head, his eyes twinkling. "By the way, sir, what was it about? What was the mystery of the second cucumber?"

"Ah, there you have me," said Anthony. "It's that second cucumber that's at the bottom of this trouble."

Carter was looking at him intently. Suddenly he shook his head and tapped his forehead significantly.

"Balmy, poor young fellow," he murmured in an audible aside.

"Now, gentlemen," said Mr. Eastwood briskly, "to business. Here are letters addressed to me, my bankbook, communications from editors. What more do you want?"

Verrall examined the papers that Anthony thrust upon him.

"Speaking for myself, sir," he said respectfully, "I want nothing more. I'm quite convinced. But I can't take the responsibility of releasing you upon myself. You see, although it seems positive that you have been residing here as Mr. Eastwood for some years, yet it is possible that Conrad Fleckman and Anthony Eastwood are one and the same person. I must make a thorough search of the flat, take your fingerprints, and telephone to headquarters."

"That seems a comprehensive program," remarked Anthony. "I can assure you that you're welcome to any guilty secrets of mine you may lay your hands on."

The inspector grinned. For a detective he was a singularly human person.

"Will you go into the little end room, sir, with Carter, while I'm getting busy?"

"All right," said Anthony unwillingly. "I suppose it couldn't be the other way about, could it?"

"Meaning?"

"That you and I and a couple of whiskies and sodas should occupy the end room while our friend, the sergeant does the heavy searching."

"If you prefer it, sir?"

"I do prefer it."

They left Carter investigating the contents of the desk with business-like dexterity. As they passed out of the room, they heard him take down the telephone and call up Scotland Yard.

"This isn't so bad," said Anthony, settling himself with a whisky and soda by his side, having hospitably attended to the wants of Inspector Verrall. "Shall I drink first, just to show you that the whisky isn't poisoned?"

The inspector smiled.

"Very irregular, all this," he remarked. "But we know a thing or two in our profession. I realized right from the start that we'd made a mistake. But of course one had to observe all the usual forms. You can't get away from red tape, can you, sir?"

"I suppose not," said Anthony regretfully. "The sergeant doesn't seem very matey yet, though, does he?"

"Ah, he's a fine man, Detective-Sergeant Carter. You wouldn't find it easy to put anything over on him."

"I have noticed that," said Anthony. "By the way, Inspector," he added, "is there any objection to my hearing something about myself?"

"In what way, sir?"

"Come, now, don't you realize that I'm devoured by curiosity? Who was Anna Rosenborg, and why did I murder her?"

"You'll read all about it in the newspapers tomorrow, sir."

" 'Tomorrow I may be Myself with Yesterday's ten thousand years,' " quoted Anthony. "I really think you might satisfy my perfectly legitimate curiosity, Inspector. Cast aside your official reticence, and tell me all."

"It's quite irregular, sir."

"My dear Inspector, when we are becoming such fast friends?"

"Well, sir, Anna Rosenborg was a German who lived at Hampstead. With no visible means of livelihood, she grew yearly richer and richer."

"I'm just the opposite," commented Anthony. "I have a visible means of livelihood and I get yearly poorer and poorer. Perhaps I should do better if I lived in Hampstead. I've always heard Hampstead is very bracing."

"At one time," continued Verrall, "she was a second-hand clothes dealer—"

"That explains it," interrupted Anthony. "I remember selling my uniform after the war—not khaki, the other stuff. The whole flat was full of red trousers and gold lace, spread out to best advantage. A fat man in a check suit arrived in a Rolls Royce with a factotum complete with bag. He bid one pound ten for the lot. In the end I threw in a hunting coat and some Zeiss glasses and at a given signal the factotum opened the bag and shoveled the goods inside, and the fat man tendered me a ten-pound note and asked me for change."

"About ten years ago," continued the inspector, "there were several Spanish political refugees in London—among them a certain Don Fernando Ferrarez with his young wife and child. They were very poor, and the wife was ill. Anna Rosenborg visited the place where they were lodging and asked if they had anything to sell. Don Fernando was out, and his wife decided to part with a very wonderful Spanish shawl, embroidered in a marvelous manner, which had been one of her husband's late presents to her before flying from Spain. When Don Fernando returned, he flew into a terrible rage on hearing the shawl had been sold, and tried vainly to recover it. When he at last succeeded in finding the second-hand clothes woman in question, she declared that she had resold the shawl to a woman whose name she did not know. Don Fernando was in despair. Two months later he was stabbed in the street and died as a result of his wounds. From that time onward, Anna Rosenborg seemed suspiciously flush of money. In the ten years that followed, her house at Hampstead was burgled no less than eight times. Four of the attempts were frustrated and nothing was taken; on the other four occasions, an embroidered shawl of some kind was among the booty."

The inspector paused, and then went on in obedience to an urgent gesture from Anthony.

"A week ago, Carmen Ferrarez, the young daughter of Don Fernando, arrived in this country from a convent in France. Her first action was to seek out Anna Rosenborg at Hampstead. There she is reported to have had a violent scene with the old woman, and her words at leaving were overheard by one of the servants.

" 'You have it still,' she cried. 'All these years you have grown rich on it—but I say to you solemnly that in the end it will bring you bad luck. You have no moral right to it, and the day will come when you will wish you had never seen the Shawl of the Thousand Flowers.'

"Three days after that, Carmen Ferrarez disappeared mysteriously from the hotel where she was staying. In her room was found a name and address—the name of Conrad Fleckman, and also a note from a man purporting to be an antique dealer, asking if she were disposed to part with a certain embroidered shawl which he believed she had in her possession. The address given on the note was a false one.

"It is clear that the shawl is the center of the whole mystery. Yesterday morning Conrad Fleckman called upon Anna Rosenborg. She was shut up with him for an hour or more, and when he left she was obliged to go to bed, so white and shaken was she by the interview. But she gave orders that, if he came to see her again, he was always to be admitted. Last night she got up and went out about nine o'clock, and did not return. She was found this morning in the house occupied by Conrad Fleckman, stabbed through the heart. On the floor beside her was—what do you think?"

"The shawl?" breathed Anthony. "The Shawl of a Thousand Flowers."

"Something far more gruesome than that. Something which explained the whole mysterious business of the

shawl and made its hidden value clear. . . . Excuse me, I
fancy that's the chief—"

There had indeed been a ring at the bell. Anthony contained his impatience as best he could, and waited for the
inspector to return. He was pretty well at ease about his
own position now. As soon as they took his fingerprints
they would realize their mistake.

And then, perhaps Carmen would ring up. . . .

The Shawl of a Thousand Flowers! What a strange story
—just the kind of story to make an appropriate setting for
the girl's exquisite dark beauty.

Carmen Ferrarez. . . .

He jerked himself back from day dreaming. What a time
that inspector fellow was. He rose and pulled the door
open. The flat was strangely silent. Could they have gone?
Surely not without a word to him.

He strode out into the next room. It was empty—so was
the sitting-room. Strangely empty! It had a bare, dishev-
elled appearance. Good heavens! His enamels—the silver!

He rushed wildly through the flat. It was the same tale
everywhere. The place had been denuded. Every single
thing of value, and Anthony had a very pretty collector's
taste in small things, had been taken.

With a groan Anthony staggered to a chair, his head in
his hands. He was aroused by the ringing of the front door
bell. He opened it to confront Rogers.

"You'll excuse me, sir," said Rogers. "But the gentlemen
fancied you might be wanting something."

"The gentlemen?"

"Those two friends of yours, sir. I helped them with the
packing as best I could. Very fortunately I happened to
have them two good cases in the basement." His eyes
dropped to the floor. "I've swept up the straw as best I
could, sir."

"You packed the things in here?" groaned Anthony.

"Yes, sir. Was that not your wishes, sir? It was the tall
gentleman told me to do so, sir, and seeing as you were
busy talking to the other gentleman in the little end room,
I didn't like to disturb you."

"I wasn't talking to him," said Anthony. "He was talking to me—curse him."

Rogers coughed.

"I'm sure I'm very sorry for the necessity, sir," he murmured.

"Necessity?"

"Of parting with your little treasures, sir."

"Eh? Oh, yes. Ha, Ha!" He gave a mirthless laugh. "They're driven off by now, I suppose. Those—those friends of mine, I mean?"

"Oh, yes, sir, some time ago. I put the cases on the taxi and the tall gentleman went upstairs again, and then they both came running down and drove off at once. . . . Excuse me, sir, but is anything wrong, sir?"

Rogers might well ask. The hollow groan which Anthony emitted would have aroused surmise anywhere.

"Everything is wrong, thank you, Rogers. But I see clearly that you were not to blame. Leave me, I would commune a while with my telephone."

Five minutes later saw Anthony pouring his tale into the ears of Inspector Driver, who sat opposite to him, notebook in hand. An unsympathetic man, Inspector Driver, and not (Anthony reflected) nearly so like a real inspector! Distinctly stagey, in fact. Another striking example of the superiority of Art over Nature.

Anthony reached the end of his tale. The inspector shut up his notebook.

"Well?" said Anthony anxiously.

"Clear as paint," said the inspector. "It's the Patterson gang. They've done a lot of smart work lately. Big fair man, small dark man, and the girl."

"The girl?"

"Yes, dark and mighty good-looking. Acts as decoy usually."

"A—a Spanish girl?"

"She might call herself that. She was born in Hampstead."

"I said it was a bracing place," murmured Anthony.

"Yes, it's clear enough," said the inspector, rising to depart. "She got you on the phone and pitched you a tale—

she guessed you'd come along all right. Then she goes along to old Mother Gibson's, who isn't above accepting a tip for the use of her room for them as finds it awkward to meet in public—lovers, you understand, nothing criminal. You fall for it all right, they get you back here, and while one of them pitches you a tale, the other gets away with the swag. It's the Pattersons all right—just their touch."

"And my things?" asked Anthony anxiously.

"We'll do what we can, sir. But the Pattersons are uncommon sharp."

"They seem to be," said Anthony bitterly.

The inspector departed, and scarcely had he gone before there came a ring at the door. Anthony opened it. A small boy stood there, holding a package.

"Parcel for you, sir."

Anthony took it with some surprise. He was not expecting a parcel of any kind. Returning to the sitting-room with it, he cut the string.

It was a liqueur set!

He noticed that at the bottom of one of the glasses there was a tiny artificial rose. His mind flew back to the upper room in Kirk Street.

"I do like you—yes, I do like you. You will remember that whatever happens, won't you?"

That was what she had said. Whatever happens. . . . Did she mean—

Anthony took hold of himself sternly.

"This won't do," he admonished himself.

His eye fell on the typewriter, and he sat down with a resolute face.

## THE MYSTERY OF THE SECOND CUCUMBER

His face grew dreamy again. The Shawl of a Thousand Flowers. What was it that was found on the floor beside the dead body? The gruesome thing that explained the whole mystery?

Nothing, of course, since it was only a trumped-up tale to hold his attention, and the teller had used the old Arabian Nights' trick of breaking off at the most interesting point.

But couldn't there be a gruesome thing that explained the whole mystery? Couldn't there? If one gave one's mind to it?

Anthony tore the sheet of paper from his typewriter and substituted another. He typed a headline:

### THE MYSTERY OF THE SPANISH SHAWL

He surveyed it for a moment or two in silence.
Then he began to type rapidly. . . .

# THE CORNISH MYSTERY

"MRS. PENGELLEY," announced our landlady, and withdrew discreetly.

Many unlikely people came to consult Poirot, but to my mind, the woman who stood nervously just inside the door, fingering her feather neck-piece, was the most unlikely of all. She was so extraordinarily commonplace—a thin, faded woman of about fifty dressed in a braided coat and skirt, some gold jewelry at her neck, and with her gray hair surmounted by a singularly unbecoming hat. In a country town, you pass a hundred Mrs. Pengelleys in the street every day.

Poirot came forward and greeted her pleasantly, perceiving her obvious embarrassment.

"Madame! Take a chair, I beg of you. My colleague, Captain Hastings."

The lady sat down, murmuring uncertainly: "You are M. Poirot, the detective?"

"At your service, madame."

But our guest was still tongue-tied. She sighed, twisted her fingers, and grew steadily redder and redder.

"There is something I can do for you, eh, madame?"

"Well, I thought—that is—you see—"

"Proceed, madame, I beg of you—proceed."

Mrs. Pengelley, thus encouraged, took a grip on herself.

"It's this way, M. Poirot—I don't want to have anything to do with the police. No, I wouldn't go to the police for anything! But all the same, I'm sorely troubled about something. And yet I don't know if I ought—"

She stopped abruptly.

"Me, I have nothing to do with the police. My investigations are strictly private."

Mrs. Pengelley caught at the word.

"Private—that's what I want. I don't want any talk or fuss, or things in the papers. Wicked it is, the way they write things, until the family could never hold up their heads again. And it isn't as though I was even sure—it's just a dreadful idea that's come to me, and put it out of my head I can't." She paused for breath. "And all the time I may be wickedly wronging poor Edward. It's a terrible thought for any wife to have. But you do read of such, dreadful things nowadays."

"Permit me—it is of your husband you speak?"

"Yes."

"And you suspect him of—what?"

"I don't like even to say it, M. Poirot. But you *do* read of such things happening—and the poor souls suspecting nothing."

I was beginning to despair of the lady's ever coming to the point, but Poirot's patience was equal to the demand made upon it.

"Speak without fear, madame. Think what joy will be yours if we are able to prove your suspicions unfounded."

"That's true—anything's better than this wearing uncertainty. Oh, M. Poirot, I'm dreadfully afraid I'm being *poisoned.*"

"What makes you think so?"

Mrs. Pengelley, her reticence leaving her, plunged into a full recital more suited to the ears of her medical attendant.

"Pain and sickness after food, eh?" said Poirot thoughtfully. "You have a doctor attending you, madame? What does he say?"

"He says it's acute gastritis, M. Poirot. But I can see that he's puzzled and uneasy, and he's always altering the medicine, but nothing does any good."

"You have spoken of your—fears, to him?"

"No, indeed, M. Poirot. It might get about in the town. And perhaps it *is* gastritis. All the same, it's very odd that whenever Edward is away for the week-end, I'm quite all right again. Even Freda noticed that—my niece, M. Poirot. And then there's that bottle of weed-killer, never used, the gardener says, and yet it's half empty."

She looked appealingly at Poirot. He smiled reassuringly at her, and reached for a pencil and notebook.

"Let us be businesslike, madame. Now, then, you and your husband reside—where?"

"Polgarwith, a small market town in Cornwall."

"You have lived there long?"

"Fourteen years."

"And your household consists of you and your husband. Any children?"

"No."

"But a niece, I think you said?"

"Yes, Freda Stanton, the child of my husband's only sister. She has lived with us for the last eight years—that is, until a week ago."

"Oho, and what happened a week ago?"

"Things hadn't been very pleasant for some time; I don't know what had come over Freda. She was so rude and impertinent, and her temper something shocking, and in the end she flared up one day, and out she walked and took rooms of her own in the town. I've not seen her since. Better leave her to come to her senses, so Mr. Radnor says."

"Who is Mr. Radnor?"

Some of Mrs. Pengelley's initial embarrassment returned.

"Oh, he's—he's just a friend. Very pleasant young fellow."

"Anything between him and your niece?"

"Nothing whatever," said Mrs. Pengelley emphatically.

Poirot shifted his ground.

"You and your husband are, I presume, in comfortable circumstances?"

"Yes, we're very nicely off."

"The money, is it yours or your husband's?"

"Oh, it's all Edward's. I've nothing of my own."

"You see, madame, to be businesslike, we must be brutal. We must seek for a motive. Your husband, he would not poison you just *pour passer le temps!* Do you know of any reason why he should wish you out of the way?"

"There's the yellow-haired hussy who works for him," said Mrs. Pengelley, with a flash of temper. "My husband's a dentist, M. Poirot, and nothing would do but he must have a smart girl, as he said, with bobbed hair and a white overall, to make his appointments and mix his fillings for him."

"This bottle of weed-killer, madame, who ordered it?"

"My husband—about a year ago."

"Your niece, now, has she any money of her own?"

"About fifty pounds a year, I should say. She'd be glad enough to come back and keep house for Edward if I left him."

"You have contemplated leaving him, then?"

"I don't intend to let him have it all his own way. Women aren't the downtrodden slaves they were in old days, M. Poirot."

"I congratulate you on your independent spirit, madame; but let us be practical. You return to Polgarwith today?"

"Yes, I came up by an excursion. Six this morning the train started, and the train back goes at five this afternoon."

"*Bien!* I have nothing of great moment on hand. I can devote myself to your little affair. Tomorrow I shall be in Polgarwith. Shall we say that Hastings, here, is a distant relative of yours, the son of your second cousin? Me, I am his eccentric foreign friend. In the meantime, eat only what is prepared by your own hands, or under your eye. You have a maid whom you trust?"

"Jessie is a very good girl, I am sure."

"Till tomorrow then, madame, and be of good courage."

Poirot bowed the lady out, and returned thoughtfully to his chair. His absorption was not so great, however, that he failed to see two minute strands of feather scarf wrenched off by the lady's agitated fingers. He collected them carefully and consigned them to the wastepaper basket.

"What do you make of the case, Hastings?"

"A nasty business, I should say."

"Yes, if what the lady suspects be true. But is it? Woe betide any husband who orders a bottle of weed-killer nowadays? If his wife suffers from gastritis, and is inclined to be of a hysterical temperament, the fat is in the fire."

"You think that is all there is to it?"

"Ah—*voilà*—I do not know, Hastings. But the case interests me—it interests me enormously. For, see you, it has positively no new features. Hence the hysterical woman. Yes, if I mistake not, we have here a very poignant human drama. Tell me, Hastings, what do you consider Mrs. Pengelley's feelings toward her husband to be?"

"Loyalty struggling with fear," I suggested.

"Yes, ordinarily, a woman will accuse anyone in the world—but not her husband. She will stick to her belief in him through thick and thin."

"The 'other woman' complicates the matter."

"Yes, affection may turn to hate, under the stimulus of jealousy. But hate would take her to the police—not to me. She would want an outcry—a scandal. No, no, let us exercise our little gray cells. Why did she come to me? To have her suspicions proved wrong? Or—to have them proved *right*? Ah, we have here something I do not understand—an unknown factor. Is she a superb actress, our Mrs. Pengelley? No, she was genuine, I swear that she was genuine, and therefore I am interested. Look up the trains to Polgarwith, I pray you."

The best train of the day was the one-fifty from Paddington which reached Polgarwith just after seven o'clock. The journey was uneventful, and I had to rouse myself from a pleasant nap to alight upon the platform of the bleak little station. We took our bags to the Duchy Hotel, and after a light meal, Poirot suggested our stepping round to pay an after-dinner call on my so-called cousin.

The Pengelleys' house stood a little way back from the road with an old-fashioned cottage garden in front. The smell of stocks and mignonette came sweetly wafted on the evening breeze. It seemed impossible to associate thoughts of violence with this Old World charm. Poirot rang and knocked. As the summons was not answered, he rang again. This time, after a little pause, the door was opened by a disheveled-looking servant. Her eyes were red, and she was sniffing violently.

"We wish to see Mrs. Pengelley," explained Poirot. "May we enter?"

The maid stared. Then, with unusual directness, she answered:

"Haven't you heard, then? She's dead. Died this evening —about half an hour ago."

We stood staring at her, stunned.

"What did she die of?" I asked at last.

"There's some as could tell." She gave a quick glance over her shoulder. "If it wasn't that somebody ought to be in the house with the missus, I'd pack my box and go to-night. But I'll not leave her dead with no one to watch by her. It's not my place to say anything, and I'm not going to say anything—but everybody knows. It's all over the town. And if Mr. Radnor don't write to the 'Ome Secretary, some one else will. The doctor may say what he likes. Didn't I see the master with my own eyes a-lifting down of the weed-killer from the shelf this very evening? And didn't he jump when he turned round and saw me watching of him? And the missus' gruel there on the table, all ready to take to her? Not another bit of food passes my lips while I am in this house! Not if I dies for it."

"Where does the doctor live who attended your mistress?"

"Dr. Adams. Round the corner there in High Street. The second house."

Poirot turned away abruptly. He was very pale.

"For a girl who was not going to say anything, that girl said a lot," I remarked dryly.

Poirot struck his clenched hand into his palm.

"An imbecile, a criminal imbecile, that is what I have been, Hastings. I have boasted of my little gray cells, and now I have lost a human life, a life that came to me to be saved. Never did I dream that anything would happen so soon. May the good God forgive me, but I never believed

anything would happen at all. Her story seemed to me
artificial. Here we are at the doctor's. Let us see what he
can tell us."

Dr. Adams was the typical genial red-faced country doctor of fiction. He received us politely enough, but at a hint
of our errand, his red face became purple.

"Nonsense! Nonsense, every word of it! Wasn't I in at-
tendance on the case? Gastritis—gastritis pure and simple.
This town's a hotbed of gossip—a lot of scandal-monger-
ing old women get together and invent Heaven knows
what. They read these scurrilous rags of newspapers, and
nothing will suit them but that some one in their town shall
get poisoned too. They see a bottle of weed-killer on a
shelf—and *hey presto!*—away goes their imagination with
the bit between its teeth. I know Edward Pengelley—he
wouldn't poison his grandmother's dog. And why should
he poison his wife? Tell me that?"

"There is one thing, M. le Docteur, that perhaps you do
not know."

And, very briefly, Poirot outlined the main facts of Mrs.
Pengelley's visit to him. No one could have been more astonished than Dr. Adams. His eyes almost started out of
his head.

"God bless my soul!" he ejaculated. "The poor woman
must have been mad. Why didn't she speak to me? That
was the proper thing to do."

"And have her fears ridiculed?"

"Not at all, not at all. I hope I've got an open mind."

Poirot looked at him and smiled. The physician was evidently more perturbed than he cared to admit. As we left
the house, Poirot broke into a laugh.

"He is as obstinate as a pig, that one. He has said it is
gastritis; therefore it is gastritis! All the same, he has the
mind uneasy."

"What's our next step?"

"I return to the Inn, and a night of horror upon one of
your English provincial beds, *mon ami*. It is a thing to
make pity, the cheap English bed!"

"And tomorrow?"

"*Rien à faire.* We must return to town and await developments."

"That's very tame," I said, disappointed. "Suppose there are none?"

"There will be! I can promise you that. Our old doctor may give as many certificates as he pleases. He cannot stop several hundred tongues from wagging. And they will wag to some purpose, I can tell you that!"

Our train for town left at eleven the following morning. Before we started for the station, Poirot expressed a wish to see Miss Freda Stanton, the niece mentioned to us by the dead woman. We found the house where she was lodging easily enough. With her was a tall, dark young man whom she introduced in some confusion as Mr. Jacob Radnor.

Miss Freda Stanton was an extremely pretty girl of the old Cornish type—dark hair and eyes and rosy cheeks. There was a flash in those same dark eyes which told of a temper that it would not be wise to provoke.

"Poor Auntie," she said, when Poirot had introduced himself, and explained his business. "It's terribly sad. I've been wishing all the morning that I'd been kinder and more patient."

"You stood a great deal, Freda," interrupted Radnor.

"Yes, Jacob, but I've got a sharp temper, I know. After all, it was only silliness on Auntie's part. I ought to have just laughed and not minded. Of course, it's all nonsense her thinking that Uncle was poisoning her. She *was* worse after any food he gave her—but I'm sure it was only from thinking about it. She made up her mind she would be, and then she was."

"What was the actual cause of your disagreement, mademoiselle?"

Miss Stanton hesitated, looking at Radnor. That young gentleman was quick to take the hint.

"I must be getting along, Freda. See you this evening. Good-by, gentlemen; you're on your way to the station, I suppose?"

Poirot replied that we were, and Radnor departed.

"You are affianced, is it not so?" demanded Poirot, with a sly smile."

Freda Stanton blushed and admitted that such was the case.

"And that was really the whole trouble with Auntie," she added.

"She did not approve of the match for you?"

"Oh, it wasn't that so much. But you see, she—" The girl came to a stop.

"Yes?" encouraged Poirot gently.

"It seems rather a horrid thing to say about her—now she's dead. But you'll never understand unless I tell you. Auntie was absolutely infatuated with Jacob."

"Indeed?"

"Yes, wasn't it absurd? She was over fifty, and he's not quite thirty! But there it was. She was silly about him! I had to tell her at last that it was me he was after—and she carried on dreadfully. She wouldn't believe a word of it, and was so rude and insulting that it's no wonder I lost my temper. I talked it over with Jacob, and we agreed that the best thing to do was for me to clear out for a bit till she came to her senses. Poor Auntie—I suppose she was in a queer state altogether."

"It would certainly seem so. Thank you, mademoiselle, for making thing so clear to me."

A little to my surprise, Radnor was wating for us in the street below.

"I can guess pretty well what Freda has been telling you," he remarked. "It was a most unfortunate thing to happen, and very awkward for me, as you can imagine. I need hardly say that it was none of my dòing. I was pleased at first, because I imagined the old woman was helping on things with Freda. The whole thing was absurd —but extremely unpleasant."

"When are you and Miss Stanton going to be married?"

"Soon, I hope. Now, M. Poirot, I'm going to be candid with you. I know a bit more than Freda does. She believes her uncle to be innocent. I'm not so sure. But I can tell you one thing: I'm going to keep my mouth shut about what I

do know. Let sleeping dogs lie. I don't want my wife's uncle tried and hanged for murder."

"Why do you tell me all this?"

"Because I've heard of you, and I know you're a clever
man. It's quite possible that you might ferret out a case
against him. But I put it to you—what good is that? The
poor woman is past help, and she'd have been the last person to want a scandal—why, she'd turn in her grave at the
mere thought of it."

"You are probably right there. You want me to—hush it
up, then?"

"That's my idea. I'll admit frankly that I'm selfish about
it. I've got my way to make—and I'm building up a good
little business as a tailor and outfitter."

"Most of us are selfish, Mr. Radnor. Not all of us admit
it so freely. I will do what you ask—but I tell you frankly
you will not succeed in hushing it up."

"Why not?"

Poirot held up a finger. It was market day, and we were
passing the market—a busy hum came from within.

"The voice of the people—that is why, Mr. Radnor. Ah,
we must run, or we shall miss our train."


"Very interesting, is it not, Hastings?" said Poirot, as the
train steamed out of the station.

He had taken out a small comb from his pocket, also a
microscopic mirror, and was carefully arranging his mustache, the symmetry of which had become slightly im-
paired during our brisk run.

"You seem to find it so," I replied. "To me, it is all
rather sordid and unpleasant. There's hardly any mystery
about it."

"I agree with you; there is no mystery whatever."

"I suppose we can accept the girl's rather extraordinary
story of her aunt's infatuation? That seemed the only fishy
part to me. She was such a nice, respectable woman."

"There is nothing extraordinary about that—it is completely ordinary. If you read the papers carefully, you will
find that often a nice respectable woman of that age leaves

a husband she has lived with for twenty years, and sometimes a whole family of children as well, in order to link her life with that of a young man considerably her junior. You admire *les femmes*, Hastings; you prostrate yourself before all of them who are good-looking and have the good taste to smile upon you; but psychologically you know nothing whatever about them. In the autumn of a woman's life, there comes always one mad moment when she longs for romance, for adventure—before it is too late. It comes none the less surely to a woman because she is the wife of a respectable dentist in a country town!"

"And you think—"

"That a clever man might take advantage of such a moment."

"I shouldn't call Pengelley so clever," I mused. "He's got the whole town by the ears. And yet I suppose you're right. The only two men who know anything, Radnor and the doctor, both want to hush it up. He's managed that somehow. I wish we'd seen the fellow."

"You can indulge your wish. Return by the next train and invent an aching molar."

I looked at him keenly.

"I wish I knew what you considered so interesting about the case."

"My interest is very aptly summed up by a remark of yours, Hastings. After interviewing the maid, you observed that for anyone who was not going to say a word, she had said a good deal."

"Oh!" I said doubtfully; then I harped back to my original criticism: "I wonder why you made no attempt to see Pengelley?"

"*Mon ami*, I give him just three months. Then I shall see him for as long as I please—in the dock."

For once I thought Poirot's prognostications were going to be proved wrong. The time went by, and nothing transpired as to our Cornish case. Other matters occupied us, and I had nearly forgotten the Pengelley tragedy when it was suddenly recalled to me by a short paragraph in the paper which stated that an order to exhume the body of Mrs. Pengelley had been obtained from the Home Secretary.

A few days later, and "The Cornish Mystery" was the topic of every paper. It seemed that gossip had never entirely died down, and when the engagement of the widower to Miss Marks, his secretary, was announced, the tongues burst out again louder than ever. Finally a petition was sent to the Home Secretary; the body was exhumed; large quantities of arsenic were discovered; and Mr. Pengelley was arrested and charged with the murder of his wife.

Poirot and I attended the preliminary proceedings. The evidence was much as might have been expected. Dr. Adams admitted that the symptoms of arsenical poisoning might easily be mistaken for those of gastritis. The Home Office expert gave his evidence; the maid Jessie poured out a flood of voluble information, most of which was rejected, but which certainly strengthened the case against the prisoner. Freda Stanton gave evidence as to her aunt's being worse whenever she ate food prepared by her husband. Jacob Radnor told how he had dropped in unexpectedly on the day of Mrs. Pengelley's death, and found Pengelley replacing the bottle of weed-killer on the pantry shelf, Mrs. Pengelley's gruel being on the table close by. Then Miss Marks, the fair-haired secretary, was called, and wept and went into hysterics and admitted that her employer had promised to marry her in the event of anything happening to his wife. Pengelley reserved his defense and was sent for trial.

Jacob Radnor walked back with us to our lodgings.

"You see, M. Radnor," said Poirot, "I was right. The voice of the people spoke—and with no uncertain voice. There was to be no hushing up of this case."

"You were quite right," sighed Radnor. "Do you see any chance of his getting off?"

"Well, he has reserved his defense. He may have something—up the sleeve, as you English say. Come in with us, will you not?"

Radnor accepted the invitation. I ordered two whiskies

and sodas and a cup of chocolate. The last order caused consternation, and I much doubted whether it would ever put in an appearance.

"Of course," continued Poirot, "I have a good deal of experience in matters of this kind. And I see only one loophole of escape for our friend."

"What is that?"

"That you should sign this paper."

With the suddenness of a conjuror, he produced a sheet of paper covered with writing.

"What is it?"

"A confession that *you* murdered Mrs. Pengelley."

There was a moment's pause; then Radnor laughed.

"You must be mad!"

"No, no, my friend, I am not mad. You came here; you started a little business; you were short of money. Mr. Pengelley was a man very well to do. You met his niece; she was inclined to smile upon you. But the small allowance that Pengelley might have given her upon her marriage was not enough for you. You must get rid of both the uncle and the aunt; then the money would come to her, since she was the only relative. How cleverly you set about it! You made love to the plain middle-aged woman until she was your slave. You implanted in her doubts of her husband. She discovered first that he was deceiving her—then, under your guidance, that he was trying to poison her. You were often at the house; you had opportunities to introduce the arsenic into her food. But you were careful never to do so when her husband was away. Being a woman, she did not keep her suspicions to herself. She talked to her niece; doubtless she talked to other women friends. Your only difficulty was keeping up separate relations with the two women, and even that was not so difficult as it looked. You explained to the aunt that, to allay the suspicions of her husband, you had to pretend to pay court to the niece. And the younger lady needed little convincing—she would never seriously consider her aunt as a rival.

"But then Mrs. Pengelley made up her mind, without saying anything to you, to consult *me*. If she could be really assured, beyond any possible doubt, that her husband was trying to poison her, she would feel justified in leaving him, and linking her life with yours—which is what she imagined you wanted her to do. But that did not suit your book at all. You did not want a detective prying around. A favorable minute occurs. You are in the house when Mr. Pengelley is getting some gruel for his wife, and you introduce the fatal dose. The rest is easy. Apparently anxious to hush matters up, you secretly foment them. But you reckoned without Hercule Poirot, my intelligent young friend."

Radnor was deadly pale, but he still endeavored to carry off matters with a high hand.

"Very interesting and ingenious, but why tell me all this?"

"Because, monsieur, I represent—not the law, but Mrs. Pengelley. For her sake, I give you a chance of escape. Sign this paper, and you shall have twenty-four hours' start —twenty-four hours before I place it in the hands of the police."

Radnor hesitated.

"You can't prove anything."

"Can't I? I am Hercule Poirot. Look out of the window, monsieur. There are two men in the street. They have orders not to lose sight of you."

Radnor strode across to the window and pulled aside the blind, then shrank back.

"You see, monsieur? Sign—it is your best chance."

"What guarantee have I—"

"That I shall keep faith? The word of Hercule Poirot. You will sign? Good. Hastings, be so kind as to pull that left-hand blind halfway up. That is the signal that Mr. Radnor may leave unmolested."

White, muttering, Radnor hurried from the room. Poirot nodded gently.

"A coward! I always knew it."

"It seems to me, Poirot, that you've acted in a criminal manner," I cried angrily. "You always preach against sentiment. And here you are letting a dangerous criminal escape out of sheer sentimentality."

"That was not sentiment—that was business," replied Poirot. "Do you not see, my friend, that we have no shadow of proof against him? Shall I get up and say to twelve stolid Cornishmen that *I*, Hercule Poirot, *know?* They would laugh at me. The only chance was to frighten him and get a confession that way. Those two loafers that I noticed outside came in very useful. Pull down the blind again, will you, Hastings? Not that there was any reason for raising it. It was part of the *mise en scène.*

"Well, well, we must keep our word. Twenty-four hours, did I say? So much longer for poor Mr. Pengelley—and it is no more than he deserves; for mark you, he deceived his wife. I am very strong on the family life, as you know. Ah, well, twenty-four hours—and then? I have great faith in Scotland Yard. They will get him, *mon ami;* they will get him."

# THE WITNESS FOR THE PROSECUTION

MR. MAYHERNE adjusted his pince-nez and cleared his throat with a little dry-as-dust cough that was wholly typical of him. Then he looked again at the man opposite him, the man charged with willful murder.

Mr. Mayherne was a small man, precise in manner, neatly, not to say foppishly dressed, with a pair of very shrewd and piercing gray eyes. By no means a fool. Indeed, as a solicitor, Mr. Mayherne's reputation stood very high. His voice, when he spoke to his client, was dry but not unsympathetic.

"I must impress upon you again that you are in very grave danger, and that the utmost frankness is necessary."

Leonard Vole, who had been staring in a dazed fashion at the blank wall in front of him, transferred his glance to the solicitor.

"I know," he said hopelessly. "You keep telling me so. But I can't seem to realize yet that I'm charged with murder —*murder*. And such a dastardly crime, too."

Mr. Mayherne was practical, not emotional. He coughed again, took off his pince-nez, polished them carefully, and replaced them on his nose. Then he said, "Yes, yes, yes. Now, my dear Mr. Vole, we're going to make a determined effort to get you off—and we shall succeed— we shall succeed. But I must have all the facts. I must know just how damaging the case against you is likely to be. Then we can fix upon the best line of defense."

Still the young man looked at him in the same dazed, hopeless fashion. To Mr. Mayherne the case had seemed black enough, and the guilt of the prisoner assured. Now, for the first time, he felt a doubt.

"You think I'm guilty," said Leonard Vole, in a low voice. "But I swear I'm not! It looks pretty black against me, I know that. I'm like a man caught in a net—the meshes of it all round me, entangling me whichever way I turn. But I didn't do it, Mr. Mayherne, I didn't do it!"

In such a position a man was bound to protest his innocence. Mr. Mayherne knew that. Yet, in spite of himself, he was impressed. It might be, after all, that Leonard Vole was innocent.

"You are right, Mr. Vole," he said gravely. "The case does look very black against you. Nevertheless, I accept your assurance. Now, let us get to facts. I want you to tell me in your own words exactly how you came to make the acquaintance of Miss Emily French."

"It was one day in Oxford Street. I saw an elderly lady crossing the road. She was carrying a lot of parcels. In the middle of the street she dropped them, tried to recover them, found a bus was almost on top of her, and just managed to reach the curb safely, dazed and bewildered by people having shouted at her. I recovered her parcels, wiped the mud off them as best I could, retied the string of one, and returned them to her."

"There was no question of your having saved her life?"

"Oh, dear me, no! All I did was to perform a common act of courtesy. She was extremely grateful, thanked me warmly, and said something about my manners not being those of most of the younger generation—I can't remember the exact words. Then I lifted my hat and went on. I never expected to see her again. But life is full of coincidences. That very evening I came across her at a party at a friend's house. She recognized me at once and asked that I should be introduced to her. I then found out that she was a Miss Emily French and that she lived at Cricklewood. I talked to her for some time. She was, I imagine, an old lady who took sudden and violent fancies to people. She took one to me on the strength of a perfectly simple action which anyone might have performed. On leaving, she shook me warmly by the hand and asked me to come and see her. I replied, of course, that I should be very pleased to do so, and she then urged me to name a day. I

did not want particularly to go, but it would have seemed
churlish to refuse, so I fixed on the following Saturday. After
she had gone, I learned something about her from my
friends. That she was rich, eccentric, lived alone with one
maid, and owned no less than eight cats."

"I see," said Mr. Mayherne. "The question of her being
well off came up as early as that?"

"If you mean that I inquired—" began Leonard Vole
hotly, but Mr. Mayherne stilled him with a gesture.

"I have to look at the case as it will be presented by the
other side. An ordinary observer would not have supposed
Miss French to be a lady of means. She lived poorly, almost
humbly. Unless you have been told the contrary, you
would in all probability have considered her to be in poor
circumstances—at any rate to begin with. Who was it exactly who told you that she was well off?"

"My friend, George Harvey, at whose house the party
took place."

"Is he likely to remember having done so?"

"I really don't know. Of course it is some time ago
now."

"Quite so, Mr. Vole. You see, the first aim of the prosecution will be to establish that you were in low water financially—that is true, is it not?"

Leonard Vole flushed.

"Yes," he said, in a low voice. "I'd been having a run of
infernal bad luck just then."

"Quite so," said Mr. Mayherne again. "That being, as I
say, in low water financially, you met this rich old lady and
cultivated her acquaintance assiduously. Now if we are in a
position to say that you had no idea she was well off, and
that you visited her out of pure kindness of heart—"

"Which is the case."

"I dare say. I am not disputing the point. I am looking at
it from the outside point of view. A great deal depends on
the memory of Mr. Harvey. Is he likely to remember that
conversation or is he not? Could he be confused by counsel
into believing that it took place later?"

Leonard Vole reflected for some minutes. Then he said
steadily enough, but with a rather pale face, "I do not think

that that line would be successful, Mr. Mayherne. Several of those present heard his remark, and one or two of them chaffed me about my conquest of a rich old lady."

The solicitor endeavored to hide his disappointment with a wave of the hand.

"Unfortunate," he said. "But I congratulate you upon your plain speaking, Mr. Vole. It is to you I look to guide me. Your judgment is quite right. To persist in the line I spoke of would have been disastrous. We must leave that point. You made the acquaintance of Miss French, you called upon her, the acquaintanceship progressed. We want a clear reason for all this. Why did you, a young man of thirty-three, good-looking, fond of sport, popular with your friends, devote so much of your time to an elderly woman with whom you could hardly have anything in common?"

Leonard Vole flung out his hands in a nervous gesture.

"I can't tell you—I really can't tell you. After the first visit, she pressed me to come again, spoke of being lonely and unhappy. She made it difficult for me to refuse. She showed so plainly her fondness and affection for me that I was placed in an awkward position. You see, Mr. Mayherne, I've got a weak nature—I drift—I'm one of those people who can't say no. And believe me or not, as you like, after the third or fourth visit I paid her I found myself getting genuinely fond of the old thing. My mother died when I was young, an aunt brought me up, and she, too, died before I was fifteen. If I told you that I genuinely enjoyed being mothered and pampered, I dare say you'd only laugh."

Mr. Mayherne did not laugh. Instead he took off his pince-nez again and polished them, a sign with him that he was thinking deeply.

"I accept your explanation, Mr. Vole," he said at last. "I believe it to be psychologically probable. Whether a jury would take that view of it is another matter. Please continue your narrative. When was it that Miss French first asked you to look into her business affairs?"

"After my third or fourth visit to her. She understood very little of money matters, and was worried about some investments."

Mr. Mayherne looked up sharply.

"Be careful, Mr. Vole. The maid, Janet Mackenzie, declares that her mistress was a good woman of business and transacted all her own affairs, and this is borne out by the testimony of her bankers."

"I can't help that," said Vole earnestly. "That's what she said to me."

Mr. Mayherne looked at him for a moment or two in silence. Though he had no intention of saying so, his belief in Leonard Vole's innocence was at the moment strengthened. He knew something of the mentality of elderly ladies. He saw Miss French, infatuated with the good-looking young man, hunting about for pretexts that would bring him to the house. What more likely than that she would plead ignorance of business, and beg him to help her with her money affairs? She was enough of a woman of the world to realize that any man is slightly flattered by such an admission of his superiority. Leonard Vole had been flattered. Perhaps, too, she had not been averse to letting this young man know that she was wealthy. Emily French had been a strong-willed old woman, willing to pay her price for what she wanted. All this passed rapidly through Mr. Mayherne's mind, but he gave no indication of it, and asked instead a further question.

"And did you handle her affairs for her at her request?"

"I did."

"Mr. Vole," said the solicitor, "I am going to ask you a very serious question, and one to which it is vital I should have a truthful answer. You were in low water financially. You had the handling of an old lady's affairs—an old lady who, according to her own statement, knew little or nothing of business. Did you at any time, or in any manner, convert to your own use the securities which you handled? Did you engage in any transaction for your own pecuniary advantage which will not bear the light of day?" He quelled the other's response. "Wait a minute before you answer. There are two courses open to us. Either we can make a feature of your probity and honesty in conducting her affairs while pointing out how unlikely it is that you would commit murder to obtain money which you might have obtained by such infinitely easier means. If, on the other hand, there is anything in your dealings which the prosecution will get hold of—if, to put it badly, it can be proved that you swindled the old lady in any way, we must take the line that you had no motive for the murder, since she was already a profitable source of income to you. You perceive the distinction. Now, I beg of you, take your time before you reply."

But Leonard Vole took no time at all.

"My dealings with Miss French's affairs were all perfectly fair and above board. I acted for her interests to the very best of my ability, as anyone will find who looks into the matter."

"Thank you," said Mr. Mayherne. "You relieve my mind very much. I pay you the compliment of believing that you are far too clever to lie to me over such an important matter."

"Surely," said Vole eagerly, "the strongest point in my favor is the lack of motive. Granted that I cultivated the acquaintanceship of a rich old lady in the hopes of getting money out of her—that, I gather, is the substance of what you have been saying—surely her death frustrates all my hopes?"

The solicitor looked at him steadily. Then, very deliberately, he repeated his unconscious trick with his pince-nez. It was not until they were firmly replaced on his nose that he spoke.

"Are you not aware, Mr. Vole, that Miss French left a will under which you are the principal beneficiary?"

"What?" The prisoner sprang to his feet. His dismay was obvious and unforced. "What are you saying? She left her money to me?"

Mr. Mayherne nodded slowly. Vole sank down again, his head in his hands.

"You pretend you know nothing of this will?"

"Pretend? There's no pretense about it. I knew nothing about it."

"What would you say if I told you that the maid, Janet

Mackenzie, swears that you *did* know? That her mistress told her distinctly that she had consulted you in the matter, and told you of her intentions?"

"Say? That she's lying! No, I go too fast. Janet is an elderly woman. She was a faithful watchdog to her mistress, and she didn't like me. She was jealous and suspicious. I should say that Miss French confided her intentions to Janet, and that Janet either mistook something she said, or else was convinced in her own mind that I had persuaded the old lady into doing it. I dare say that she herself believes now that Miss French actually told her so."

"You don't think she dislikes you enough to lie deliberately about the matter?"

Leonard Vole looked shocked and startled.

"No, indeed! Why should she?"

"I don't know," said Mr. Mayherne thoughtfully. "But she's very bitter against you."

The wretched young man groaned again.

"I'm beginning to see," he muttered. "It's frightful. I made up to her, that's what they'll say, I got her to make a will leaving her money to me, and then I go there that night, and there's nobody in the house—they find her the next day—oh, it's awful!"

"You are wrong about there being nobody in the house," said Mr. Mayherne. "Janet, as you remember, was to go out for the evening. She went, but about half past nine she returned to fetch the pattern of a blouse sleeve which she had promised to a friend. She let herself in by the back door, went upstairs and fetched it, and went out again. She heard voices in the sitting-room, though she could not distinguish what they said, but she will swear that one of them was Miss French's and one was a man's."

"At half past nine," said Leonard Vole. "At half past nine—" He sprang to his feet. "But then I'm saved—saved —"

"What do you mean, saved?" cried Mr. Mayherne, astonished.

"By half past nine I was at home again! My wife can prove that. I left Miss French about five minutes to nine. I arrived home about twenty past nine. My wife was there

waiting for me. Oh, thank God—thank God! And bless
Janet Mackenzie's sleeve pattern."

In his exuberance, he hardly noticed that the grave
expression on the solicitor's face had not altered. But the
latter's words brought him down to earth with a bump.

"Who, then, in your opinion, murdered Miss French?"

"Why, a burglar, of course, as was thought at first. The
window was forced, you remember. She was killed with a
heavy blow from a crowbar, and the crowbar was found
lying on the floor beside the body. And several articles
were missing. But for Janet's absurd suspicions and dislike
of me, the police would never have swerved from the right
track."

"That will hardly do, Mr. Vole," said the solicitor. "The
things that were missing were mere trifles of no value, tak-
en as a blind. And the marks on the window were not at all
conclusive. Besides, think for yourself. You say you were
no longer in the house by half past nine. Who, then, was
the man Janet heard talking to Miss French in the sitting-
room? She would hardly be having an amicable conversation with a burglar."

"No," said Vole. "No—" He looked puzzled and dis-
couraged. "But, anyway" he added with reviving spirit, "it
lets me out. I've got an alibi. You must see Romaine—my
wife—at once."

"Certainly," acquiesced the lawyer. "I should already
have seen Mrs. Vole but for her being absent when you were
arrested. I wired to Scotland at once, and I understand that
she arrives back tonight. I am going to call upon her immediately I leave here."

Vole nodded, a great expression of satisfaction settling
down over his face.

"Yes, Romaine will tell you. It's a lucky chance that."

"Excuse me, Mr. Vole, but you are very fond of your
wife?"

"Of course."

"And she of you?"

"Romaine is devoted to me. She'd do anything in the
world for me."

He spoke enthusiastically, but the solicitor's heart sank a

little lower. The testimony of a devoted wife—would it gain credence?

"Was there anyone else who saw you return at nine-twenty. A maid, for instance?"

"We have no maid."

"Did you meet anyone in the street on the way back?"

"Nobody I knew. I rode part of the way in a bus. The conductor might remember."

Mr. Mayherne shook his head doubtfully.

"There is no one, then, who can confirm your wife's testimony?"

"No. But it isn't necessary, surely?"

"I dare say not. I dare say not," said Mr. Mayherne hastily. "Now there's just one thing more. Did Miss French know that you were a married man?"

"Oh, yes."

"Yet you never took your wife to see her. Why was that?"

For the first time, Leonard Vole's answer came halting and uncertain.

"Well—I don't know."

"Are you aware that Janet Mackenzie says her mistress believed you to be single, and contemplated marrying you in the future?"

Vole laughed. "Absurd! There was forty years' difference in age between us."

"It has been done," said the solicitor dryly. "The fact remains. Your wife never met Miss French?"

"No—" Again the constraint.

"You will permit me to say," said the lawyer, "that I hardly understand your attitude in the matter."

Vole flushed, hesitated, and then spoke.

"I'll make a clean breast of it. I was hard up, as you know. I hoped that Miss French might lend me some money. She was fond of me, but she wasn't at all interested in the struggles of a young couple. Early on, I found that she had taken it for granted that my wife and I didn't get on— were living apart. Mr. Mayherne—I wanted the money— for Romaine's sake. I said nothing, and allowed the old lady to think what she chose. She spoke of my being an adopted son to her. There was never any question of marriage—that must be just Janet's imagination."

"And that is all?"

"Yes—that is all."

Was there just a shade of hesitation in the words? The lawyer fancied so. He rose and held out his hand.

"Good-by, Mr. Vole." He looked into the haggard young face and spoke with an unusual impulse. "I believe in your innocence in spite of the multitude of facts arrayed against you. I hope to prove it and vindicate you completely."

Vole smiled back at him.

"You'll find the alibi is all right," he said cheerfully.

Again he hardly noticed that the other did not respond.

"The whole thing hinges a good deal on the testimony of Janet Mackenzie," said Mr. Mayherne. "She hates you. That much is clear."

"She can hardly hate me," protested the young man.

The solicitor shook his head as he went out. *Now for Mrs. Vole*, he said to himself. He was seriously disturbed by the way the thing was shaping.

The Voles lived in a small shabby house near Paddington Green. It was to this house that Mr. Mayherne went.

In answer to his ring, a big slatternly woman, obviously a charwoman, answered the door.

"Mrs. Vole? Has she returned yet?"

"Got back an hour ago. But I dunno if you can see her."

"If you will take my card to her," said Mr. Mayherne quietly. "I am quite sure that she will do so."

The woman looked at him doubtfully, wiped her hand on her apron, and took the card. Then she closed the door in his face and left him on the step outside.

In a few minutes, however, she returned with a slightly altered manner.

"Come inside, please."

She ushered him into a tiny drawing-room. Mr. Mayherne, examining a drawing on the wall, started up suddenly to face a tall, pale woman who had entered so quietly that he had not heard her.

"Mr. Mayherne? You are my husband's solicitor, are

you not? You have come from him? Will you please sit down?"

Until she spoke he had not realized that she was not English. Now, observing her more closely, he noticed the high cheekbones, the dense blue-black of the hair, and an occasional very slight movement of the hands that was distinctly foreign. A strange woman, very quiet. So quiet as to make one uneasy. From the very first Mr. Mayherne was conscious that he was up against something that he did not understand.

"Now, my dear Mrs. Vole," he began, "you must not give way—"

He stopped. It was so very obvious that Romaine Vole had not the slightest intention of giving way. She was perfectly calm and composed.

"Will you please tell me about it?" she said. "I must know everything. Do not think to spare me. I want to know the worst." She hesitated, then repeated in a lower tone, with a curious emphasis which the lawyer did not understand, "I want to know the worst."

Mr. Mayherne went over his interview with Leonard Vole. She listened attentively, nodding her head now and then.

"I see," she said, when he had finished. "He wants me to say that he came in at twenty minutes past nine that night?"

"He did come in at that time?" said Mr. Mayherne sharply.

"That is not the point," she said coldly. "Will my saying so acquit him? Will they believe me?"

Mr. Mayherne was taken aback. She had gone so quickly to the core of the matter.

"That is what I want to know," she said. "Will it be enough? Is there anyone else who can support my evidence?"

There was a suppressed eagerness in her manner that made him vaguely uneasy.

"So far there is no one else," he said reluctantly.

"I see," said Romaine Vole.

She sat for a minute or two perfectly still. A little smile played over her lips.

The lawyer's feeling of alarm grew stronger and stronger.

"Mrs. Vole—" he began. "I know what you must feel—"

"Do you?" she asked. "I wonder."

"In the circumstances—"

"In the circumstances—I intend to play a lone hand."

He looked at her in dismay.

"But, my dear Mrs. Vole—you are overwrought. Being so devoted to your husband—"

"I beg your pardon?"

The sharpness of her voice made him start. He repeated in a hesitating manner, "Being so devoted to your husband—"

Romaine Vole nodded slowly, the same strange smile on her lips.

"Did he tell you that I was devoted to him?" she asked softly. "Ah! yes, I can see he did. How stupid men are! Stupid—stupid—stupid—"

She rose suddenly to her feet. All the intense emotion that the lawyer had been conscious of in the atmosphere was now concentrated in her tone.

"I hate him, I tell you! I hate him. I hate him. I hate him! I would like to see him hanged by the neck till he is dead."

The lawyer recoiled before her and the smoldering passion in her eyes.

She advanced a step nearer and continued vehemently.

"Perhaps I shall see it. Supposing I tell you that he did not come in that night at twenty past nine, but at twenty past ten? You say that he tells you he knew nothing about the money coming to him. Supposing I tell you he knew all about it, and counted on it, and committed murder to get it? Supposing I tell you that he admitted to me that night when he came in what he had done? That there was blood on his coat? What then? Supposing that I stand up in court and say all these things?"

Her eyes seemed to challenge him. With an effort he

concealed his growing dismay, and endeavored to speak in a rational tone.

"You cannot be asked to give evidence against your husband—"

"I should like you to tell me one thing," said Mr. Mayherne. He contrived to appear as cool and unemotional as ever. "Why are you so bitter against Leonard Vole?"

She shook her head, smiling a little.

"Yes, you would like to know. But I shall not tell you. I will keep my secret."

Mr. Mayherne gave his dry little cough and rose.

"There seems no point in prolonging this interview," he remarked. "You will hear from me again after I have communicated with my client."

She came closer to him, looking into his eyes with her own wonderful dark ones.

"Tell me," she said, "did you believe—honestly—that he was innocent when you came here today?"

"I did," said Mr. Mayherne.

"You poor little man." She laughed.

"And I believe so still," finished the lawyer. "Good evening, madam."

He went out of the room, taking with him the memory of her startled face. *This is going to be the devil of a business,* said Mr. Mayherne to himself as he strode along the street.

Extraordinary, the whole thing. An extraordinary woman. A very dangerous woman. Women were the devil when they got their knife into you.

What was to be done? That wretched young man hadn't a leg to stand upon. Of course, possibly he did commit the crime.

*No,* said Mr. Mayherne to himself. *No—there's almost too much evidence against him. I don't believe this woman. She was trumping up the whole story. But she'll never bring it into court.*

He wished he felt more conviction on the point.

The police court proceedings were brief and dramatic. The principal witnesses for the prosecution were Janet

Mackenzie, maid to the dead woman, and Romaine Heilger.

Mr. Mayherne sat in court and listened to the damning story that the latter told. It was on the lines she had indicated to him in their interview.

The prisoner reserved his defense and was committed for trial.

Mr. Mayherne was at his wits' end. The case against Leonard Vole was black beyond words. Even the famous K.C. who was engaged for the defense held out little hope.

"If we can shake that woman's testimony, we might do something," he said dubiously. "But it's a bad business."

Mr. Mayherne had concentrated his energies on one single point. Assuming Leonard Vole to be speaking the truth, and to have left the murdered woman's house at nine o'clock, who was the man Janet heard talking to Miss French at half past nine?

The only ray of light was in the shape of a scapegrace nephew who had in bygone days cajoled and threatened his aunt out of various sums of money. Janet Mackenzie, the solicitor learned, had always been attached to this young man, and had never ceased urging his claims upon her mistress. It certainly seemed possible that it was this nephew who had been with Miss French after Leonard Vole left, especially as he was not to be found in any of his old haunts.

In all other directions, the lawyer's researches had been negative in their result. No one had seen Leonard Vole entering his own house, or leaving that of Miss French. No one had seen any other man enter or leave the house in Cricklewood. All inquiries drew blank.

It was the eve of the trial when Mr. Mayherne received the letter which was to lead his thoughts in an entirely new direction.

It came by the six-o'clock post. An illiterate scrawl, written on common paper and enclosed in a dirty envelope with the stamp stuck on crooked.

Mr. Mayherne read it through once or twice before he grasped its meaning.

*Dear Mister:*

*Youre the lawyer chap wot acts for the young feller. If you want that painted foreign hussy showd up for wot she is an her pack of lies you come to 16 Shaw's Rents Stepney tonight It ull cawst you 2 hundred quid Arsk for Missis Mogson.*

The solicitor read and reread this strange epistle. It might, of course, be a hoax, but when he thought it over, he became increasingly convinced that it was genuine, and also convinced that it was the one hope for the prisoner. The evidence of Romaine Heilger damned him completely, and the line the defense meant to pursue, the line that the evidence of a woman who had admittedly lived an immoral life was not to be trusted, was at best a weak one.

Mr. Mayherne's mind was made up. It was his duty to save his client at all costs. He must go to Shaw's Rents.

He had some difficulty in finding the place, a ramshackle building in an evil-smelling slum, but at last he did so, and on inquiry for Mrs. Mogson was sent up to a room on the third floor. On this door he knocked, and getting no answer, knocked again.

At this second knock, he heard a shuffling sound inside, and presently the door was opened cautiously half an inch and a bent figure peered out.

Suddenly the woman, for it was a woman, gave a chuckle and opened the door wider.

"So it's you, dearie," she said, in a wheezy voice. "Nobody with you, is there? No playing tricks? That's right. You can come in—you can come in."

With some reluctance the lawyer stepped across the threshold into the small, dirty room, with its flickering gas jet. There was an untidy unmade bed in a corner, a plain deal table, and two rickety chairs. For the first time Mr. Mayherne had a full view of the tenant of this unsavory apartment. She was a woman of middle age, bent in figure, with a mass of untidy gray hair and a scarf wound tightly round her face. She saw him looking at this and laughed again, the same curious, toneless chuckle.

"Wondering why I hide my beauty, dear? He, he, he.

Afraid it may tempt you, eh? But you shall see—you shall see."

She drew aside the scarf, and the lawyer recoiled involuntarily before the almost formless blur of scarlet. She replaced the scarf again.

"So you're not wanting to kiss me, dearie? He, he, I don't wonder. And yet I was a pretty girl once—not so long ago as you'd think, either. Vitriol, dearie, vitriol—that's what did that. Ah! but I'll be even with 'em—"

She burst into a hideous torrent of abuse which Mr. Mayherne tried vainly to quell. She fell silent at last, her hands clenching and unclenching themselves nervously.

"Enough of that," said the lawyer sternly. "I've come here because I have reason to believe you can give me information which will clear my client, Leonard Vole. Is that the case?"

Her eyes leered at him cunningly.

"What about the money, dearie?" she wheezed. "Two hundred quid, you remember."

"It is your duty to give evidence, and you can be called upon to do so."

"That won't do dearie. I'm an old woman, and I know nothing. But you give me two hundred quid, and perhaps I can give you a hint or two. See?"

"What kind of hint?"

"What should you say to a letter? A letter from *her*. Never mind how I got hold of it. That's my business. It'll do the trick. But I want my two hundred quid."

Mr. Mayherne looked at her coldly, and made up his mind.

"I'll give you ten pounds, nothing more. And only that if this letter is what you say it is."

"Ten pounds?" She screamed and raved at him.

"Twenty," said Mr. Mayherne, "and that's my last word."

He rose as if to go. Then, watching her closely, he drew out a pocketbook, and counted out twenty one-pound notes.

"You see," he said. "That is all I have with me. You can take it or leave it."

But already he knew that the sight of the money was too much for her. She cursed and raved impotently, but at last she gave in. Going over to the bed, she drew something from beneath the tattered mattress.

"Here you are," she snarled. "It's the top one you want."

It was a bundle of letters that she threw to him, and Mr. Mayherne untied them and scanned them in his usual cool, methodical manner. The woman, watching him eagerly, could gain no clue from his impassive face.

He read each letter through, then returned again to the top one and read it a second time. Then he tied the whole bundle up again carefully.

They were love letters, written by Romaine Heilger, and the man they were written to was not Leonard Vole. The top letter was dated the day of the latter's arrest.

"I spoke true, dearie, didn't I?" whined the woman. "It'll do for her, that letter?"

Mr. Mayherne put the letters in his pocket, then he asked a question.

"How did you get hold of this correspondence?"

"That's telling," she said with a leer. "But I know something more. I heard in court what that hussy said. Find out where she was at twenty past ten, the time she says she was at home. Ask at the Lion Road Cinema. They'll remember —a find upstanding girl like that—curse her!"

"Who is the man?" asked Mr. Mayherne. "There's only a Christian name here."

The other's voice grew thick and hoarse, her hands clenched and unclenched. Finally she lifted one to her face.

"He's the man that did this to me. Many years ago now. She took him away from me—a chit of a girl she was then. And when I went after him—and went for him, too—he threw the cursed stuff at me! And she laughed! I've had it in for her for years. Followed her, I have, spied upon her. And now I've got her! She'll suffer for this, won't she, Mr. Lawyer? She'll suffer?"

"She will probably be sentenced to a term of imprisonment for perjury," said Mr. Mayherne quietly.

"Shut away—that's what I want. You're going, are you? Where's my money? Where's that good money?"

Without a word, Mr. Mayherne put down the notes on the table. Then, drawing a deep breath, he turned and left the squalid room. Looking back, he saw the old woman crooning over the money.

He wasted no time. He found the cinema in Lion Road easily enough, and, shown a photograph of Romaine Heilger, the commissionaire recognized her at once. She had arrived at the cinema with a man some time after ten o'clock on the evening in question. He had not noticed her escort particularly, but he remembered the lady who had spoken to him about the picture that was showing. They stayed until the end, about an hour later.

Mr. Mayherne was satisfied. Romaine Heilger's evidence was a tissue of lies from beginning to end. She had evolved it out of her passionate hatred. The lawyer wondered whether he would ever know what lay behind that hatred. What had Leonard Vole done to her? He had seemed dumfounded when the solicitor had reported her attitude to him. He had declared earnestly that such a thing was incredible—yet it had seemed to Mr. Mayherne that after the first astonishment his protests had lacked sincerity.

He did know. Mr. Mayherne was convinced of it. He knew, but he had no intention of revealing the fact. The secret between those two remained a secret. Mr. Mayherne wondered if some day he should come to learn what it was.

The solicitor glanced at his watch. It was late, but time was everything. He hailed a taxi and gave an address.

"Sir Charles must know of this at once," he murmured to himself as he got in.

The trial of Leonard Vole for the murder of Emily French aroused widespread interest. In the first place the prisoner was young and good-looking, then he was accused of a particularly dastardly crime, and there was the further interest of Romaine Heilger, the principal witness for the prosecution. There had been pictures of her in many papers, and several fictitious stories as to her origin and history.

The proceedings opened quietly enough. Various technical evidence came first. Then Janet Mackenzie was called. She told substantially the same story as before. In cross-examination counsel for the defense succeeded in getting her to contradict herself once or twice over her account of Vole's association with Miss French; he emphasized the fact that though she had heard a man's voice in the sitting-room that night, there was nothing to show that it was Vole who was there, and he managed to drive home a feeling that jealousy and dislike of the prisoner were at the bottom of a good deal of her evidence.

Then the next witness was called.

"Your name is Romaine Heilger?"

"Yes."

"You are an Austrian subject?"

"Yes."

"For the last three years you have lived with the prisoner and passed yourself off as his wife?"

Just for a moment Romaine Heilger's eyes met those of the man in the dock. Her expression held something curious and unfathomable.

"Yes."

The questions went on. Word by word the damning facts came out. On the night in question the prisoner had taken out a crowbar with him. He had returned at twenty minutes past ten, and had confessed to having killed the old lady. His cuffs had been stained with blood, and he had burned them in the kitchen stove. He had terrorized her into silence by means of threats.

As the story proceeded, the feeling of the court which had, to begin with, been slightly favorable to the prisoner, now set dead against him. He himself sat with downcast head and moody air, as though he knew he were doomed.

Yet it might have been noted that her own counsel sought to restrain Romaine's animosity. He would have preferred her to be more unbiased.

Formidable and ponderous, counsel for the defense arose.

He put it to her that her story was a malicious fabrication from start to finish, that she had not even been in her own house at the time in question, that she was in love with another man and was deliberately seeking to send Vole to his death for a crime he did not commit.

Romaine denied these allegations with superb insolence.

Then came the surprising denouement, the production of the letter. It was read aloud in court in the midst of a breathless stillness.

"Max, beloved, the Fates have delivered him into our hands! He has been arrested for murder—but, yes, the murder of an old lady! Leonard, who would not hurt a fly! At last I shall have my revenge. The poor chicken! I shall say that he came in that night with blood upon him—that he confessed to me. I shall hang him, Max—and when he hangs he will know and realize that it was Romaine who sent him to his death. And then—happiness, Beloved! Happiness at last!"

There were experts present ready to swear that the handwriting was that of Romaine Heilger, but they were not needed. Confronted with the letter, Romaine broke down utterly and confessed everything. Leonard Vole had returned to the house at the time he said, twenty past nine. She had invented the whole story to ruin him.

With the collapse of Romaine Heilger, the case for the Crown collapsed also. Sir Charles called his few witnesses, the prisoner himself went into the box and told his story in a manly straightforward manner, unshaken by cross-examination.

The prosecution endeavored to rally, but without great success. The judge's summing up was not wholly favorable to the prisoner, but a reaction had set in and the jury needed little time to consider their verdict.

"We find the prisoner not guilty."

Leonard Vole was free!

Little Mr. Mayherne hurried from his seat. He must congratulate his client.

He found himself polishing his pince-nez vigorously, and

checked himself. His wife had told him only the night before that he was getting a habit of it. Curious things, habits. People themselves never knew they had them.

An interesting case—a very interesting case. That woman, now, Romaine Heilger.

The case was dominated for him still by the exotic figure of Romaine Heilger. She had seemed a pale, quiet woman in the house at Paddington, but in court she had flamed out against the sober background, flaunting herself like a tropical flower.

If he closed his eyes he could see her now, tall and vehement, her exquisite body bent forward a little, her right hand clenching and unclenching itself unconsciously all the time.

Curious things, habits. That gesture of hers with the hand was her habit, he supposed. Yet he had seen someone else do it quite lately. Who was it now? Quite lately—

He drew in his breath with a gasp as it came back to him. The woman in Shaw's Rents—

He stood still, his head whirling. It was impossible—impossible—Yet, Romaine Heilger was an actress.

The K.C. came up behind him and clapped him on the shoulder.

"Congratulated our man yet? He's had a narrow shave, you know. Come along and see him."

But the little lawyer shook off the other's hand.

He wanted one thing only—to see Romaine Heilger face to face.

He did not see her until some time later, and the place of their meeting is not relevant.

"So you guessed," she said, when he had told her all that was in his mind. "The face? Oh! that was easy enough, and the light of that gas jet was too bad for you to see the make-up."

"But why—why—"

"Why did I play a lone hand?" She smiled a little, remembering the last time she had used the words.

"Such an elaborate comedy!"

"My friend—I had to save him. The evidence of a woman devoted to him would not have been enough—you hinted as much yourself. But I know something of the psychology of crowds. Let my evidence be wrung from me, as an admission, damning me in the eyes of the law, and a reaction in favor of the prisoner would immediately set in."

"And the bundle of letters?"

"One alone, the vital one, might have seemed like a—what do you call it?—put-up job."

"Then the man called Max?"

"Never existed, my friend."

"I still think," said little Mr. Mayherne, in an aggrieved manner, "that we could have got him off by the—er—normal procedure."

"I dared not risk it. You see you thought he was innocent—"

"And you knew it? I see," said little Mr. Mayherne.

"My dear Mr. Mayherne," said Romaine, "you do not see at all. I knew—he was guilty!"